AN INCIDENT AT BLOODTIDE

By George C. Chesbro

The Mongo novels

An Incident at Bloodtide
Dark Chant in a Crimson Key
The Fear in Yesterday's Rings
In the House of Secret Enemies (novellas)
The Language of Cannibals
Second Horseman Out of Eden
The Cold Smell of Sacred Stone
Two Songs This Archangel Sings
The Beasts of Valhalla
An Affair of Sorcerers
City of Whispering Stone
Shadow of a Broken Man

Other novels

Bone
Jungle of Steel and Stone
The Golden Child
Veil
Turn Loose the Dragon
King's Gambit

Writing as David Cross

Chant
Chant: Torture Island
Chant: Code of Blood

AN INCIDENT AT BLOODTIDE

GEORGE C. CHESBRO

THE MYSTERIOUS PRESS

New York · Tokyo · Sweden

Published by Warner Books

 A Time Warner Company

Mysterious Press books are published by
Warner Books, Inc., 1271 Avenue of the Americas, New York, NY 10020.

 A Time Warner Company

The Mysterious Press name and logo are trademarks of Warner Books, Inc.
Printed in the United States of America
First printing: May 1993

10 9 8 7 6 5 4 3 2 1

Library of Congress Cataloging-in-Publication Data

Chesbro, George C.
    An incident at bloodtide / George C. Chesbro.
      p. cm.
    ISBN 0-89296-464-2
    I. Title.
    PS3553.H359I53   1993
    813'.54—dc20   92-50270
                                                  CIP

For Nancy,
my favorite Captain

AN INCIDENT AT BLOODTIDE

CHAPTER ONE

My brother, stretched out diagonally across the trampoline with his ankles crossed and his hands locked behind his head, said, "There's a metaphor here someplace, Mongo."

I was draped across the fourteen-foot catamaran's steel bow support, dangling my hands in the warm, murky water that looked still, but was in fact anything but. I looked around at the vast expanse of water surrounding us, a three-mile-wide section of the Hudson River the first Dutch settlers had dubbed the "Tappan Sea." To the west, the setting sun was not so much crimson as the softer shade of a strawberry lollipop that was about to drop out of the sky behind Hook Mountain in Upper Nyack, the model for "Skull Island" in the original version of *King Kong*. To the east, the huge banks of windows fronting the General Motors plant in Tarrytown reflected the sun's rays, making the entire building appear like one giant, rectangular stoplight, and bathing the normally mud-colored river in a red glow that was heightened by a recent bloom of microorganisms, a relatively rare and short-lived phenomenon I had heard local sailors and fishermen refer to as "bloodtide." To the south, the serpentine span of the Tappan Zee Bridge and the particular dangers it represented were slowly but inexorably drawing closer. The water felt close to body temperature; bodies lost in the river's depths would quickly rot and fill with gas and bob to the surface.

"A metaphor," I replied. "Damn, I missed it. It passed without a ripple. Did it go by to port or starboard?"

"Tide will tell, Mongo."

"Ho ho ho. Tide will tell what?"

"When there's no wind, tide will tell."

"That's not a metaphor, it's basic earth science."

"When venturing out on the river of life in a sailboat with no motor, don't count on the wind to always get you where you want to go."

"I think your metaphor needs some work, brother. It isn't going to float with Mary, assuming she ever sees us again. She's going to say we're the boats with no motors. She warned us when we went out that what little wind we had was going to die, remember? But no, you said it would be really swell to take a little sail before dinner."

"I didn't hear any demurrals from you. In fact, I seem to recall you being downright enthusiastic at the prospect."

"Hey, I don't live year-round in a house on the Hudson; I don't get that many opportunities to go sailing. Besides, you know how impressionable I am; I count on the wisdom of my big brother when it comes to situations like this. I actually think you've left us both to drift aimlessly downriver."

"Well, we can always just sit tight and wait until we get to New York. The river's narrower there. We'll just paddle to shore, tie up the cat, and spend the night in the brownstone."

"New York's twenty-five miles away. The tide will change before we get there, and in the meantime we'll die of thirst and exposure."

"Jesus, Mongo, you've become such a worrywart since I moved out. In any case, we're more likely to die of acute embarrassment when somebody takes pity on us and pulls over to ask what the hell we're doing out here on a fourteen-foot catamaran with no motor."

"I'm simply going to tell them it was your idea to take a quick sail before dinner. That was four hours ago."

"When caught up in the swift and unpleasant currents of life, with no help from above—"

"Not to mention from the north, south, east, or west."

"—the wise man applies the paddle."

"Now, *there's* a metaphor," I said, rolling over and sitting up. "For 'tis better to struggle with two little paddles than to get run over by a barge in the dark."

I removed the two plastic paddles from where they were secured in the webbing connecting the two halves of the trampoline, handed one to Garth, then climbed down onto the starboard pontoon of the Hoby Cat, straddling it. Garth positioned himself on the port side and we began to paddle, angling toward the western shore where the bright lights festooning the docks of the various boat clubs had already come on.

If we'd started paddling just after the wind had died and while we were still north of Hook Mountain, we probably would have stood a reasonable chance of getting to shore within reasonable walking distance of Garth's home in Cairn, or perhaps even have caught one of the faint breezes that sometimes waft off the land at dusk. However, choosing the path of lazy optimism and least resistance, we had decided to "sail the tide" for a while and wait for the wind to come up. Two hours later we'd still been sailing the tide, which had carried us right into the center of the deep channel marked by buoys and used by the mammoth tankers and barges that plied the river, servicing the dozens of companies that were located on both shores of the river between New York City and Albany. Tankers and tug-drawn barges had right-of-way over everything else on the river, and for good reason: even if the pilot or captain of one of these floating behemoths did manage to spot a tiny vessel like ours in his path, there wouldn't be much he or she could do about it, inasmuch as it can take up to five miles for a tanker or barge to come to a stop. By the time a captain managed to change course, we would long since have been reduced to flotsam of floating bits of steel, fiberglass, canvas, Mylar, and flesh. The first order of business was to get out of the channel, and so we proceeded apace, huffing and puffing, making agonizingly slow progress at an angle against the combined forces of tide and current carrying us toward the sea.

"Where to?" I asked.

"Let's go for Petersen's."

I glanced to my right, at the floodlit buildings and docks that were the old and venerable Petersen's Boat Yard in Nyack. We were almost abreast of the landmark shelter, and still at least a mile and a half from shore. "We're never going to make Petersen's, Garth."

"Well, we aim for it, and hope we at least hit the outer edge of Nyack Boat Club's parking lot. If we can just get to one of the boats on an outside mooring, we can rest up, then work our way in from mooring to mooring. They'll let us tie up, and we can take a cab home."

"I don't know about you, but my arms already feel like they're ready to drop. Why don't we just take an angle toward Memorial Park? There's a ramp there. We can call Mary, have her drive down with the pickup and trailer. Then we don't have to worry about coming back to get the cat in the morning."

"Mary won't be home. Believe it or not, we'd actually planned to eat early. She's got a church meeting tonight that's supposed to resolve a big hassle they've been into for months. She won't be back until late. Don't worry about the cat. You can drop me off on your way back into the city, and I'll sail her home."

I felt a little flutter of anxiety, a tightening in my stomach. I stopped paddling, looked back at Garth. "What about Vicky? I'm not sure she's ready to set foot again in any place with crosses on the walls, no matter how benign."

Garth nodded. "Agreed. Mary knows the situation, even if she doesn't quite understand the problem; you had to be there. But I've made it clear that there is a problem. We've got lots of friends among the neighbors, and I'm almost certain she'll have dropped Vicky off with one of them."

Garth had every reason to be as upset as I was at the prospect of our young charge being taken into a church, and so if he was comfortable with whatever decision Mary might have made, there was no reason why I shouldn't be. I turned back and resumed

4

paddling. My pause for a little *tête-à-tête* had cost us a good twenty-five yards.

Vicky Brown was a very cute nine-year-old girl with blond hair, green eyes, and freckles, whose physical beauty was marred only by her reluctance to smile or laugh, and belied by the fierce, poisonous invective that would still, even after two years of what I considered to be the very best therapy available, spew from her mouth in moments of stress or anger; when Vicky couldn't get what she wanted, the person denying her was very likely to be labeled a "nigger," "kike," or "mud person." Her severe emotional disturbance was perfectly understandable in view of the fact that she had been born into and reared in a home that was an incubator of paranoia and hatred, her mind molded into a twisted shape by a combination of parents who were over-the-top Christian fundamentalists whose fundamental belief was that ninety-nine percent of the world's population were servants of Satan bound for Hell, and savage sexual abuse visited upon her by one Rev. William Kenecky, now very much deceased, who had been the leader of the band of zealots to which Vicky's parents had belonged. The cult had not only believed that the world was about to end in nuclear holocaust but had gone to considerable lengths to bring about that goal in order to hasten the Second Coming of Christ. Global nuclear war had been a bit beyond their reach, but they'd damn near succeeded in frying a number of cities and a few million people.

Garth and I had been sucked into the lives, and conspiracy, of these decidedly strange and dangerous people as the result of a plea for help Vicky had written to Santa Claus. Most members of the cult had died horribly in a hysterical act of mass suicide inside a sealed plastic bubble world they'd called Eden, where they'd gone to await "Rapturing" while the rest of the world burned and was invaded by demons. Despite their best efforts to exterminate themselves and their daughter, we'd managed to rescue Vicky and her parents. The courts had granted my brother and me custody of the child for an indefinite length of time, inasmuch as the parents were currently committed to a psychiatric hospital. Our responsibility was to care for the child until such time as the parents were deemed sufficiently mentally healthy to regain custody of their daughter. I wondered then, and still wondered, if that time would ever come.

I also wondered if Vicky herself could ever be made emotionally and spiritually whole. Children raised in an atmosphere of hate who are also victims of severe sexual abuse rarely ever fully recover to lead normal lives, and Vicky had suffered the extremes of both these crimes against her. But Garth and I loved the girl, and we were determined to provide an atmosphere and emotional support system that would promote healing to the greatest extent possible. We knew we could never give her back her childhood, or erase the Hieronymus Bosch horror of her memories; our goal was to at least nurture the closing of the wounds in her, to help her build emotional scar tissue strong enough to support a reasonably integrated and happy adult no more neurotic than the rest of the general population.

To that end we had bypassed the horde of child psychiatrists and assorted other therapists practicing in New York City and appealed for help to the happiest and most integrated person I knew, and the one person we both thought might do Vicky some good. April Marlowe was one of many women I had loved, but she occupied a special place in my life. She had once saved my mind with her love, after I had survived a nasty bout with sensory deprivation, and it had been this woman who had given me the courage, for the first time in my life, to accept the love of a woman. That had not been an insignificant accomplishment. The fact that April, who now lived with her husband in upstate New York, was a practicing witch might not have sat too well with the judge who had granted us temporary custody, or with any child welfare agency, but we were not answerable to anyone when it came to decisions regarding Vicky, who had to learn to perceive the world, and her place in it, in a totally new way. April Marlowe was the person to do that, to afford Vicky a fresh way of perceiving nature, literally from the ground up. April might be a witch, but—as always with the hopelessly complicated and bizarre hash of human belief systems—it was the singer, not the song, that made the difference.

For much of the year Vicky lived with April and her husband

on their farm and attended a very special and highly accredited private school run by April and other members of her Church of Wicca. Summers and vacations she spent with us, either with me in New York or with Garth and his wife at their home on the river in Cairn. Between the rusticity of the farm, the deep understanding of April, the incredible empathy of my brother with the world's walking wounded, and the richness of New York's culture that I could share with her, we hoped there was a process of spiritual detoxification taking place that would eventually give Vicky a new sense of oneness with the world, and with the many different kinds of human beings who inhabited it. The jury was still out, but then we'd only had her less than two years, and there was a lot of poison that had to be leeched from her very young soul.

Now it was the influence, however subtle, of Mary Tree, Garth's beautiful wife who also happened to be a world-famous folksinger, that was giving me pause. Mary and I adored each other, and she had brought to Vicky the invaluable gift of music. In almost every way, Mary was an ideal role model for Vicky. What concerned me was the recent interest Mary had been showing in a kind of not-quite-born-again brand of Christianity, a predilection I couldn't fathom. The fact that I couldn't understand Mary's spiritual needs was of no consequence, but what concerned me was that it was just such a taste for the supernatural that had ground up Vicky in the first place. Mary certainly didn't proselytize, and—at Garth's insistence—never brought up the subject of religion with the child, but I was still anxious about what unconscious signals Mary might be sending to the girl. Vicky had to learn to have faith in herself, the soundness of her own senses, and the people around her, not in any gods even remotely resembling the savage, merciless deity that had ruled the world of her parents and the Reverend Kenecky.

The muscles in my arms and shoulders burned, and were starting to cramp. It was growing darker. We had made it out of the deep channel, which meant we weren't going to be run over by a barge or tanker, but there was still the danger of getting whacked by one of the large powerboats that roared up and down the river, even at night. The lights of the Nyack Boat Club were slipping away off to starboard. We weren't going to make it to that point of landing, and it was doubtful we could even make Memorial Park, a half mile or so further down the shoreline. With luck, we might still be able to park the cat on the beach of one of the riverfront mansions in South Nyack, just before the bridge.

"What do you hear from the lovely Dr. Harper Rhys-Whitney?" my brother asked.

"Nothing," I replied curtly, digging into the water with my paddle and trying to ignore the stabbing pains in my arms and shoulders. The woman whose absence I was suffering as a kind of persistent, dull ache in my chest was off on one of her annual pilgrimages to the Amazon to hunt for new species of venomous snakes. I missed her terribly, and it was a subject I did not care to discuss. "They don't have that many phones or mailboxes in the rain forest. What's the hassle at Mary's church?"

Garth grunted. "A little clash of cultures and a big dose of politics. Church versus State, arguments over worshipping false idols, that sort of thing. They hired this young assistant pastor a few months ago, and he wasn't there a week before he announced that it was inappropriate to display the American flag on the altar. He said it was wrong to display a symbol of nationalism in a place where the business is supposed to be worship of the Creator of the universe. So he took the flag off the altar and locked it away."

"Oh-oh. Bad move politically."

"You've got that right. The congregation's been at each other's throats ever since, with the flag-removers a distinct minority. I don't have to tell you which side Mary's on. They're being called unpatriotic, and they accuse the other side of worshipping false gods. It's gotten ugly."

"The pastor sounds hopelessly naive. They should have taught him in the seminary that patriotism is just another form of religion, and hate is what most politics are about. Theologically, of course, he's absolutely right."

Garth laughed. "My brother the theologian. I love it."

"Why don't you turn on the radio and call for help?"

"We don't have a radio."

"Oh, that's right. I forgot. Then how about turning on our running lights so we don't get rammed?"

"We don't have any lights."

"Tell me again whose idea this was."

"You thought it was a great idea."

"I'm just a city boy. What do I know about these things?"

"You're the one who taught me how to sail."

"Mary's on the assistant pastor's side, naturally."

"Naturally. The other side's led by a big poo-bah by the name of Bennett Carver—who, incidentally, happens to own half the tankers that go up and down this river. After the assistant pastor took the flag down, Carver put a new one back on the altar; the kid took it down, Carver put another up. It went on like that for a while."

"So tonight they're going to make a final decision on what to do with the flag?"

"Nope. The flag is back on the altar. Bennett Carver's not a man to mess with. The meeting's about whether or not to fire the assistant pastor, and maybe the pastor as well for letting things get out of hand."

I stopped paddling, leaned forward on the pontoon. "Shit, brother, I don't know about you, but I am one tired puppy."

"Yeah. But unless—"

We both turned at the sound of a powerful engine behind us, saw a rack of very bright lights on the bridge of what appeared to be a commercial fishing boat, or maybe the Coast Guard. Both the red and green running lights on the bow were visible, which meant the boat was coming directly at us, and at high speed. I tossed my paddle onto the canvas trampoline, stood up on the pontoon, and gripped one of the steel shrouds. The small mountain of lights and rising cascade of sound kept coming on the same course—directly toward us. At the rate he was going, he would be on us in less than a minute. He was going to be close—too close. Even if the captain of the boat saw the cat in time to turn away, there was a good chance he would pass close enough for his wake to capsize us.

I said, "It may be about time to abandon ship, brother."

Garth held up his hand. "Wait. If we jump off, and he veers away in the wrong direction, we're in trouble."

"It looks to me like we're in trouble right now."

Suddenly the roar of the boat's engine became a purr as the captain cut back on the throttle and veered sharply to his right. A few seconds later his wake arrived, but it was directly to our stern and rolled harmlessly under us. We bounced up and down a half dozen times, and then the water became still again. The brightly lighted boat, its engine thrumming in idle, had stopped, and was positioned about thirty yards off our port beam. One of the spotlights on the bridge swiveled in our direction, bathing us in a blinding, white glow. We shielded our eyes with our hands and squinted, trying to see who was on the boat. Garth saluted tentatively. If it was the Coast Guard, we were going to get a ticket for being on the river at night without lights, but at least we'd get towed to shore.

Very slowly, so as not to create too much of a wake, the boat circled around and came alongside us on the port beam. Then the spotlight that had been kept aimed on us was turned off. I blinked and rubbed my eyes. When I looked up again I was able to make out the figure of a burly black man, about six feet tall, standing at the stern of the boat, one hand on the helm and the other resting on his starboard gunwale as he stared down at us, a big grin on his face. The boat was a trawler, perhaps thirty feet long, with a phalanx of tires strung along the side to act as fenders. The man was dressed in baggy khaki shorts and a tank-top T-shirt that emphasized his athletic build. He had sharply chiseled features, piercing black eyes, and gray hair and beard that made him older than his well-muscled body would indicate.

"Help is at hand, brother," Garth said to me, then turned and waved to the man at the helm of the trawler. "Hello, Tom. You're probably thinking that we're happy to see you."

"Yeah, I might think that," the man replied drily in a deep, rich baritone that could easily be heard over the subterranean murmur of his boat's engine. "You're a long way from home, Garth. How the hell'd you get way down here?"

Garth shrugged. "Expert seamanship. What else?"

"Want a tow?"

"I thought you'd never ask."

The man pulled ahead slightly, then reached down and picked up a coiled line. He attached one end of the line to a cleat on the stern on his boat, then tossed the coil onto the center of the trampoline. I took the other end, tied it around the bow frame, at the base of the mast, with a bowline knot. Garth lowered the sail and tied it around the boom, then raised the flippers. Thus secured, the cat would track fairly straight in the calm water, with minimal risk of pitchpoling.

"Mongo, meet Captain Tom Blaine," Garth continued as we clambered up over the stern of the trawler. "Riverkeeper, relentless scourge of polluters, and on occasions like this a friend indeed."

The man smiled, revealing even, white teeth that shone in the bright lights. His grip was very firm, that of a man who'd spent a good part of his life working with his hands. "You must be Garth's famous brother, Robert," he said. "I've heard a lot about you, and it's a pleasure to meet you."

"Well, I'll plead guilty to being Garth's brother, Captain, and my friends call me Mongo. This rescue at sea definitely qualifies you as a friend. Glad to meet you."

Tom Blaine nodded, then leaned over the stern to check the rigging and knot I'd used to secure the catamaran. Apparently satisfied, he turned back to the helm, put the engine into gear, and brought the throttle up. He slowly brought the trawler around, pointing upriver. With its flippers out of the water, the cat swung wide as we turned, but then obediently fell into line behind us as we headed north.

"There's a jug of iced tea and a thermos with a little coffee in the galley. Sorry I can't offer you hydraulic sandwiches. I don't believe in taking alcohol out on the river."

"Iced tea sounds just about right to me," Garth said. "I'm so dehydrated that I'd probably pass out if I drank a beer right now. Mongo?"

"Actually, I could use a double Scotch, but I'll have some of the coffee, if there's enough. Otherwise, make it two iced teas."

Garth nodded, then ducked down into the galley while I seated myself on a large, coiled hawser. To my right were three green plastic jugs, scuba gear, and a black rubber diver's wetsuit that was sitting in a puddle of water, as if it had been recently used.

"You dive in the river, Tom?" I asked. "I wouldn't think there'd be much to see."

The big black man grunted, then half turned his head and spoke to me over his shoulder. "The Hudson ain't the Caribbean, and that's for sure. It's got a silt bottom, always stirred up by current and tides. You can't see a damn thing, but sometimes you have to go underwater to get what you've gotta get. As long as you know exactly what you're looking for, where and when to go down, and which way is up, you'll be all right."

"Garth called you a riverkeeper. That's an official title? This is your job, patrolling the river?"

"Between Palisades and West Point, yeah."

"You work for the state?"

Tom Blaine's response was a humorless laugh. "Hardly. The Cairn Fishermen's Association pays me. It's my job to monitor pollution."

"You've got a lot of territory to cover."

"You're telling me. I put in seventy, sometimes eighty, hours a week." He paused, then added, "But it's good work. I love it. I like to think I make a difference, which isn't something too many people in this world we live in can say. I've lived on this river all my life. Grew up in what used to be a shantytown just south of Haverstraw. That's when the river was used as a dumping ground and toilet by all the rich people who hadn't figured out yet how nice it could be living next to the water. They all had their big mansions inland, and we lived off the river, fishing and crabbing. Sometimes we'd find shit—I mean that literally—washed up on the shore when the tide went out. It's taken a lot to get this river back to where it is now. I was with Pete Seeger when he and some other folks were organizing to build the *Clearwater,* and working to clean up the river. I used to do this kind of thing on my own, as a volunteer, but after I retired, the Fishermen's Association hired me to do it full-time. I keep my eyes open, watch out for polluters, and turn over evidence to the

12

association to use in court when they sue to stop the sons-of-bitches. You'd be amazed at the attitudes of some of these people. They seem to believe—no, they *do* believe—that God put this river here for their private use, to pour shit into and take money out." He paused, half turned to look at me, then nodded in the direction of the green jugs sitting next to me. "Some people's attitudes are worse than others'. Those are the bastards I love to get."

I glanced at the jugs and diving gear. "What do you have to dive for that you can't find on the surface, Tom?"

He again looked around at me. He seemed about to speak, but then glanced in the direction of the galley, where Garth had gone, and apparently had second thoughts about answering my question specifically. "Some of the crap-dumping bastards are tricky, Mongo. Or they think they're being tricky. You've got to be a little tricky yourself in order to catch them, and prove them guilty in court. It takes time to build a case, and it's not a good idea to talk too much about it before you turn what you've got over to the lawyers."

Which, I thought, was a polite way of telling me to mind my own business—or there was something he didn't want Garth to know, which I found unlikely, unless it had something to do with the fact that Garth was now a local resident.

Garth must have overheard the last part of our conversation, because he was laughing when he emerged from the galley, a glass of iced tea in one hand and a cup of coffee in the other. "And nobody's trickier than Tom," he said, handing me the coffee. "He's a polluter's nightmare. If he got even a small percentage of what he's cost some of these companies in fines, lawyers' fees, and court costs, he'd be a rich man. Powerful men in certain factories along this river have been known to tremble in terror when Tom's boat comes into sight."

Tom Blaine raised one hand off the helm and waved it at Garth in a self-deprecating gesture. "Your brother's a sailing fool, Mongo. You should have known better than to go out with him on that little toy you've got back there. You know, this isn't the first time I've had to tow him home, either because there wasn't enough wind, or too much of it."

13

Garth laughed again. "Watch what you say there, Captain. You're talking to the man who taught me how to sail."

"Really?" the gray-haired, gray-bearded man replied, apparently surprised. "Where'd you learn to sail, Mongo?"

"In the library, and out here. Hey, Captain, I live in the city. When my brother and sister-in-law bought a house right on the Hudson, complete with boathouse, you'd better believe I was going to take advantage of it. I'd always wanted to learn to sail, so I bought them that used Hoby Cat as a housewarming present."

The riverkeeper again looked around at me. "No lessons?"

"Lots of books. And the Hudson River is a great teacher."

"But a tough one," the other man replied evenly. "A guy can get killed out here if he doesn't know what he's doing."

"Oh, Mongo knows what he's doing, all right," Garth said drily. "He's a classic overachiever. Once he takes it into his head that he's going to do something, there's no stopping him until he's done it—and usually well. He's pretty damn good on that cat. Give him a stiff breeze that would blow me over, and he's out there flying a hull."

I offered my brother a pained grimace, spoke again to the riverkeeper. "Tom, you say you work for a private organization, doing work that benefits all of us. I would think that monitoring pollution levels would be the job of the state or federal government."

Tom Blaine grunted derisively. "That it is, Mongo. On paper. Both have monitoring and enforcement responsibilities. The problem is getting either the state or federal government to do its job—they spend more time arguing about turf than taking care of the river. A lot of it has to do with politics. Things weren't so bad when Shannon was President, but then he went and got himself thrown out of office, and now the right-wingers are back in power. To them, their business buddies can do no wrong, and people who care about air and water are just pains in the ass out to wreck the economy. The result is that the monitoring and protective agencies get no money, and not a whole lot of effort is put into enforcement. Even when workers do see violations, their bosses won't let them do anything about it. Hell, we actually get tips from state workers asking us to go after some shit-dumper because they can't do it themselves. So we do—which means I do. Sometimes we'll go to the Coast Guard, which is supposed to be the big gun on the river, but they'd rather play soldier than sheriff. It seems they're on the lookout for terrorists sailing up the river to blow up Poughkeepsie. I used to try to prod them into doing what they're supposed to do, but I finally gave up. Now I just turn any evidence I find over to the Fishermen's Association, and their lawyers go after the pricks in court. That works. The fines are usually a joke, but the bad publicity embarrasses the bastards, and they usually stop whatever it is they've been doing—for a time anyway. When they start up again, we sue them again. It's a constant battle. But damned if the river doesn't continue to get cleaner. I'm in a position to know." He paused, turned to look at the green jugs next to the coil of rope on which I sat. "It's the unbelievable arrogance of the sons-of-bitches that gets to me; that, and their hypocrisy. You'll hear these people carrying on in church about all the wonderful things in God's world, and then they go out on Monday morning and virtually shit in one of the most beautiful rivers God ever created. You'll hear them yammering about what a great country this is; they cry when they sing 'America the Beautiful,' and they tell you flag burners should be shot. And then they spend their working hours spitting on America's face. It's unbelievable."

It was now dark on the river, except for the lights of the towns and anchorages on both shores, our running lights, and those of the other boats on the water. Tom Blaine must have seen something floating in the water ahead, for he eased back on the throttle, veered off to starboard. Garth and I got to our feet, looked over the side as a large log drifted past. It bumped gently against one of the catamaran's pontoons, then disappeared into the darkness.

The riverkeeper's anger and passion now seemed at least banked, if not spent, and he fell silent and attentive as the three of us gazed out over the river. Garth and I remained at the rail, enjoying the special thrill and beauty of being on the Hudson at night—specks of light on black velvet, the lapping sounds of the water passing under us, the reassuring purr of the trawler's engine. Behind us, the lights of the Tappan Zee Bridge, a necklace of emeralds and white gold, were rapidly growing fainter, like last night's dream receding into memory. We'd had our adventure for the day, and it felt good to be going home.

CHAPTER TWO

Tom Blaine brought us to within a hundred yards of the beach on Garth's property. We hopped back on the catamaran, untied the towline, thanked him profusely, then proceeded to make our way to shore. It was high tide, and we paddled our way under the overhang that was both a family music room and a state-of-the-art recording studio where Mary and her musician friends laid down many of the tracks for her best-selling albums. We pulled the cat up on the beach, in front of the original boathouse on which the main house had been built, then walked up the path leading to the side door. I was thoroughly exhausted, but it was a healthy fatigue, free of mental stress. Being out on the water always did wonders for my head. The mellow high I was enjoying would last until at least midmorning on Monday. Now I was ready for a hot shower, a good stiff Scotch, and some music—live music, if Mary felt like playing her guitar or the piano—dinner, and then sleep. I knew I was going to feel good driving into the city in the morning.

As we came to the side of the house, I noticed a late-model

green Cadillac parked in the driveway behind Mary's Wagoneer. I said, "It looks like you've got company."

Garth merely shrugged, then led the way through the screen door at the side of the house. "Mary?" he called cheerfully. "Guess who's back? It's just like Mongo says: there's nothing like a short sail before dinner to whet your appetite. Mary?"

There was no response, and we walked into the spacious living room with its pine walls and fireplaces at the north and south ends. "Mary?" Garth called again. "You home?"

"We're in here, Garth." Mary's voice, coming from the music room off to our left, sounded strained, nervous.

Garth and I exchanged glances, and then I followed him into the music room, which was essentially a large, enclosed deck overlooking the river. It was my favorite room; despite the clutter of cables, amplifiers, and huge, studio-quality speakers, I found it comfortable and cozy, a place where you could sit in an easy chair and look out over the river through the wraparound windows, read, or listen to music, or just think.

But now the room was filled with an almost palpable atmosphere of tension apparently generated by the lanky stranger who was slumped in Garth's favorite chair, a leather recliner, with his long legs stretched out and crossed at the ankles.

Mary was seated on a straight-backed chair between two five-foot-high floor speakers. Her back was stiff, not touching the chair, and both feet were flat on the floor. Her large hands with their long fingers were clenched tightly in her lap. She was wearing her waist-length, gray-streaked yellow hair in a ponytail that was pulled back tightly from her face and held in place with a calico ribbon. As usual when she was home, she wore no makeup, and her flesh, normally a golden brown in the summer from the sun, now looked pale, almost translucent, like delicate china. Her blue eyes seemed cloudy, and she appeared to be very tense, perhaps afraid.

The man in Garth's recliner did not rise, but instead stared intently at my brother and me with cold, black eyes that were bright with intelligence, but also tinted with cruelty. I judged he would be six-four or six-five if he were standing, a couple of inches taller than Garth, but much thinner. He wore jeans, the bottoms tucked into the tops of highly polished black cowboy boots with silver chains draped around the ankles. His black T-shirt was too large for him and hung loosely on his tall frame. Crawling out onto his flesh from both sleeves were black tattoos that appeared to be the clawed, hairy legs of some creature, perhaps a spider that might be tattooed on his chest. He had angular features, with high cheekbones, long nose, and pronounced chin. His hair was black—too black, with a flat, matte appearance that made me think the color had come out of a bottle. I put his age at around forty-five. His thin lips were slightly parted in what seemed to me an insouciant, arrogant smile. I instantly disliked the man and was certain that his presence in the house meant trouble. He was obviously in no hurry to introduce himself, and Mary was too distracted, or fearful, to do the honors.

Garth walked to the center of the room, stopped. "Who are you?" he asked in a soft, even tone.

Now Mary rose to her feet in a quick, jerky motion. Her hands remained clasped together. "Garth," she said nervously, "this is Sacra Silver, an old . . . acquaintance. Sacra was in town, and he stopped by to say hello. Sacra, this is my husband, Garth, and his brother, Robert."

The man Mary had introduced as Sacra Silver pointed a long index finger at me. "Brother Robert is the famous one, isn't he?" he said in a raspy, nasal voice. "Former circus star, unlikely martial arts expert, Ph.D. in criminology, ace private investigator, and darling of the media. Mongo the Magnificent."

Having delivered this pronouncement in his gravelly voice, the man ran both hands through his long, bottle-black hair and smirked. Sacra Silver was a man who could insult you without half trying, and was obviously willing to go out of his way to do so. "You've got quite a stage name there yourself, Sacra Silver," I replied. "I can't say I've heard of you. What's your act?"

"You don't want to know."

"Actually, you're right," I said. The dislike I had instinctively felt for this sour man was rapidly turning to anger, and I didn't like that. I felt I was somehow being emotionally manipulated, although I couldn't, for the life of me, understand what would motivate somebody, a guest in a couple's home, to go over-the-top obnoxious immediately. Most obnoxious people take at least a minute or two to get properly warmed up, but Sacra Silver had seemed full-bore intent on offending Garth and me from the moment we'd walked into the room. I wondered why, and I wondered where Mary knew him from. I shrugged, continued, "Just trying to be polite. It's always a pleasure to meet one of Mary's friends."

His response was to laugh; it was an unpleasant, grating sound. I glanced at Mary, waiting for her to say something, anything, that might short-circuit the tension that was rapidly building in the room, but she seemed almost paralyzed with fear or anxiety. She remained mute, lips tightly compressed, looking at the far end of the room.

"So you're Mary's latest old man," the man who called himself Sacra Silver said to Garth. "Looking at you, I wouldn't think you're her type."

Finally Mary spoke. "Sacra," she said quickly in a tight, anxious voice, "Garth is my husband."

"It's true, babe," Silver said with a dismissive wave of his hand. "He certainly does not look like your type, and you know exactly what I mean."

"Sacra, please . . ."

Garth walked the rest of the way across the room, to his wife, pointedly turning his back on the tall man sitting in the leather recliner. My brother's movements were slow, lazy, almost to the point of exaggeration. If I'd been Sacra Silver, I'd have begun giving quick and serious thought to abandoning my present position. He obviously had no idea at all of what type Garth really was. I did. I knew the warning signals when I saw them, and when Garth spoke, it only confirmed my suspicions that Mr. Sacra Silver was shortly about to encounter more trouble than he was likely to know how to handle. I wasn't inclined to warn him. Silver remained serenely stretched out in the chair, his fingertips pressed together and forming a tent under his chin as he stared at my brother's broad back.

"What is it, Mary?" Garth asked in a soft, perfectly calm voice.

"Talk to me. Who is this man, and what does he want? Tell me what's going on."

"Sacra and I have known each other a long time, Garth," Mary said in a voice that trembled. "He and I—"

Suddenly the man in the recliner snapped his fingers, producing a loud, popping sound. Mary immediately fell silent, turned away from Garth, and covered her face with her hands. Her reaction startled me.

Garth didn't appear to react at all. His movement as he turned to face Sacra Silver was even more exaggeratedly slow. "Tell me why you're here," he said to the man in a voice that was only a half decibel above a whisper.

"I'm going to cut through all this bullshit," Silver announced to my brother, not even bothering to look at him. "It will save us all a lot of trouble and aggravation. Mary and I go back a long time. You may be her husband now, but believe me when I tell you that doesn't mean jack shit—not to her, and certainly not to me. We've shared more than she and you ever could. She may be married to you, hiding out here in Cairn, but all the time she's really been waiting for me to come back around. Well, I have. I'm here. If I know Mary, she's never even mentioned my name. But I can tell you that there hasn't been a moment of your life together that she hasn't been thinking of me. She belongs to me, Frederickson. That's it. Nobody's going to sneak around doing anything behind your back. I've given it to you straight and up front; she's mine, and I'm here to reclaim her. It's very simple, so don't make the mistake of trying to make anything complicated about it. You're out of the picture, out of this house. She doesn't want you here any longer. Now, let me hear you say you understand what I've just said."

Well. Let it be said for Sacra Silver that he had chutzpah, if not a keen sensitivity to the danger inherent in irritating my brother. For a moment, it occurred to me that this might all be an elaborate practical joke: Sacra Silver, an old friend of Mary's, perhaps a character actor specializing in playing outrageous, creepy types, had dropped by, and they had decided it might be fun to play a little trick on Garth. But, of course, it wasn't that at all. Mary was clearly terrified of the man. Sacra Silver was a wild card.

"Now I understand the stage name," I said cheerfully to the man in the chair. "You're a comedian."

"Shut up," Silver said in a perfunctory tone, continuing to stare at the opposite wall. "This is between Mary, her old man, and me. Butt out."

"Mary," Garth said in the same soft tone, "I'm asking you to tell me what's going on here. Who is this man?"

"Garth," Mary stammered, "it isn't . . . I don't . . . I'm so sorry. I'm just . . ."

"He's your guest, Mary, so it's up to you to tell him it's time to leave. I think you should do it now. Then we can talk."

Garth waited perhaps five seconds, just long enough to watch his wife helplessly glance back and forth between him and the man in the chair. Mary seemed incapable of speaking or moving. Then Garth abruptly turned, walked over to Silver, grabbed the front of the man's shirt, and pulled him to his feet. The T-shirt ripped, baring Silver's chest, revealing an enormous, grotesque tattoo of a black, spiderlike creature with large emerald eyes in a tortured human face.

"You're in my chair," Garth said in the same mild tone he had used with his wife. "I want you out of it, and I want you out of—"

Sacra Silver reached back with his right hand to his hip pocket, drew something out. There was a sharp, ominous click. I started to shout a warning, but there was no need. Mary screamed when the multi-bladed butterfly knife glinted in the bright lights of the room, but Garth was ready. He released his grip on the man's tattered shirt just in time, and the blades sliced through the empty air where his wrist had been a moment before. Garth popped him with a left jab to the nose, then hit him hard with a right hand to the stomach, doubling Silver over. He grabbed the wrist of the hand holding the knife, twisted. The weapon clattered to the floor. Then Garth stepped around behind the man, grabbed the nape of his neck with one hand and his belt with the other. Garth turned him around, marched him unceremoniously to the open window at the front of the room, and tossed him out headfirst, just beyond the edge of the outside deck. I nodded appreciatively. There hadn't been a wasted motion.

I had heard no sound behind me, but perhaps that was understandable considering all the commotion in front of me. I started when I felt a small hand touch my back. I turned, and was startled and alarmed to see Vicky, barefoot and sleepy-eyed, staring up at me. I did not think we had been making that much noise, but it had obviously carried to the bedrooms in the west wing of the house.

"Mr. Mongo?" the child said.

Garth was Garth to the child, and Mary simply Mary. But I was still "Mr. Mongo," a title I had bestowed upon myself when I had first met her, under rather perilous circumstances, and had made a desperate bid for her trust—and all-important silence— by telling her I was Santa's chief helper. "Hello, sweetie," I said, quickly stepping in front of her and stroking her cheek. "What are you doing up?"

"What's wrong, Mr. Mongo?"

What was wrong was the spectacle of violence. In the two years since we had taken responsibility for her, Garth, April, and I had gone to great pains to insulate Vicky from all kinds of violent images; the girl had seen enough death and suffering, and heard enough screaming, to last more than a lifetime. Now I swept her up in my arms, cradled her head on my chest, and turned so that she could not see the expression of terror and shock on Mary's face. "Nothing's wrong, sweetheart," I whispered in her ear. "Garth just dropped something."

Garth stood very still in front of the window, watching me, his face impassive, but his eyes gleaming with anxiety. The child in my arms was breathing regularly, and her eyes were closed. I nodded reassuringly to my brother, and only then did he turn, lean out the open window, and look down at the water below. He remained there for almost a minute, but apparently didn't see anything, for he finally turned away and headed for the door.

"Don't go down there, Garth," Mary said in a low voice that vibrated with tension. "It's a trick. You don't know anything about him. He's a very dangerous man."

Garth stopped and stared at his wife, and I could see in his soulful brown eyes the same surprise and confusion I felt at Mary's curious behavior. Garth and I had seen Mary shot at, and we had witnessed her instantly turn away from a lifelong faith in pacifism to shoot a man who had been about to kill Garth. Mary Tree was certainly no coward, and yet she appeared to be totally intimidated by the man Garth had just thrown out the window. Finally Garth simply shook his head, turned, and walked out of the room. Mary put one hand to her mouth and looked at me in alarm. I didn't know what to do, and so I merely shrugged as best I could with the girl in my arms. After a few more moments of hesitation, Mary bolted for the door to go after Garth.

Satisfied that Vicky was asleep, I carried her back to her bedroom. I put her to bed, tucked her in, then went out, closing the door quietly behind me. I went back to the music room, walked over to the window, leaned over, and looked down. Garth was almost directly below me, slowly paddling his canoe in the area where Sacra Silver would have fallen. The river's surface was placid, reflecting the light from the full moon overhead. Mary was out of sight, and I assumed she was standing up on the section of beach beneath the overhang. Garth looked up, saw me at the window.

"Can you see anything from up there?" my brother asked.

I shook my head, then turned away from the window and headed for the door.

Garth stayed out on the river almost forty minutes, paddling the canoe in ever-widening circles in a systematic search for our departed guest. Finally he paddled back to shore, pulled the craft up onto the beach in front of the boathouse, then came over to where I was standing next to a silent, pensive Mary. I noticed that Garth did not look at his wife.

"He's not dead, Garth," Mary blurted suddenly, turning and gripping Garth's right forearm with both hands. "He just wants you to think he's dead, make you worry. I know him." She paused and sucked in a deep breath, screwed her eyes shut, and rapidly shook her head back and forth. "Damn him. *Damn him!*"

"I'm not worried," Garth said in an even tone. "If he's dead, so be it. I'll take the consequences. If he's not dead, he'd better stop playing possum pretty damn quick and get his goddamn car out of the driveway."

My brother abruptly turned and headed up the path to the side door. Mary and I followed. Inside the house, he went directly to the telephone in his office, called the Cairn police. He calmly, without any hesitation, told whoever was on the other end of the line what had happened. When I noticed that Mary was no longer standing beside me, I went out of Garth's office, returned to the music room. Mary was standing at the open window, staring out into the night. I went to her, placed my hand gently on her back; her muscles were hard, knotted.

"So?" I said to my brother as he entered the room.

"Harry's coming over to check it out and take a statement."

"Did you tell Harry he pulled a knife on you?" I asked, glancing over to the spot on the floor beside the recliner where the butter-fly knife had fallen.

"I did."

Now there was a long, uncomfortable silence. Both Garth and I glanced over at Mary, who, for the first time since I had known her, looked all of her forty-five years of age, even older. She still seemed afraid, but in addition now appeared confused, as if she could not quite come to grips with what had happened—whatever that might be. The visit of her decidedly strange friend had apparently ended in tragedy. I wanted to go to her, to find words to bridge the gap that had suddenly opened between her and my brother and me, but did not feel it was my place.

"I'm going back to the city now," I said to Garth. "I'll take Vicky with me; I think it's better that she be gone before Harry gets here and starts asking questions. She could wake up, and I don't think she needs to hear any of this."

"Agreed," Garth replied simply.

"Please don't go, Mongo," Mary said in a small voice. "Not . . . yet. I want to explain." She paused, looked at Garth. "With Sacra Silver, I just don't know where to begin."

I went over to the woman, took her hands in mine, kissed them. "You don't have to explain anything to me, Mary. I'm not the one who needs to understand. Aside from the fact that I don't want Vicky to know about any of this, it's really not my place to be here now. This is between you and Garth. I hope you understand."

Mary did not reply. When I let go of her hands, they dropped limply to her sides. I went to the guest room, quickly packed my clothes into my duffel bag. When I came out, Garth was waiting for me in the hallway. He had wrapped the sleeping girl in a blanket and was holding her in his arms. It was a wonderful picture. I felt awful.

"You've got enough clothes for her at the brownstone?" Garth asked.

"Yeah."

My brother carried Vicky out of the house, to the car, and gently laid her on the backseat. Garth now looked withdrawn, deeply troubled.

"I'm doing the right thing, aren't I, Garth? I'll stick around if you think it would help."

Garth shook his head. "No. You were absolutely right when you told Mary I'm the one she has to talk to. If Harry needs a statement from you, I'll have him call you in an hour or so."

"*You* call me if you need anything."

"Yeah."

"Good luck, Garth."

"Yeah."

As I pulled around the green Cadillac and out of the driveway, I could see Garth standing in a patch of bright moonlight, staring after me. Then the moon passed behind a cloud, and he was shrouded in darkness. I headed for the Palisades Parkway, and New York City.

CHAPTER THREE

Garth showed up at the brownstone on West Fifty-sixth Street three days later, a Wednesday morning. I was in my office on the first floor going over a file in preparation for a lunch meeting with a client, with Vicky sitting next to me on the floor, reading a book. The door opened, and Garth leaned in. He was carrying a large suitcase.

Garth said simply, "I'm back, Mongo."

"Garth!" Vicky shrieked with delight when she saw my brother. She put her book to one side, jumped up, and ran to him with outstretched arms. "Are you going to take me back to your house?"

"Nope," Garth replied as he swept up the child with his free hand. "I'm going to stay with you and Mongo here in the city for a while. Want to help me unpack?"

Vicky nodded eagerly, and Garth said to me, "See you later, brother," before turning away, closing the door behind him.

I waited ten minutes, impatiently drumming my fingers on the top of my desk, and then I got up and went into the adjoining office to give some instructions to Francisco Gonzalez, my secretary. Then I went upstairs to Garth's apartment on the fifth floor. I found him and Vicky in the bedroom, unpacking his suitcase.

"Vicky," I said to the girl, "Francisco knows how you like to work with his computer, and he wants to give you another lesson. But you have to go down right now, while he has the time."

The child gave a little squeal of delight. She ran to the door, then suddenly stopped and looked back, a pensive expression on her face. "Is it all right, Garth? I said I'd help you unpack."

Garth nodded. "It's all right, sweetheart. I'm almost finished. Go ahead."

I waited until I heard Vicky's footsteps recede down the stairway, then went and closed the bedroom door. Garth resumed unpacking his suitcase, transferring shorts and handkerchiefs to the top drawer of his dresser. It was the largest suitcase he owned, and he'd brought a lot of clothes. I did not think that boded well.

"Garth, I didn't call because I didn't want to intrude."

"I know that," my brother replied in a flat tone.

"When I didn't hear from Harry, I figured there was no problem with the police, and I didn't think that whatever else was going on was any of my business. It's not that I wasn't concerned."

"I know that too, Mongo. I should have called you. I'm sorry. I . . . just didn't feel like talking."

"Do you feel like talking now?"

"Not particularly."

"All right, *will* you talk? Mary means something to me too, you know. I love both of you, and I've never met a couple who looked more in love than the two of you. I can't believe this is happening."

"I know the feeling," Garth replied drily as he picked up a handful of ties, then walked to the closet and began to drape them over a tie rack. "What do you want to know, Mongo?"

"For openers, what's the story on the guy you threw through the window?"

"They haven't found a body in the river, he hasn't shown up anywhere else, and, so far, nobody's filed a missing persons report. As far as the cops are concerned, if there's no body and no missing persons report, there's no problem. Mary backed up my story of what happened, and Harry took the knife with him. I pushed the Cadillac out onto the street. That's about it."

"Who the hell was the guy, Garth?"

It seemed to me Garth hesitated just a moment before answering. "An old boyfriend."

"How old? Where the hell did he come from?"

Garth had finished hanging up his ties, but he remained standing in the doorway of the closet, with his back to me. "I don't know the answer to either of those questions, Mongo. Mary freezes up whenever she tries to talk about him. As close as I can figure, she got involved with the guy twelve or thirteen years ago, before she got involved with the Fellowship of Conciliation and moved to Cairn."

"Christ, Garth, it's hard for me to imagine Mary hooking up with such a weirdo—an obnoxious weirdo, to boot."

"To you and me, maybe, but apparently not to her. Who knows? What I do know is that she's very much afraid of him."

"Why?"

"I don't know, Mongo. I get the impression he has something on her that she doesn't want me to know."

"Jesus, Garth, it's been three days. You haven't been able to talk this out?"

"No. She can't seem to talk about her past with this man without ending up crying hysterically, or just clamming up and staring off into space. She did manage to tell me that they were lovers back then, and that they met at a time when her career was at its low ebb. She says he left her, but she can't—or won't—tell me why he should show up again after all this time."

"Now that she's on top again, maybe he wants her back for her celebrity value. Not to mention her money."

Garth shrugged his broad shoulders. "There's also the question of how he found out she lives in Cairn."

"Mary Tree may not be listed in the phone book, but you are, and it's no big secret that Mary Tree lives in Rockland County, or that she's married to you. Garth, you think Mary still carries a torch for this guy? Is that what this is all about?"

"I don't know how she feels about him romantically; I only know she's afraid of him. She doesn't think he's dead."

"Assuming he didn't land the wrong way and break his neck, and that he's a good swimmer, he could have stayed underwater after you threw him in the river, swum up under the overhang out of your line of sight, and then split before you got down there. The question is, why would he do it? And, once out of the water, why not just get in his car and drive away, or at least come back for it later? It seems silly to disappear and let his car sit out on the street collecting tickets. What would be the point?"

Still with his back to me, Garth began rummaging around among his suits, then began rearranging the ties he had just put on the rack. "I don't know," he said at last. "Mary said something about it being his way of trying to do a number on our heads. She called it a magical attack. It didn't mean anything to me, and, like I said, Mary hasn't been very good at explaining things."

I felt a tightening in my throat. The words meant something to me, not only as a result of the time I had spent with the decidedly good witch, April, but as the legacy of a deadly confrontation, many years before, with a decidedly evil band of self-described super-witches, so-called ceremonial magicians, in New York.

"Mary ever into the occult?" I asked quietly, watching my brother's back.

"You know she's heavily involved with her church."

"I'm not talking about Christianity. I'm talking about witchcraft, voodoo, astrology, that sort of thing."

My brother grunted. "When did you start making such fine distinctions between beliefs in the supernatural?"

"I'm making them for purposes of this discussion. What about it? Was Mary ever into witchcraft?"

"What's your point, Mongo?"

"You said she used the words 'magical attack' to describe Sacra Silver's disappearing act. That's a wicca concept and term. One difference between wicca and the big-time religions is that wicca isn't centered around one deity. Witches don't pray to get what they want, they manipulate; they *do* things, for good or bad. They try to shape events by, in one way or another, enforcing their will on others. To wit, Silver tried to get Mary away from you, and you out of her life, through sheer intimidation. That didn't work; you threw him out the window. So what does he do? Give up? No. Disappearing like that could be his way of making sure that he remains the focus of your lives, that he stays between you. You have to be able to think like a witch. Going away like he did could be his means of *not* going away. It's a very witchy thing to do."

"You're putting me on, right, Mongo?"

"He hasn't really gone away, has he? *You* went away, which is all Sacra Silver wanted from the beginning."

Garth's reply was a halfhearted shrug.

"Right now Mary presumably believes in Holy Trinities, virgin births, messiahs, life after death, and various other tenets of Christianity. What notions do you suppose she had thirteen years ago, when she became involved with Silver?"

"I don't know, Mongo," Garth said wearily. "When you get right down to it, I just don't really know all that much about my wife's background, outside of her music and career. She doesn't talk about her past, except for the things everybody knows. I didn't—don't—care who she was with, or what she did, before we met. I just loved her. As far as I was concerned, everything important in our lives together started on the day you brought me those tapes she'd given you to give to me."

"Garth," I sighed, "I have to say something. And then I have to ask you a question."

"Mongo, I guess maybe I wish you wouldn't do either."

"By your own admission, Mary's very disturbed about Sacra Silver, dead or alive. In your own words, she's damn well afraid of him. If you'd found them in bed together, or if she'd tossed you out because she said she wanted to go back with her old boyfriend, that would be one thing. But that's not what happened. She's so upset, so afraid, that she can't even bring herself to talk about who he is, or what it is about him that so terrifies her. Your wife's in a lot of trouble, Garth. My question is, what are you and your damn suitcase doing here?"

Garth remained unmoving and silent for what seemed to me to be a very long time, but probably wasn't. It would be understandable if he was offended, considering what I had just said, but I'd felt I'd had to tell him what was on my mind. Then he slowly turned around to face me, and I could see that he wasn't offended; he was crying. Garth didn't cry like other people; there was no sobbing, no facial distortion, no strangled speech, virtually nothing changed in his speech or appearance, except for the tears that welled in his bloodshot eyes and streamed down his cheeks.

"I can't help her, Mongo," he said evenly as he walked back across the room and sat down on the bed.

"Who says?"

"She won't let me. I guess you may be right about his disappearing the way he did being his way of making sure he wouldn't go away. Like you pointed out, it sure as hell worked. These last three days have been hell, with him right there between us whenever we looked at each other, or when I tried to get her to talk about it. I'll tell you something I do know, Mongo. She's afraid, all right, but she's not afraid for herself; she never was. She's afraid for me. She really does seem to believe that this creep is some kind of sorcerer who's sold his soul to the devil in exchange for special powers over people; she believes he can hurt me in some terrible way if he chooses to, and that he can't be stopped."

"I thought you said she couldn't talk about him."

"Put together enough incomplete sentences and sometimes you'll get a whole thought or two."

"Witchcraft and Satanism are two different things, brother, and Silver could be into either, or both. The principle is the same: you work on people's heads. I'd say Mr. Silver has worked on Mary's head real good in the past, because he certainly has power over her. All he has to do is show up after thirteen years, and she falls to pieces. But I still don't understand why the hell you're here, and not there."

"My being there only makes matters worse. That night and the next morning, it was only her past and Sacra Silver that Mary couldn't talk about. By yesterday morning, she didn't seem to be able to talk about anything at all. You could see the strain just continuing to build up in her. And then she said something that . . . bothered me. She told me he wouldn't hurt her, but that he

32

would hurt me, and you, and everybody else she and I care about until he got what he wanted, namely her. She said she would never go back with him, but that I should maybe go away. Mongo, she wanted me to run away from a man who's probably dead. That's how little faith she has in my ability to handle this thing. Can you understand how *small* that made me feel? That's when I felt myself slipping back to the . . . *nothing* I felt inside myself when I was poisoned with the NPD. Just by walking into our house, this man took away Mary's faith in me, and maybe my own in myself."

I stood and stared at my brother, feeling very uncomfortable. His alluding to the emptiness he had felt when he'd been poisoned sounded alarm bells. Years before, when Garth had still been a New York cop, somebody had slipped him a dose of a mysterious and potent chemical called nitrophenyldienal, "spy dust," the properties of which were still classified top secret by the government. He had not only nearly "lost" himself, but I'd thought I'd lost him. He'd survived, but the experience had changed him forever. However, none of the changes he'd undergone had made him weaker, less strong-willed. Quite the contrary.

"Are you going to be all right, Garth?" I asked tightly.

He nodded. "I'm all right now. I'm just explaining why I had to leave."

"Sacra Silver didn't do this to you, Garth; Mary did. I love her too, but obviously not the way you do. When you give of yourself like you have, it makes you vulnerable; it gives to the person you love the power to hurt you very deeply. In your case, I'm thinking that kind of hurt could literally be fatal."

My brother shook his head. "I don't know how to fight him. I can punch him out, throw him in the river, maybe even kill him, but none of that seems to make the slightest impression on my wife. She's still afraid of him—afraid for me. She believes Silver is a man I can't handle, and it's that *attitude* I can't handle."

"She loves you, Garth, and she doesn't want you hurt. You have to give her points for that."

He nodded, but tears continued to stream down his cheeks. "It doesn't matter, Mongo. If she loves me so much that she pushes me away and humiliates me in an effort to save me from ghosts that exist only in her mind, then it would be better if she didn't love me; if we were just friends, at least she might be able to confide in me. I'd rather she hated me than loved me and . . . do this. I tried to explain that to her this morning, but by then I wasn't able to talk too well myself. I can't fight ghosts, Mongo; I can't help her fight her terror if she won't let me. I couldn't— can't—deal with it. That's why I'm here, and not there."

I glanced at my watch. I had to leave for my luncheon meeting, and after that I had to zip down to Foley Square to give a deposition. With luck, I would be finished by four-thirty; assuming rush-hour traffic wasn't hopelessly snarled on the West Side Highway or George Washington Bridge, I figured I could be in Cairn by early evening. "I'd like your permission to drive up and talk to her."

The tears had abruptly stopped. Garth rose from the bed, closed his suitcase, carried it to the closet. "You don't need my permission to talk to Mary, brother. Like you said, she's your friend too. You introduced us to each other."

"I don't want my brother to think I'm butting into his business."

Garth, completely clear-eyed now, turned to face me. "I don't think you're butting into my business, Mongo. As a matter of fact, it looks like my wife and I could use your help now. She's in trouble, in her head, and she won't let me help her, which gives me trouble with *my* head. Whatever Sacra Silver has on her, if he does have anything on her, doesn't matter. It's her fear that's tearing us apart, not Sacra Silver. She has to trust me and our love enough to let us work this out together."

"I'll give her the message." I walked to the door of the bedroom, turned back. "I'm thinking that dealing with Mary's haunts may keep us preoccupied for a while. Maybe we should cut Vicky's visit with us short."

Garth nodded curtly. "I'll call April."

"You want me to call? It might be easier for me to explain."

"No, Mongo; I'll call. I don't have any trouble explaining the situation to other people. It's my wife I can't talk to."

•   •   •

Sacra Silver's car was back in the driveway. I pulled my Volkswagen Rabbit up behind it. I got out, walked up the flagstone path to the front door, knocked. There was no answer, and I knocked again. I hadn't called first, because I hadn't been sure what I wanted to say over the phone; also, considering Mary's state of mind, I had been concerned that she might simply refuse to see me. As a result, it could very well turn out that I was wasting my time. I knocked a third time. When there was still no answer, I tried the door. It was open, and I went in.

"Hello?" I called. "Mary, you home? It's Mongo."

I walked through the living room and down a connecting corridor to the music room, where I found Sacra Silver, to all appearances quite alive, sitting in Garth's chair. He was wearing new boots, brown, the same jeans, and a new T-shirt, this one yellow. He was sipping at what looked like Scotch or bourbon on the rocks, and he lifted the tumbler to me in a mock salute as I entered the room. His cold, piercing black eyes glittered with amusement, and his thin lips curled back in a sneer that was for him probably a genuine, heart-felt smile. He was obviously enjoying what he considered to be his little reincarnation joke, but he was going to be disappointed if he expected any reaction from me.

"How you doing there, big fella?" I said casually. "I was looking for Mary. Is she around?"

He was definitely disappointed at my lack of response to seeing him not only alive and well but back in Garth's home, and back in Garth's leather recliner. His smile, what little there had been of it, vanished. "If she was here, Frederickson, she'd most likely have answered the door, wouldn't she? Do you always walk into other people's homes uninvited?"

"No, but in this case the home happens to belong to my brother and sister-in-law. In the absence of an owner to tell me I'm not welcome, I guess I have as much right to be here as you do."

"What do you want?"

"Like I said, I want to talk to Mary."

35

"What if she doesn't want to talk to you?"

"Then I'll go home."

"She's at the hospital. I don't know when she'll be back."

"Who's hurt?"

The simulated smile returned to his face. "The assistant pastor at her church. The dumb schmuck was skulking around trying to hide a flag, of all things—something to do with an argument over whether it should be on the altar. The bozo was taking the sucker down into the basement; he tripped, fell down the stairs, and broke his back." Now Silver laughed, a kind of nasal bray that grated on my nerves. The image of a man breaking his back obviously amused him. "There must be a moral there someplace."

"If there is, I'm sure you'll tell me what it is."

Silver drained off his drink, set the tumbler down on the small, glass-topped table to his left, smacked his lips. "The moral of your story is that it doesn't make any difference whether or not you get to talk to Mary; there's nothing you can say that will make her change her mind about anything. She belongs to me, and she knows it. The sooner your brother realizes that and accepts it, the sooner he'll be able to get on with his life. Maybe he already has, because I understand he walked out of here this morning. Smart move. He doesn't know shit about Mary. For Christ's sake, they've been married two years, and he doesn't even realize she's queer, or that she spent six months in a mental hospital after she almost baked her brains on peyote. She and I have done things together she probably doesn't even remember."

"You know what Robin Williams says about the sixties," I replied with a shrug. "If you remember them, you probably weren't there. What's your point?"

He rattled the melting ice cubes, then leaned back in the chair, studying me through narrowed lids. He was obviously not getting the audience response he wanted, and now looked even more disappointed. "I'm saying that you're wasting your time if you came here to try to get Mary to change her mind."

I retrieved a straight-backed chair from across the room, pushed a microphone out of the way, and sat down across from the other man. "Big fella, you seem to be under the mistaken impression that I give a shit about what you, Mary, or Garth decide to do. I care what *happens* to my brother and Mary, and I wish them happiness, but I have enough trouble managing my own life and times without trying to tell other people how to manage theirs. I may think you're a prick for surfacing in their lives and disrupting them like you have, but you're Mary and Garth's problem, not mine. This matter is between the three of you, and it's none of my damn business."

I watched him watching me as he reached out with one of his long arms and began to absently turn his empty tumbler on the glass-topped table beside him. I knew he was trying to gauge my sincerity, and so I gazed back at him with my most sincere expression—which in this case was meant to project profound indifference. Finally he asked, "If you don't think it's any of your business, why are you here?"

"Just to touch base, say hello, and hear her tell me she's all right. Mary's more than just a sister-in-law, big fella, she's my friend. She talks to me. Does that make you nervous?"

Sacra Silver didn't like that, and he flushed slightly. "Nothing you could do or say would make me nervous, Frederickson. The fact of the matter is that I'll be surprised if she wants to talk to you about anything."

"We'll see, won't we?" I replied, leaning forward slightly in my chair. "I take it Sacra Silver is a witch name. You fancy yourself a ceremonial magician, or are you a member of a coven?"

That startled him. He recovered quickly, but not before I had seen the surprise reflected in his eyes, and watched him tense slightly. "What are you talking about?"

"Oh, come on, Sacra. Don't be coy. I can read your aura. You think you can practice the craft."

"You don't see shit," he said, but his tone was wary. "Where did you get that idea?"

"Oh, I don't know. The notion might have come up in a conversation between Garth and me, which means it probably came up in a conversation between Garth and Mary."

His response was to shake his head. "Mary would never say . . . Your brother didn't hear anything like that from Mary."

"If you say so. Then I must have heard it someplace else."

"How do you know the term 'ceremonial magician'? What do you know about the craft?"

Feigning indifference in Sacra Silver and all his works, I had apparently managed to pique his interest, and in the past I had often been downright amazed at how much curious people will reveal about themselves as they attempt to probe the lives of another person. I wasn't interested in killing this particular cat, only hooking him. I figured I had done that, and that it was time to play him on the line for a while to see if I might not be able to cast a little spell of my own. I flashed what I hoped was an enigmatic smile, rose. "I think I'll have a drink," I said, and started for the door. Then, in what I hoped was an Oscar-winning characterization of debonair indifference laced with graciousness, I paused, turned back, and pointed to his empty glass. I asked casually, "You want another one?"

Sacra Silver was either too distracted to question this rather odd gesture of subservience or just too lazy to get up and get his own drink. He only thought about it for a second or two, then picked up his glass and held it out to me. "Yeah," he said somewhat absently. "Dewar's."

Holding the tumbler by the base, I went to the kitchen, headed directly for the cabinet where Mary kept her plastic wrap. I had already taken note of the license plate of the car in the driveway, but somehow Sacra Silver didn't seem to me to be a green Cadillac kind of guy, and I thought the vehicle might be a company car or borrowed; besides, I wanted more than what I could get from Motor Vehicles—assuming there was more to get. I tore off a sheet of the plastic, wrapped it around the tumbler, which I placed at the back of the shelf, behind a jar of spaghetti sauce. Then I went to the bar in the living room, put some ice into an identical tumbler, splashed in some Dewar's. I poured myself a Jack Daniel's on the rocks, then headed back to the spider in the music room.

"Ceremonial magic is a bit different from garden-variety witch-craft, isn't it, pal?" I said easily as I handed him his fresh drink. "More dangerous. The ceremonial magician works alone. You don't have other members of a coven to help you absorb the

38

rebound you're going to get if you attack somebody you shouldn't, namely a person who can reflect the bad news back at you."

"You're very well read, Frederickson," Silver said in a neutral tone.

"Oh, I'm more than well read. Let's see what *you* know about ceremonial magic and other aspects of the craft. Here's a witch name for you: Esobus. Ever hear that one?"

He did not reply, but he moved his chair back an inch or two, and pulled his chin in slightly, as if to protect himself. His jet-black eyes now reflected not only surprise but growing caution, perhaps even concern.

"Okay," I continued, "that one stumped you. Let's try a few more. Sandor Peth? John Krowl? Daniel? Who's buried in Aleister Crowley's tomb?"

"Peth, Krowl, and Daniel are legendary ceremonial magicians," Silver replied tightly.

"Dead legendary ceremonial magicians. I could mention a few more names you might recognize, and they're dead too. Actually, they were mostly legends in their own minds—and yours, I guess. Except for Daniel and Esobus, they were real idiots, preying on idiots."

"You're full of shit, Frederickson."

"Oh, no, I'm not. You know I know what I'm talking about."

I could see that he was struggling not to say the word, but it came out anyway. "How?"

"I was once in love with a witch, who happened to save my life. Also, I once spent a few months dancing around with a bunch of creeps who had the same belief system I suspect you have. I picked up a few things. Those people I mentioned caught the biggest, damnedest rebound of all—death. Esobus, by the way, also saved my life, and I was sorry I couldn't return the favor. I was with her when she died."

"She?"

"Oh, yes. Esobus was a woman, and she happened to be a good friend of mine."

"I still say you're full of shit."

"Sure I am."

39

"Who was Esobus? What was her real name?"

"You sure as hell don't know, and you're not going to find out from me. When she died, she and I were the only two people who knew her secret. I think I'll keep it that way. I will tell you that she was a respected scientist who was trying to do a number on people like you who do numbers on other people. She looked on what she was doing as a research project, and she was under the mistaken impression that she was going to learn something valuable from the experience. All it did was kill her. I also knew Daniel, who happened to be a very good man. I can assure you the rest were idiots. I guess my point is that you should be careful who you choose as role models. I think I'm also offering you a little friendly advice about who you choose to throw bad spells at, because they're liable to bounce back and hit you right between the eyes. My experience has been that witches and ceremonial magicians who try to work the dark side of the craft are usually shits-for-brains. But hey, I'm not offending you, am I? We're just having a casual conversation about a particularly loony belief system, right? I mean, I know you don't think I'm suggesting that you're a shit-for-brains. If I did think that, I might try to catch you off guard and do a number on your head like you've done to Mary's—assuming, of course, that I cared one way or another."

"I can inflict great suffering on you, Frederickson," the other man said in a low, tense voice.

"The last man who said that to me died with blood running out of his mouth, nose, eyes, ears, and ass, and I didn't lay a finger on him. In a sense, he self-destructed. Just like you, he'd bought into a particularly dangerous belief system. Sure, you can hurt me, but I'm in no more danger from you than from any other pain in the ass who might come at me with a knife or gun. You're in more danger from what you believe than I am, because I don't believe it."

"I hope I never have to prove you wrong, Frederickson. I can make very bad things happen to you, and I don't need a knife or gun."

"For sure. You've already made something bad happen in this

house, but that's because one of the people involved, Mary, *believed* you could make bad things happen. The healthy response when she found you on her doorstep would have been to slam the door in your face, but her faith in your powers wouldn't permit her to do that. She let you into her home, and back into her life, and both she and the man who had faith in *her* are now suffering because of it. Mary's wound is self-inflicted, but the pain ends up shared. You control Mary because Mary believes you have the power to control her; by believing it, she makes it happen. It's a very sad, but simple, self-fulfilling prophecy."

"What's your faith, Frederickson? What do you believe in?"

"Gravity, mathematics, and mystery."

"What about God? Do you believe in God?"

"Now, there's a mystery."

Sacra Silver, squinting slightly, stared hard at me. I stared back. "You believe in yourself," he said at last. "And you believe in your brother. That's your faith. You believe that the two of you, working individually or together, can overcome virtually any difficulty."

"No, I don't believe that at all. I do imagine things, and one of the things I imagine is that I have enough sense not to let your imagination get the better of me. Imagination, of course, is the third leg of the Witch's Triangle, along with will and secrecy. I don't know how much will you have, because, so far, the only person I've seen you manipulate is Mary, and Mary's very impressionable. As for power you derive from secrecy, that remains to be seen. You use a witch name in your everyday life, which interests me. Most witches don't, you know. I imagine that if I nosed around enough to find out who you really are, your background and all that, the information might go a long way toward helping people who have let your imagination get the better of them."

He didn't like that at all. His black eyes flashed with anger, and his thin lips drew back from his teeth. "I tend to imagine horrible things happening to people who make themselves my enemies, Frederickson. Very horrible things. And sometimes the things I've imagined actually do happen to those people."

"That could easily be construed as a threat," I replied evenly, and smiled at him. "It's hard for me to believe that you take risks like that."

He frowned slightly. "What risk am I taking?"

"It's lucky for you I don't take your shade prince act too seriously, big fella. Let's just suppose I did. Suppose I believed that the next bad thing that happens to me is your fault, because you imagined it—cast a spell, so to speak. Naturally that would make me paranoid, and the focus of my paranoia would be you. Considering you responsible for the bad thing that's happened to me, I take the very unimaginative and unmagical step of walking up to you with a gun and blowing your brains out. A nonbeliever like me would call that poetic justice, but a witch would call it rebound. See what I mean about risk-taking? If I were you, I'd be downright careful about threatening anybody with as wispy a weapon as Sacra Silver's imagination."

"I don't make idle threats, Frederickson."

"Oh, *have* you been threatening me? I thought we were just having a casual conversation about having to be careful what you believe, because you tend to become what you believe."

"You said I was none of your business."

"I did say that, but just out of idle curiosity I'd like to know what brought you to Cairn in the first place. Was it because of Mary, or did you have some other business in town and then just happened to find out that she lives here now? Thirteen years is a long time to stay out of touch. And what do you really want from her? Money? Or do you just want to get your face on television at the next Grammy awards? What's the inside scoop on this sudden visitation?"

"Curiosity killed the cat, Frederickson."

"Funny, but I was thinking along those exact same lines not ten minutes ago."

"What the hell does that mean?"

I wasn't about to tell him what the hell that meant, any more than he was likely to tell me anything I really wanted to know, but I was spared the trouble of coming up with an evasive answer when Mary suddenly appeared at the door. She looked terrible;

the color was gone from her face, and her skin was blotchy. She had a tic in her left cheek.

"Hello, Mary," I said, rising to my feet.

Seeing me made her look even more stricken, and I suspected it had more than a little to do with the fact that I had found Sacra Silver in her house. She swallowed hard, glanced back and forth between Silver and me. "Mongo, I didn't know . . . Sacra's only been here since this afternoon."

She was trying to tell me Silver wasn't sleeping in Garth's bed, and I was glad to hear it. I raised my hand, shook my head. "You don't owe me any explanations, Mary. I just came by to see if you were all right. Mr. Silver and I have been passing the time with a pleasant conversation about witchcraft, ceremonial magic, imagination, and how bad things can happen to people who expect bad things to happen to them. Now, can you and I talk?"

Once again, she glanced uncertainly back and forth between the other man and me. "Mongo," she said in a small voice, "I don't think you can understand. I don't want anything to happen . . ."

"Mary, believe it or not, I think I do understand. You don't want anything bad to happen to Garth, or to me. I think you're trying very hard to protect Garth from harm. It's all right." I paused, turned to Silver. "Is it all right if I talk to Mary, big fella? You're not worried about anything, are you?"

"I'm not worried about a damn thing, Frederickson."

"Good," I said, taking Mary's hand and leading her toward the door. "See you later. Don't let anything bad happen to you while we're gone."

Chapter Four

How's your assistant pastor?" I asked as I stroked, then feathered with my paddle to keep the canoe on a steady course as we headed upriver, against the current. We were about thirty yards from shore. It was a clear, warm night, and the river was unusually still, at least on the surface. I was a firm believer in the calming influence of large bodies of water, and when we had come out of the house I had suggested that we go out on the river. When Mary hadn't objected, I'd dragged the large, steel Grumman down the beach, seated Mary in the bow, then sat in the stern, along with a bottle of wine, corkscrew, and two glasses I'd snatched from the bar and wine rack on our way out. From her position in the bow, Mary stroked regularly and with power, her back muscles rippling beneath the light sweater she wore.

Mary shrugged. "Sacra told you about it?"

"He said something about the man falling down some stairs and breaking his back while he was looking for someplace to hide a flag."

"He thinks somebody pushed him."

44

"Thinks? Wouldn't he know if he was pushed?"

"He's in a great deal of pain, and very depressed. He can't remember things clearly right now."

"I thought that issue had been resolved a while ago."

Mary was quiet for some time. Finally she said, "It was; the flag was to remain on the altar. Tim—our assistant pastor—just felt it was wrong, blasphemous. It ate at him. He wanted to remove it one more time, as a symbolic gesture. He believed it was what God wanted him to do. Now he's not only in the hospital, but I think the congregation is going to vote to fire him. I wish he hadn't done it."

I imagined the assistant pastor also wished now he hadn't done it, but I didn't say so. Instead, I steered us out another fifteen yards to where two buoys constructed from plastic soda bottles marked the ends of a drift net that had either been set for the night or not picked up during the day. I grabbed hold of the closest buoy, tied on with the painter attached to the stern of the canoe. "Time for some refreshment," I said.

Mary set her paddle down, turned around, then sat in the bottom of the canoe, resting her arms on the gunwales. I slid down, opened the wine, filled two glasses, and handed one to her. Mary sipped at her wine, then gazed out over the moon-washed river, which was still tinted red with bloodtide.

"You don't look good, Mary," I continued quietly. "You don't look good at all."

"I've got things on my mind."

"Sacra Silver."

Now she looked at me, her blue eyes glittering in the moon-light. "I know you came in and found Sacra there, Mongo, but he'd only come to the house a few hours before. Things aren't what they seem."

"How do you know how things seem to me, Mary?"

I waited for a reply, but there was none. She again looked out over the river. In the distance, out in the deep channel, an enor-mous tanker was making its way downriver, its dark bulk silhou-etted against the bright lights on the Westchester shore.

"It seems to me that you and Garth love each other," I contin-ued. "It seems to me that the two of you were building a fine life

45

together here in Cairn. Then one day somebody out of your past shows up, and you fall to pieces. You let the guy run off at the mouth about you belonging to him, and telling Garth he should leave so that you and the guy can take up where you left off thirteen years ago. It seems to me that you may think you're doing what you're doing to protect Garth. Sacra Silver just isn't your type, Mary."

"I hate him!" she snapped with an abruptness that startled me, arching her neck and spitting out the words. "I *hate* him!"

"Then why—?"

"Sacra *can* make very bad things happen to people, Mongo."

"Like what? Does he beat them up? Write nasty letters? Make obscene phone calls?"

"You don't take him seriously."

"I take you seriously. What does Sacra Silver do to make bad things happen to people? I saw him draw a knife on my brother, and we both watched Garth take it away from him, in a manner of speaking. Don't you think Garth can take care of himself?"

Mary shook her head. "Mongo, I love Garth more than I've ever loved any man. I don't think I ever really knew what love was all about until I met Garth. If anything ever happened to him, I think I'd die."

"That doesn't jibe with the way you've been acting."

"Garth has never met anyone like Sacra, Mongo. Neither have you."

"You're quite wrong, Mary, but that's beside the point. I'm not about to bore you with stories about the kinds of people Garth has dealt with, real bad guys who would eat Mr. Silver for lunch."

Again, she shook her head. "Sacra doesn't hurt people himself, at least not with his hands, or with weapons. He just *makes* bad things happen."

"You mean he can will things to happen?"

She nodded.

"That's your first mistake, Mary—believing that Silver can just will things to happen, or that he has special powers. Right now he has power, but it's over *you*, and you've given him that power by believing his bullshit. The terrible irony is that something bad certainly has happened, to you and Garth. I suppose you could argue that Silver made it happen, but that isn't true. He *wanted* to come between you and Garth, but *you* granted his wish by your reaction to him. That's how witchcraft works. Garth can fight Silver, but he can't fight you; he loves you way too much for that. By trying to protect him by preventing him from protecting you, you've caused him great hurt. You've made it appear that you believe negatively in Silver more than you believe positively in Garth, and that hurt him terribly. It hurt him so much that he had to leave. Presto. Silver gets what he wants. But there's nothing magical about it, is there?"

The wake from a passing powerboat hit us, causing the canoe to bob and the plastic bottles to scrape against the canoe's metal skin. I braced my arms on the gunwales to steady us as I met Mary's gaze. There was a different light in her eyes now, perhaps reflecting understanding, a different set to her mouth. I thought I might finally be getting her attention.

"Does Garth think I want to be with Sacra?" she asked quietly.

"I'm not sure. Garth isn't thinking too clearly right now. You've certainly made it appear that way. Garth isn't a jealous man, Mary, but he is a very proud man. He loves you dearly. He would fight for you, die for you without a moment's hesitation. What he won't do is fight to *keep* you; he would figure that it's up to you to decide who you want to be with. If you wanted to be with somebody else, he would simply accept that decision. I suspect he's thinking along those lines now, because, at best, you've been sending him very mixed signals by what you've done and not done. You've hurt his pride. He sees that you're deeply troubled, but he feels that you pushed him away when he tried to help. That's what he can't abide."

Mary sighed deeply, gazed down at the bottom of the canoe. "Sacra can bring harm to people, Mongo. It isn't something I believe, it's something I know. You have a point when you say that Sacra has already hurt Garth through me, but it's not that simple. Sacra controls other people too; there are a number of men and women who will do whatever Sacra tells them to do. There are people who will kill for him; he doesn't have to do it himself. That's why I've . . . done what I've done. I can't bear the thought of Sacra and his people harming Garth. If the price I pay is having him leave me, then I'd rather pay it than have Garth hurt—or dead. That's what could happen if Sacra doesn't get his way."

Now it was my turn to sigh. "Mary, you can't shut out Garth. The price you're paying is worse than wasted, worse than if you were simply getting nothing in return. What you've bought so far is misery for the two of you. Again, I'm not going to bore you with war stories, but I can absolutely assure you that your old boyfriend is a pussycat compared to some of the people my brother has handled in the past. But don't *you* defeat Garth. You've got to have faith in him."

Once again, Mary was silent for a long time. I poured some more wine, watched her watching the river. The tanker in the deep channel was well past us now, heading for the large, central span beneath the Tappan Zee Bridge. We would soon be bobbing up and down again when its bow wave and wake reached us.

"Talking to you makes me feel better, Mongo."

"Thank you, Mary. That's a nice compliment."

"I lose myself when Sacra is around. He's always had that effect on me. I just . . . get lost. He's a manipulator, and I know it, but I just can't seem to stop him from manipulating me. He's a spiritual terrorist; he finds out what people believe in, and then he goes to work on their hearts."

"Mary, I don't understand what you mean. I don't understand just what it is you perceive that he can do to people, aside from rounding up some gang to beat on somebody. You're saying it's more than that."

"Garth wouldn't understand either. That's because you and Garth have no faith."

The bow wave from the passing tanker finally reached us, and the thick, lazy swell rolled under the canoe, lifting us up, dropping us down in its trough. The strands of the drift net scraped against the gunwale beneath my right arm. I sipped at my wine, asked quietly, "Why do you say that?"

"Neither of you believe in God. You're not religious."

"I believe in mystery. So does Garth."

"Now I'm the one who doesn't understand."

"Mary, there's nothing mysterious about religions—any of them. They all try to give you recipes, recipe religion; cook your life like our priests tell you, and God will reward you. I don't remember exactly when it was, but I wasn't very old. I was sitting in church one Sunday, and I suddenly realized that I didn't buy any of it; I didn't believe any of the things that my parents and those other people there presumably believed that was prompting them to worship and pray to some all-powerful, invisible thing. When that thought first occurred to me, when I first realized I didn't believe in the God I thought everybody in the world believed in, I got real scared. For just a moment, I thought I was going to die, to be punished by that God for not believing in messiahs, miracles, and all that other stuff I know you believe in. Then it occurred to me that, if God was omniscient, if He or She already knew what I was thinking anyway, then it didn't make any difference. There was no point in trying to hide what I thought. And I wasn't afraid anymore. After all, I was only using the brain God had presumably given me in the first place. What replaced the fear was a sense of indescribable *awe* in the face of the universe, of eternity. I couldn't feel that while I was preoccupied with trying to learn a recipe for living, which in my case just happened to be of the Christian variety. Religions *demystify,* Mary. They consistently trivialize the notion of God."

"Does what you just said mean you do believe in God?"

"It doesn't mean I believe or disbelieve, Mary. It means that I consider God, whatever that may be, irrelevant. There's no value in thinking about gods one way or another. Being distracted about what some god does or doesn't want leads as often to hatred and murder as it does to anything beneficial; that's not a belief or opinion, it's history. And so I believe in mystery, which is much more self-evident than any deity. Look at this river, the moon; think of the sun, and the planets, and billions more like them, but mostly look at this river, and *feel* its power passing beneath you. Hey, what do you want for your nickel? You want to live forever? How about living right now? For all the beauty and wonder surrounding you right now, there is no power in the river, or sea, compared to the tides of the human heart. I don't mean to sound disrespectful, Mary, but do you really think a god who created this river, the moon overhead, and the human heart is really going to give a shit what you eat, or anything else you do? Give me a break. There is no magic in life, no miracles. But there is a whole lot of mystery, and God is just a metaphor for the mystery. Humans diminish themselves, and miss the mystery, when they worship the metaphor. Love, my friend, is the greatest mystery of all."

"I love Garth very much, Mongo."

"I'm not the one you should be telling that to. Start believing in your love, and stop believing in the magical powers of Sacra Silver. Garth will survive if you fail to do that, Mary, but you may not. Beliefs like the ones you seem to have can kill. Stop being a victim."

"I met him at a time when my whole life was in ruins," Mary said in a tone that was soft and distant, but not strained. "The Beatles and the Rolling Stones were in, and the music I was doing was out. Bobby, he made the adjustment—he *led* the adjustment. Later, Judy did too. I couldn't. I didn't know how to do anything but sing folk songs. My records weren't selling, and finally my record company didn't bother pressing any more. I didn't have a recording contract, and I couldn't even get small-town club dates. It was like starting all over again, playing for private parties and in bars. It was a nightmare. I started drinking a lot and then doing drugs, just to get through each day. I almost died from an overdose of peyote and wound up in a mental hospital. To tell you the truth, I don't remember exactly where I met Sacra; I just woke up one morning in whatever seedy hotel I was in and found him in bed with me. At the time, I thought he was the strongest man I had ever met. He was able to take over my life because he gave me something to live for. He told me what to do, and I did it, because it was easier than having to make my own decisions. Then he started making me do things I didn't really want to do, but did because I was so used to things the way they were. Twice I tried to leave him; I got involved with other men. Those two men died, Mongo—one in a motorcycle accident and the other from bad drugs. Don't ask me how I know this, Mongo, because I can't prove it, but I *know* those men died because Sacra *wanted* them to. I kept going back to him. I went back after the first man's death because I was still ambivalent about my feelings for Sacra; after the second death, I went back to him because I was afraid. Mongo, once I entered into a lesbian relationship with another one of Sacra's girlfriends, not because I was sexually attracted to the other woman, but because Sacra was turned on by the idea, and he insisted I do it. I'm not comfortable with a lot of decisions I made during those years, and it's just not something I can calmly discuss with Garth. There are things about my past with Sacra that I don't want Garth to ever know."

"Mary, believe me when I tell you Garth wouldn't give a shit if you once made love to monkeys, much less to another woman. He might not much care for it if you did it *now,* but to him the past is past. As far as he's concerned, the best part of his life started when he met you. I might recommend that you try a similar approach. Throw out all that old, ratty baggage, starting with Sacra Silver."

"Maybe it's too late."

"Nope."

"I don't know what to do, Mongo."

"For openers, throw out Silver. Simply tell him to get the hell out of the house. If he gives you a hard time, call the cops." I paused, watching her, saw panic rise like a flash flood in her eyes, saw the color drain from her face. I continued, "It's better for you to face up to him, Mary. It's what you want, isn't it?"

"More than anything, Mongo," she answered in a small voice. "But I . . ."

Her voice trailed off, but the meaning of the words she hadn't spoken was clear: she was just not up to the job of evicting Sacra Silver from her house, much less of freeing herself from the firm grip he had on her mind, at least not by herself.

I said, "Let me give the matter some thought, Mary. Maybe I can come up with a solution. In fact, it might be better if I took care of the matter—if you give me the okay to do it. Will you let me handle it?"

She seemed startled by the suggestion, and then frightened. "Oh, Mongo, I don't want him to turn his anger on you."

"I can handle his anger. But he has no special powers, and that's the thought you have to keep in mind. Start practicing better mental hygiene."

"I don't want him to hurt you, Mongo. I couldn't bear that, any more than I could bear him hurting Garth. You still don't understand—or won't accept—what he can do to people who cross him or get in his way."

"But you'll let me take care of it?" I asked, casting a wary eye on another, larger set of waves generated by a second tanker, and heading our way.

She nodded hesitantly. "Just remember that I couldn't abide it if anything happened to you, Mongo. Please be very careful what you say to him."

"I will," I said, clenching the wine bottle between my knees and bracing my arms on the gunwales as a large bow wave, its foaming crest sparkling in the moonlight, loomed just behind me and to my right. "Incoming. Hang on."

The bow wave, a healthy four-footer, rolled under us, lifting the canoe. We dipped down, then started up the face of the following wave. The drift net scraped against the canoe, and the plastic buoy bottles rapped out a ragged tattoo on the stern, just behind my head. Up we went again, down again.

"Oh, my God!" Mary shouted hoarsely as she blanched and put both hands to her mouth. She was staring, wide-eyed, at something just behind me, over my right shoulder. The canoe dipped again, and she screamed.

I turned my head to the right, gagged, and almost vomited as the canoe rose and dipped again, and for just a brief moment a large section of the drift net was exposed. In that moment I saw the net's grisly catch—an arm, its flesh still partially covered with shreds of thick, black rubber. The arm had apparently been ripped from its owner's shoulder, because splinters of bone entangled with long threads of tissue snaked out from the gaping socket. On the limb's wrist was a large diver's watch with a red plastic strap that I had last seen being worn by the keeper of this river that now held his remains.

•   •   •

I untied the painter from the buoy, and we quickly paddled back to shore. Together, Mary and I pulled the canoe up on the beach. Then Mary turned back, wrapped both arms around her body, and began to shake as she gazed out in the direction of the horror in the net, which could not even be seen from where we were standing.

"Mary?"

"God," she murmured. "It's Tom Blaine, isn't it?"

"I think so. Listen, I'm going into the house to call the police, but I'd like you to wait for me down here for a few minutes. Will you be all right?"

When she moved her head slightly in what I took to be an assenting nod, I hurried up the path beneath the overhang, up to the house. Not surprisingly, Sacra Silver's car was still in the driveway, and so I wasn't surprised either to find him still in the music room, sitting in Garth's chair.

I went to the kitchen, picked up the telephone, and called the Cairn police to report what we had found on the river. Then I tried to call Garth to tell him that his friend was dead. He wasn't home, or he wasn't answering the phone, so I left a message on his machine. Then I went into the music room. Silver was half dozing, a magazine in his lap. He heard me come in, opened his eyes, and studied me. He seemed amused by something, probably by the way he assumed my conversation with Mary had gone. He picked up his empty glass off the side table, held it out toward me.

"Get me another drink, will you, Frederickson?"

"Sure," I replied easily as I walked toward him across the polished hardwood floor. When I reached him, I took the glass from his hand, tossed it over my shoulder, then kicked him hard in the right shin, just above his boot top. He hooted in surprise and pain, jackknifed the upper part of his body down, and grabbed hold of his hurting ankle. I grabbed two handfuls of hair, yanked him out of the chair and onto the floor, face down. He started to roll over, saving me the trouble of turning him. I kicked him again, this time directly in the solar plexus. He jack-knifed again, rolled on his other side, and retched, wheezing and

53

gasping for air. While he occupied himself with the task of trying to breathe, I went about the business of patting him down. He wasn't carrying any weapons. I squatted down in front of his face, rapped him hard on the top of his skull with my knuckles.

"Hello," I said. "Anyone home? I don't mean to be rude, big fella, but I needed to make sure I had your full attention. You're a hard man to talk to. It's time to say good night. If I knew how to get you out of the lives of my brother and sister-in-law with magic, I'd use it, but I'm not much into magic. You've got Mary shook up real good, and she's got my brother shook up real good. Neither of them is thinking clearly or behaving properly, so that leaves me in the position of acting as their champion, if you will. Mary tells me that she wants you out of her house, and out of her life, and I intend to see that her wish is granted. Now, I want you to haul your skinny ass out of here as soon as you get your wind back. You'll be pleased to know that I'm not going to thump on you anymore, because I want you to be able to drive."

"You . . . little . . . dwarf fuck. You . . . sucker-punched me."

"I didn't punch you, Sacra, I kicked you. I want you to know I'm the meanest little dwarf fuck you're ever likely to meet. I felt a demonstration was in order, because I had to show you I was serious. If you try to cause any more trouble, I'm the one you're going to have to deal with—not Mary, not Garth. Now, it seems to me that you have a limited number of options. You can go to the police and charge me with assault, but I don't advise that. What with your little disappearing act, and the illegal butterfly knife that you pulled on my brother, your credibility with the cops probably isn't at its peak right now. The cops would insist on knowing your real name, and I don't think you want to give it. Finally, you'd be laughed at; you wouldn't want it bandied about that the mighty Sacra Silver had been beaten up by a little dwarf fuck, now, would you?

"Your second option is to get up and cast a magic spell and hope that I disappear or turn into a toad. If you try that, you'd better hope that it works, because if it doesn't, I'm going to start kicking you again.

"Your third option is to do what I said, haul your ass out of here, and keep it out. This is the course of action I recommend.

You're not to contact Mary again, ever. If I hear that you've so much as sent her a postcard, I'm going to find you and resume this demonstration. I will beat the shit out of you. Do you understand?"

"There's another choice, dwarf," he said in a rasping voice as, still holding one hand to his stomach, he managed to get up on his knees. His black eyes glittered now, shimmering brightly with hatred. "I'll kill you."

"What a terrible thing to say. I'd really hoped you'd begin to show a change in attitude."

Still looking a little wobbly, he slowly rose to his feet and glared at me. Then he did just about what I'd expected him to do, which was to kick at me as if he were trying to score a field goal. I spun counterclockwise away from the kick, then stepped in close to his body and swept his supporting leg out from under him. He landed flat on his back. I hopped on his chest and sat down hard, pressing the index and middle fingers of my left hand against his eyeballs, while at the same time grabbing his throat with my right hand, applying just enough pressure on the carotid artery to discourage him from putting up too much of a fuss about my sitting on him. I squeezed the artery; his hands started to come up toward me, and I applied a little more pressure to his eyeballs. His arms froze in place, and then his hands started to tremble. Then his arms slowly sank back to his sides. When I judged that he was just about ready to pass out, I released the pressure on his throat and eyes, got up off his chest, and backed away a few paces.

"I was hoping to be able to continue our interesting conversation," I said as Silver, holding his throat with both hands, slowly sat up, "but something's come up that requires my undivided attention. I just don't have any more time for funnin' with you, so we've got to get it on here. We're going to resolve the issue. Now, if you want to take another pass at me, I'll give you a chance to rest between rounds."

He continued to glare at me, but now there was uncertainty and fear mingled with the hatred in his eyes. Finally he looked away. He was finished.

"Exercise your option of getting out of here, Silver," I continued quietly. "And stay away. If you don't, you're going to get round two with the little dwarf fuck, whether you want to or not. You know I could've put a lot more hurt on you than I did. I don't care how many bad spells you try to cast on me, as long as you do it long-distance—which should be no problem for a hotshot ceremonial magician like you. Come at me with a knife or gun, and I'll kill you and claim self-defense. Now, either take another shot at me or get out. Your choice."

He swayed slightly on his feet, still not looking directly at me, then moved unsteadily toward the door. "Your car's behind mine," he mumbled.

"There's room for you to back around it. Don't scratch the paint."

Standing just inside the screen door at the back, I waited and watched until he was gone. Then I retrieved the plastic-wrapped tumbler from the cabinet where I had hidden it. I put the tumbler in the glove compartment of my car, then went back down to the beach.

Mary was standing exactly where and as I had left her, next to the canoe, staring out over the water with her arms wrapped tightly around her midsection. Coast Guard and Cairn Police River Patrol boats had arrived on the scene, and their revolving red, green, and white lights flashed as divers carefully removed the drift net and its sad, gruesome contents from the buoys.

I put my hand in the small of Mary's back, gently kneaded the tense muscles. "He's gone," I said. "I don't think he'll bother you anymore. If he does, you let me know immediately, anytime day or night."

She turned her head to look down at me, disbelief clearly reflected in her eyes. "Sacra's . . . gone?"

"Yeah."

"Just like that?"

"Yeah. We had a talk about how tacky and rude it was for him to show up after all these years and try to come between a husband and wife. He saw my point and left. He turns out to be quite a reasonable chap after all."

Mary wasn't buying it. "Sacra has been called a lot of things," she said, shaking her head, "but I've never heard anyone describe him as reasonable."

"Well, you know what a silver-tongued devil I can be."

"What on earth did you do to him, Mongo?"

"Well, I'll admit I had to act slightly out of character, forgoing my usual patience and diplomatic aplomb. The point is that he's gone. I don't believe he'll come back, but if he does, first call the police and then me. Your job is to keep remembering that you don't have to be afraid of him. Now, speaking of people to call, why don't you go call Garth? I assume the police and Coast Guard are going to want statements from both of us, but they can start with me. I'm going to paddle out there and check in. Why don't you go start taking care of business with your husband? The machine in his apartment is on, but I think he's home, and I suspect he'll pick up the phone if he hears your voice."

Mary nodded. She hugged me hard, kissed me on the forehead, then started up to the house. I pulled the canoe back down to the water's edge, hopped in, and started paddling out toward the bobbing island of flashing lights.

CHAPTER FIVE

Tom Blaine's funeral was on Saturday. Afterward, Jessica Blaine invited the mourners back to her home for coffee and cake. The small, wood-frame house was close on the river in the south of Cairn; it had a warm, lived-in feeling, and was filled with chintz, various marine bric-a-brac and photographs, and dozens of fine pieces of sun-bleached driftwood—the best examples of nature's art culled from a lifetime of living in close harmony with the river outside the back door. Walking into the house, one had the feeling of entering a safe harbor.

According to the county medical examiner, enough pieces of the riverkeeper's body had been found to establish a fairly accurate cause and time of death. He had apparently died on Tuesday night, sometime between the hours of ten and midnight, while diving—presumably in the deep channel, since the tearing apart of his body had been caused by vortex and the knife-blade edges of spinning steel props on the engines of a very large tanker or tugboat. His boat had apparently slipped its anchor, for the trawler had been found on Thursday morning run aground in the salt marshes near Piermont. There had been no green plastic jugs found aboard; Garth and I had asked.

Nobody had yet come up with a good explanation of just why Tom Blaine would have been diving at night, considering the fact that visibility in the Hudson is limited to a few inches at high noon on a cloudless day, or why he should have been diving so far out from shore, in the deep channel, where all evidence of pollution would normally be rapidly dissipated in the huge volume of water that surges in that dredged canyon in the riverbed, a river within a river. However, an explanation for what seemed an example of extraordinarily bad judgment was not deemed necessary; whatever his reasons for being out there, he had been run over by a passing tanker, super-tug, or barge whose captain would have had no chance to see him, and he had died horribly when he had been sucked up into the vessel's enormous spinning propeller blades. His death had officially been ruled an accident.

Along with Garth and Mary, I'd been sitting on a worn sofa chatting with a small group of fishermen when I spotted Harry Tanner, whom I knew through Garth. The Cairn policeman was standing by himself over by a window that looked out on the river. I excused myself from the group, went over to him. He smiled warmly as I came up, extended his hand.

"How you doing, Mongo?"

"Okay, Harry, aside from the sadness of the occasion. Yourself?"

"Fair to middling. A shame about Tom, huh?"

"Yeah. You know he was after somebody, don't you?"

The policeman with the handlebar moustache and deep-set hazel eyes nodded. "Garth told me about what happened last Sunday night when Tom towed you guys home—the green jugs and all that."

"He said something about 'nailing the bastards.' "

"Garth told me about that too."

"And?"

"And what, Mongo?"

"I just wondered if the Cairn police were checking out the situation."

"I'm not sure there's any situation to check out, Mongo. But even if there were, it's not our jurisdiction. Cairn's only one of a number of towns along the river, and we don't know where Tom was when he was killed."

"Whose jurisdiction is it?"

"Coast Guard."

"Are they going to investigate? I mean, isn't it just a little bit suspicious that within forty-eight hours after he announces his intention to 'nail the bastards,' he winds up dead?"

Harry Tanner shrugged, smoothed the ends of his moustache. He looked slightly uncomfortable. "That's hard to say, Mongo. I'm not speaking ill of Tom when I tell you that he took that job of his pretty seriously. A lot of people called him a zealot. He was always talking about nailing some bastard or another, and you qualified as one of those bastards even if all you did was take a piss in his river."

"Maybe this time some bastard who was doing more than pissing in the river nailed him."

Harry thought about it, shook his head. "I'm no more pleased about Tom's death than you are, Mongo," he said. "He was my friend. But I just think you're looking for something that isn't there. You think somebody's going to kill a man because he's been caught dumping something in the river?"

"You're a cop, Harry, so I don't have to tell you about the petty things that will drive some people to murder. Also, in this case it might depend on what was being dumped. Besides, what would he be doing diving in the deep channel, and at night, no less? The water must be thirty or forty feet deep out there, moving all the time. What could he hope to find? Even if he did find something, how could he hope to prove where it came from? Except for keeping an eye on sail- and powerboats to make sure they don't dump their waste-holding tanks in the river, all the action in pollution monitoring is along the shoreline, where you can tell where the stuff is coming from. Right?"

"You're saying someone took Tom—or his corpse—out there and arranged for the body to be diced up by a tanker?"

"I'm saying it seems surpassingly strange that anyone, much less an experienced diver like Tom Blaine, would have been diving

60

in the deep channel of the Hudson River at night. Law enforcement agencies are supposed to investigate when people die under surpassingly strange circumstances."

"I hear what you're saying, Mongo, and I understand where you're coming from, but you'd have had to know Tom to understand why the authorities aren't going to be as suspicious as you are. Like I said, he was a zealot, and he'd pretty much worn out the Coast Guard's patience. He'd sometimes work twenty hours at a stretch, and it wasn't at all unusual for him to be out on the river at night. He found you and Garth becalmed on your catamaran at night, didn't he? Maybe he saw something suspicious in the water out there and went in after it. He got careless, and he got sucked up into the props of a tanker that passed over his position. All of the people I've talked to, including the Coast Guard, think there's no question that Tom's death was accidental. I feel the same way. Aside from Tom's reason for being where he was, everything seems pretty straightforward. I wouldn't worry about it, Mongo."

•   •   •

I wasn't worried about it; I was curious about it. So was Garth. Most of the other mourners had left, but Garth, Mary, and I remained behind. We were sitting around the riverkeeper's widow, who was slowly rocking back and forth in a worn rocking chair, eyes half closed, adrift in sorrow and memory. Garth leaned forward in his chair and took the woman's hand. "What do you think could have happened, Jessica?" he asked quietly.

Tears came to the woman's soft, gray eyes. She wiped them away, then wrapped both her hands around Garth's. "I can't imagine," she answered in a trembling voice, biting her lower lip. "It's so . . . horrible. Tom was always so safety conscious; he was a certified diving instructor. He was always so careful around the boat, and with the materials he handled. I . . . it's awfully hard for me to understand."

"Jessica, do you have any idea why Tom would have been diving in the deep channel at night?"

She shook her head, then closed her eyes as more tears welled up and ran down her cheeks.

"Garth," Mary said with quiet alarm, "maybe you shouldn't pursue this right now."

"It's all right, child," Jessica Blaine said to Mary. "I don't mind. I guess I want somebody to ask me questions; nobody else has. It's like the police just take it for granted that Tom was stupid enough to do something like that. It bothers me."

Mary nodded, then rose and put her arm around the woman's shoulders. I moved my chair closer to the rocker. "Mrs. Blaine, the night Tom towed Garth and me back here to Cairn, he'd just come from someplace where he was investigating some kind of infraction; at least we assume that, because his diver's suit was still wet, and he mentioned that he was getting the goods on somebody. Do you have any idea what he might have been investigating, or who he could have been talking about?"

Again, the woman shook her head. "Tom worked long hours, and he was usually working on a number of cases at one time. We didn't see much of each other, and so we made it a practice never to talk about his work when he got home—it would get him too aggravated. I always tried to get him to think about other things and relax when he was home."

Garth asked, "There wasn't one particular company he was more mad at than the others?"

"He was mad at all the companies he caught dumping their dirt in the river. If he was particularly angry with one company, he didn't tell me."

Garth turned to me. "I'm working on getting a list of all the companies with plants on the river in the area Tom patrolled. I should have it by Monday or Tuesday, and I'll fax you a copy at the office. It can't hurt to know the names of the outfits Tom monitored."

"It would also help to know which of them are serviced by tankers or barges."

"Just about all of them use tankers or barges in one way or another," Jessica Blaine said. "That's why they're located on the river. They use water transport for shipping goods or bringing in manufacturing supplies, and often both."

I asked, "Mrs. Blaine, is there anyone else Tom might have

talked to, anyone he might have confided in about some particularly urgent case he was investigating?"

"I really don't know. He worked for the Cairn Fishermen's
Association, of course, so someone there might know. But Tom
was given free rein by the association, and he was pretty close-
mouthed about current investigations. He liked to wait until he'd
gathered his evidence. Then he'd go directly to the Coast Guard.
If the Coast Guard didn't act, or if Tom felt they were dragging
their heels, then Tom would take the evidence to the association,
and they'd decide whether or not to go to court. Aside from that,
there isn't much I can tell you. Most nights he'd come home and
work in his office for an hour or two, then come up to be with
me."

Garth and I exchanged glances, then looked back at the woman.
Garth asked, "Tom had an office, Jessica?"

She nodded. "In the basement. That's where he kept his samples and his logs."

"Would you mind if Mongo and I looked around down there?"

Jessica Blaine slowly shook her head. "Not at all."

Tom Blaine's widow led us into the kitchen, opened a door in
the rear of a pantry area, then flipped a light switch on the wall.
Garth and I descended a short flight of wobbly, oft-repaired,
wooden steps into the basement. There was a dangling, naked
light bulb at the foot of the stairs, and Garth pulled a string to
turn it on. The stairs bisected the damp, stone basement; to our
left was an oil-burning furnace, a washer and dryer, and a floor-
to-ceiling Peg-Board filled with rusting tools that had obviously
been used only on rare occasions. To the right was Tom Blaine's
makeshift office. There was a scarred wooden desk with a green
gooseneck lamp flanked by two battered metal filing cabinets.
Secured to the concrete wall directly in front of the desk was a
corkboard covered with Polaroid photographs of tankers heading
up and down the river. Two walls were taken up with crude,
handmade wood shelving on which sat an array of labeled coffee
cans, jars, and bottles containing gooey materials of different
colors, and in varying states of desiccation, and which I wasn't
inclined to examine too closely. There were three rows of green

plastic jugs similar to the ones we had seen on his boat the evening he had towed us back to Cairn.

All of the labels on the cans, bottles, jars, and jugs were clearly marked with a date at the very top; the rest of the information on the labels was not so clear. Below the dates were a series of numbers and letters, presumably a code identifying the container's contents and where the sample had been taken. All of the containers were arranged on the shelves by date, in the order that they had been taken. Unlike the mudlike materials in most of the other containers, the contents of the green plastic jugs sloshed around when shaken. Unlike the labels on the other containers, which appeared to contain a good deal of information—including what might have been chemical formulas—the labels on the jugs carried only a date and a single letter and number code. The last three jugs on the shelf bore the dates of the preceding weekend, which meant they were probably the ones we had seen on the riverkeeper's boat. All bore an identical code: C-26Q431. The other dozen or so jugs on the shelves all bore codes preceded by the letter C, followed by a different arrangement of numbers and letters. Their dates covered the past six months.

"Hey, Mongo," Garth said quietly, "take a look at these."

I went over to where Garth was standing. He had removed three dust-covered, leather-bound ledgers from the file cabinet on the left and was looking through one of them. I picked up another from the desk, examined its cover. There was a label that gave the dates of March 1987 to June 1989; the label on the third ledger was dated even earlier. Each entry in the ledgers listed a date, a site, a suspected violator, the nature of the infraction, action taken, and final resolution—fines, cease-and-desist orders by some court, or whatever. The ledgers I was examining contained a detailed record of actions taken against polluters in Cairn and the surrounding region over a period of almost six years.

There was nothing complicated about the entries, no codes and no key to codes. It seemed the enigmatic system Tom Blaine had used for labeling the containers had only been used for purposes of security and confidentiality until the samples had been tested in some lab and the matter resolved by the Coast

Guard or in court. There was no way of telling what the liquids in the green plastic jugs were or where they came from.

"What's the date on that ledger?" I asked.

Garth closed the book, examined the cover. "It ends nine months ago."

"We need the latest one."

"Indeed."

Garth began searching through the remaining drawers of the two filing cabinets while I checked out the desk drawers. There was nothing in the desk but yellowed copies of old legal transcripts, sundry office supplies, and an ancient pack of Juicy Fruit gum. We checked all the shelves and even looked on the floor under the desk and shelving, but found nothing but cobwebs and three dead spiders. If Tom Blaine had been keeping a detailed record of his activities for the past nine months—and there was no doubt in our minds that he had—the ledger recording that activity was not in his office, and it had not been on the boat, at least not when it was found.

We turned at the sound of footsteps on the stairs, nodded as Jessica Blaine and Mary descended into the pool of light cast by the single overhead bulb at the foot of the stairway.

"Tom spent so many hours down here," the black woman with the gray eyes and silver hair said wistfully, glancing around the dusty work space. "I'm sorry it's so dirty. Tom would never let me clean down here—he said there were too many toxic chemicals, and he didn't want me near any of them. Tom was really a very tidy man. I just don't want you to think . . ."

"There's no need to apologize, Jessica," Garth said. "Tom had a lot more important things on his mind than a few cobwebs in his office."

"Is there something in particular you're looking for?"

"As a matter of fact, there is: Tom's most recent ledger. It doesn't seem to be down here. Is it possible he could have left it around someplace upstairs, and you put it away?"

The silver-haired woman shook her head. "He always kept everything down here, and he would usually take his new journal with him out on the boat. When he didn't, he always left it right there on top of his desk."

Garth and I looked at each other, and my brother grimaced slightly. I knew what he was thinking. We had the jugs he had been carrying on his trawler Sunday night, but knowing what was in them, or even where they had come from, wouldn't necessarily be of any value. We had to know who he'd caught, or what the riverkeeper had been up to on Tuesday night, and that record—along with any samples he might have taken before he died—had disappeared from his boat before it ran aground in Piermont.

"Mrs. Blaine," I said, "has anybody else been down here since Tom's death? The police, maybe?"

She looked puzzled. "No. Why would the police want to come down here?"

A good question. Harry Tanner had made it clear that the Cairn police considered the matter outside their jurisdiction, the Coast Guard was showing no interest, the state police—assuming they were potential players—hadn't even put in an appearance, and Garth and I were the only ones who thought there might be something suspicious about Tom Blaine's death in the first place.

"Mrs. Blaine, with your permission, I'd like to take the most recent samples Tom gathered, the contents of three of those green plastic jugs, back to the city to be analyzed."

"Of course, if you want to," the woman replied, then frowned slightly. "But why? Do you think what happened to Tom could have been . . . caused by somebody?"

I wasn't sure how to reply. There seemed no reason whatsoever to flog the emotions of a grieving widow further with conjecture about the possibility that her husband had been murdered. On the other hand, by asking her questions and rummaging around in her husband's office, Garth and I were openly displaying our concern, if not outright skepticism, over the manner in which the incident was being treated by the authorities; the eerie circumstances of the man's death seemed to speak for themselves, even if no one but Garth and I seemed to be listening. But I had no business raising false expectations, or committing the time and resources of Frederickson and Frederickson to an investigation that should properly be handled by the police or Coast Guard. In short, I wasn't quite sure what I was doing or wanted to do;

I didn't know how far I was willing to pursue the matter, and I didn't want to further upset Jessica Blaine.

It was Garth who came up with the right reply. "Jessica, Tom devoted his life to cleaning up the Hudson and keeping it clean, for all of us. Mary and I live on the river, and the beauty she and I enjoy every day is in no small part due to Tom's efforts. He died in the line of duty. Mongo and I would just like to find out what he was working on at the end, so that maybe we can finish his final business for him."

The woman seemed pleased, and she nodded. "Yes. Tom would like that. Thank you."

Garth walked out to the car with me, helped me load the plastic jugs in the trunk. I said, "How's it going with Mary, if I may ask?"

"You may ask." His voice was even, but his brown eyes reflected warmth, gratitude. "She's still a little nervous, but I think things are going to be all right now. I don't know what you said to her, but it seems to have straightened her head out. I owe you, brother."

"Glad to be of service," I replied, getting into the car. "I'll call you."

·   ·   ·

I dropped the jugs off at a commercial substance-testing laboratory we regularly used, then went back to the brownstone. I parked in the underground garage, then went up the stairs that led to my offices on the first floor. When I walked in, Francisco jumped up out of his chair as if someone had stuck him with a pin. My secretary's razor-cut black hair was rumpled, as if he had been running his fingers through it; he looked pale, his paisley tie was askew, and there were sweat stains around the collar and in the armpits of his blue silk shirt.

"What is it, Francisco? What's the matter?"

He grabbed a piece of paper off the top of his desk, held it out to me with a hand that trembled. "Sir, you're to call this number right away. Garth . . . Sir, your brother's dead."

CHAPTER SIX

I took the piece of paper from the slight Puerto Rican's hand and stared stupidly at the writing on it, trying to figure out just what it was I felt on hearing the news that my brother was dead. All I seemed able to identify were the things I didn't feel: I didn't feel the shock I thought I should be experiencing; I didn't feel ill; I didn't feel grief. I didn't even feel sad. I didn't feel anything at all, except stupid; suddenly I couldn't remember what day it was, or what I had been doing since I'd gotten up that morning. I couldn't even remember why I'd come into the office; I wondered if it might not be a good idea to go out and come back in again to see what would happen, as if this were a bad dream that might come out differently if I repeated some action. I busied myself with working at the details of the day and time, and why I'd asked Francisco to come in on a Saturday to help me with a backlog of paperwork, and where I'd been, and when I finally remembered it all, I found myself right back where I had been when I'd forgotten, standing beside my secretary's desk, staring vacantly at the number written on the piece of paper, my vision blurring.

Francisco tentatively reached out to touch me, then drew his hand back. "Mongo, I'm so sorry."

"Yeah," I replied in a perfectly normal tone of voice. "Me too."

"Are you all right?"

"I don't think so, Francisco. I don't think so."

"I . . . Do you want me to make the call?"

"No, Francisco."

"Mongo?"

"Yes, Francisco?"

"I, uh . . . You had four appointments on Monday morning, and you were due in court in the afternoon to testify in the Handley industrial espionage case. I've canceled the appointments, and the D.A. has agreed to reschedule your testimony. I was able to reach him at home."

"Thank you, Francisco."

"Sir, I . . . I don't know what to say."

"What's to say? You can take the rest of the day off."

"Sir?"

"You can go home now. Thanks for coming in."

"Mongo," Francisco stammered, "it's your *brother*. I want to help in some way."

"Thank you, Francisco. There's nothing to do. It's really not that big a deal. People die all the time. Living, you know, is a very risky business; like they say, nobody gets out of it alive anyway. Haven't you heard that? By rights, Garth and I should have been dead a long time ago. Hell, we've certainly been responsible for enough other people kicking off. Today was Garth's turn. No big deal."

"Mongo, you don't look or sound good at all. Please let me—"

"Please just let yourself go home, Francisco. I want to be alone, if that's all right with you. I don't need any help. I'm okay."

My secretary looked at me strangely for a few moments, then finally picked up his sports coat from the back of the chair and walked around me. I felt, rather than saw, him pause in the doorway.

I continued, "Just come in on Monday morning and run the office the way you usually do. I'll check in with you. Don't schedule anything until I give the okay. Have a nice day, Francisco."

When I heard the door close behind me, I sat down at the secretary's desk, rubbed my eyes and blew my nose, then looked again at the number he had written down on the slip of paper. Now I wished I'd had the presence of mind to ask Francisco who had called, and just what they'd said, but it was too late. It probably didn't make any difference. The number was in the 914 area code, Rockland County, but it wasn't a Cairn exchange, so it hadn't been Mary or the Cairn police who'd called. Whoever answered would undoubtedly tell me again that Garth was dead, and presumably tell me how he'd died.

Actually, it didn't—as far as I could tell—make much difference to me how he had died, only that he was dead. If Sacra Silver had killed Garth, I was going to kill Sacra Silver, but Garth would still be dead.

My hands were perfectly steady as I picked up the telephone receiver and dialed the number Francisco had written down. It was busy. For some reason that made me angrier than the news that Garth was dead or the possibility that Sacra Silver might have killed him; somebody had a lot of nerve tying up the phone line while I was trying to get through to get information about my brother's death. Some people had no manners at all.

It occurred to me that my emotional thermostat was slightly askew.

I punched the redial button. The line was still busy.

I started going over in my mind the things that would have to be done as soon as I got this stupid phone call out of the way. First, I would have to leave for Cairn as soon as possible to be with Mary and try to comfort her as best I could. Funeral arrangements would have to be made, our parents and other relatives would have to be notified. I would have to make arrangements for relatives around the country to come to the funeral, if they wished, and afterward I would have to arrange to have Garth's body shipped back to Nebraska for burial in the family plot. I would have to contact our lawyer and make arrangements for Garth's will to be read.

Dead brothers necessitate lots of arrangements.

70

Before I left for Cairn, I was going to have to make out a list of instructions for Francisco; there were clients to call, matters that had to be attended to; it would probably be a good idea to make arrangements for some of Frederickson and dead Frederickson's work load for the coming week or two to be farmed out to other agencies.

Now I was sorry I had sent Francisco home. I was suddenly hungry, with a ravenous craving for pizza. I could have sent Francisco out for pizza.

Damn Garth anyway for getting himself killed. It was all such a distraction, and there was so much to do.

But all I could do at the moment was sit and stare at the beige telephone and the number on the slip of paper in front of me. I'd already picked up the receiver and tried the number twice, so I couldn't understand why I couldn't do it again. But suddenly I felt frozen in place, paralyzed.

I was certain I would be all right if only I could eat two or three slices of pizza. Damn Francisco anyway for going home when I'd ordered him to. What kind of secretary was he? He should have known that I didn't really want him to go, that I needed help. It wasn't every day that your brother died.

I willed myself to move, to reach out for the telephone. But then I started to move too much; my hand had begun to shake uncontrollably, and I dropped it back into my lap, hunching over in an effort to keep it still.

Then the crushing weight of my grief settled over me like a black blanket of lead, and the tears came. With Garth gone, I felt less than half a person. He had carried me, both literally and figuratively, on his broad shoulders throughout a tormented childhood and had helped me to grow up reasonably whole. As things had turned out, much of my life had been defined by danger, both psychological and physical, perils I had undoubtedly, if not consciously, sought out to prove something to the world, or to myself. Always, Garth had been at my side, and he had saved my life on countless occasions. A half hour before, I'd been afraid of nothing; now it seemed I was afraid of everything, even to pick up a telephone and call a number to see what the person on the other end might have to say. Only now, with Garth dead, did I realize the extent to which my brother had been my courage, my heart, my spine.

I leaned forward on the desk, resting my head on my arms, and sobbed uncontrollably, letting the tears flow freely as my sorrow washed through me like some tidal wave of acid. When my tears were spent I didn't feel all that much better, but at least my hands had stopped shaking. I sighed, blew my nose, picked up the telephone receiver, and once again punched the redial button. The line was still busy. I redialed the number, just to make sure I had gotten it right. Busy.

I hung up the telephone and stared at it some more. When the line was still busy five minutes later, I got out my reverse directory for Rockland County and looked up the number. It was a pay phone in a shopping mall in Nanuet. Now I did what I should have done in the first place, what I probably would have done if I hadn't been just slightly unnerved. I picked up the receiver once again and called Garth and Mary's home. This line was busy also, but that didn't surprise me. I kept pushing the redial button until I finally got through.

"Hello," Garth said in a cracked voice.

I was certain there had been times in my life when I'd been happier, or felt more relieved, but at the moment I simply couldn't recall them. I closed my eyes, heaved a deep sigh. "It's Mongo, Garth."

There was silence at the other end of the line for a few seconds, then a tentative "Mongo?"

"Yep."

"Oh, Jesus, I thought you were—"

"Dead, yeah. You were out, and Mary took the message that I was dead, and you were to call a certain number to get the grisly details. The number's for a pay phone at the Nanuet Mall. The receiver must be off the hook."

"Jesus," he said again. "Just a minute. There's someone tearing at my sleeve here."

There was a brief pause, and then Mary came on the line. She was sobbing, but with joy. "Mongo! Is that really you?"

"In living color. I emphasize the word 'living.' "

"But I got a call from the police . . ."

"It was just a misunderstanding that's been cleared up. I assure you the report of my death was highly exaggerated, and all that."

"But how could the police—?"

"Just a misunderstanding, babe, like I said. A case of mistaken identity. You know all dwarves look alike to you normal-size people."

"You know," she whispered hoarsely, "I really would miss you, Mongo."

"Yeah, I'd miss me too. Can you put Garth back on the line?"

"Sure. Love you, brother-in-law."

"Love you, sister-in-law."

"Yeah," Garth said in a low voice when he came back on the line. "A pay phone at the Nanuet Mall, huh?"

"That's right—but not for publication around there, because you-know-who has to be the one who pulled this little stunt. I don't think Mary should know. Can you talk?"

"No."

"All right, I'll talk. It looks like we've got a merry prankster on our hands."

"Now I'll kill the son-of-a-bitch," Garth said quietly in his casual, matter-of-fact tone of voice that was always a danger signal.

"Shhh. That's talking. You leave him to me; he's mine. I'll take care of Sacra Silver. Your job is to take care of Mary."

"What are you going to do?"

"For openers, find out who the fuck he really is."

"Maybe that is his real name," Garth said very softly. "Mary told me she never heard him call himself anything else."

"Yeah, but he's a bullshit artist, and he's got things to hide. I've got a glass in my glove compartment with his prints on it, and I'm going to get out the old fingerprint kit as soon as I get off the line. He's close by you, maybe somewhere right in Cairn. This little prank took some careful timing to make it work. He not only knew when I left, and how long it would take me to get to New York, but also when you left the house. That was his window of opportunity, when he called Mary and Francisco to leave his message. He's watching your house—or was. The fact that he didn't just shoot us tells us something about him: he's an

73

overgrown juvenile delinquent, probably fairly bright, who tries to get his way through bluff, intimidation, and manipulation. But he apparently doesn't have the guts to kill, not even from ambush."

"Maybe he's waiting for a better opportunity."

"I don't think so. It turns out our friend is a fucking practical jokester."

"I'll show him a practical joke."

"No, *I'll* show him a practical joke. You just keep your eyes open up there. And don't discuss any of this with Mary."

"Agreed. But what if he doesn't . . . uh, show up anywhere?"

"What if he doesn't have a record?"

"Yeah."

"A dipshit like this has to have a record with somebody, somewhere, even if it's only for an arrest. If I can find out who he really is, then I'll be in a better position to take a run at him. Most of these people who are into the occult begin to believe their own bullshit, and that's a weakness. I'm going to show him a little sorcery. But you let *me* handle it. All right? Mary will get all wound up if she gets wind of this."

"I hear you."

"I'll be in touch. You keep your head low."

"Yeah. And before you tell me how low your head already is, let me tell you to keep it even lower."

"I'll talk to you, brother," I said, and hung up.

I went downstairs to the garage, took the plastic-wrapped tumbler out of the glove compartment of the Volkswagen Rabbit, brought it back up to my office. I retrieved an old fingerprint kit from the bottom of a filing cabinet and went to work dusting the glass, working carefully around the curved surface. There was, of course, no guarantee that the prints were going to be of any use at all, but, as I had told Garth, I had a strong feeling that Mr. Sacra Silver had been a bit too clever by half at least once in his life, had run afoul of the law, and that his prints would be on file somewhere.

I ended up with good prints of every finger on his right hand, including the thumb. I transferred the prints on the tumbler to plastic film, took the film to our photo lab in a back room.

There I set up our high-resolution Polaroid camera and shot the fingerprints with high-speed film against a soft gray background. When I had finished, I picked up the telephone and called a friend, a captain in the NYPD, who owed me a couple of favors.

•   •   •

"I don't know where you got this water, Mongo, but I don't see how it could have come out of the Hudson River."

I studied Frank Lemengello, the husky, bushy-haired chief chemist at the lab where I had brought the samples I had taken from Tom Blaine's basement. He was sitting on his desk, with the three green plastic jugs to his right. Beneath each jug was a computer printout of the chemical makeup of each sample.

"Actually, I didn't take the samples. They were collected by a man who's dead now, but he almost certainly did take them out of the Hudson. What's the problem with that?"

"The stuff in all three of these jugs is seawater."

"Seawater?"

"Yeah. You know, like from the ocean."

"The Hudson is an estuary, lower than sea level, all the way to Albany. It has tides, and the water in that part is saline."

"It may be saline, but it's not seawater." Frank paused, patted the jug closest to him. "This is seawater. Even at the mouth of New York Harbor you get a lot of mix with fresh water; you wouldn't have this concentration. But there's other stuff in there too."

"Like what?"

"Some heavy metals, and petrochemicals like ethyl benzene and toluene. It's all on the printout. Nasty stuff, by the way."

I thought about it, trying to figure out how a concentration of undiluted seawater laced with heavy metals and petrochemicals had found its way twenty-five miles up the Hudson River, and finally thought I had an answer. "A tanker," I said.

"Come again?"

"An oceangoing oil tanker flushing out its bilge, ballast, and holding tanks after making a delivery. That's how that stuff got in the river."

He gave me a nod, but it was tentative. "That could be the

answer, I suppose; but to get these concentrations, you'd have to collect your samples right at the port virtually as a tank was being flushed, or you'd get more dilution with river water."

Which would explain why Tom Blaine had been diving at night, in the deep channel, beneath a tanker.

It didn't explain why Tom had died, but it hinted strongly at a grisly conclusion. If a tanker was in the process of flushing its tanks, it wasn't going anywhere at the moment. But in this case the main turbines had been turned on. It seemed inconceivable to me that a captain would choose to murder a man over some bilge water, but it was beginning to look as though that was exactly what had happened.

"Frank, you don't know anything about pollution laws, fines for dumping, that sort of thing, do you?"

The chemist shook his head. "Can't say that I do, Mongo."

"Well, then," I said, gathering up the jugs and printout sheets, "I guess I'll just have to go find somebody who does."

CHAPTER SEVEN

The nearest Coast Guard Command station was located in the New York Harbor, on Governors Island. It was a short subway ride for me, but a trip into the city for Garth. Nevertheless, when I called to tell him about the lab report on the samples, and what I intended to do next, he insisted that he wanted to go with me. I hung around the office catching up on paperwork until he arrived, and then we headed for the subway.

We actually got in to see the top man himself, one Captain Richard Marley. Marley was a beefy man with a pleasant manner, curly brown hair, and light brown eyes that, to my consternation, seemed to glaze over when I explained why we had come, and started to hand him the computer printouts.

"Excuse me," he said, taking the papers from my hand, then setting them off to one side of his desk before sinking back into his leather swivel chair. "This wouldn't have any connection with that riverkeeper up in Cairn, would it?"

Garth and I looked at each other, then back at the Captain of

77

the Port of New York. Garth said, "As a matter of fact, it would. Those are laboratory analyses of water Tom Blaine took out of the Hudson north of here. He died getting those samples."

Marley blinked, sat up straight. "Died?"

"He got chewed up by the propeller blades of some tug or tanker."

Marley winced, half turned away. "Jesus. You're sure it was a tug or tanker?"

"It's what the coroner said. A normal powerboat, even a cigarette boat, would have sliced him up, but not into the sushi he ended up as."

"He could only have been run over by a big boat if he was in the deep channel. What the hell was he doing diving in the deep channel?"

"Getting those samples," I said with some impatience, pointing at the sheets of paper on the corner of his desk. "Or samples just like those. There's more than one ship involved. The samples I had analyzed came from two different ships, almost certainly tankers, and he was probably killed by a third."

"And you two have been hired to look into the death?" Marley asked in an even tone. "Or are you working on a pollution case?"

"We haven't been hired by anybody to do anything. You might call what we're doing a labor of love."

"I'm sorry to hear about Tom Blaine's death, Frederickson," the burly man said, once again leaning back in his chair. "I'll admit I considered him a pest, but he always thought he was doing the right thing, and he worked damn hard at his job. Just what is it you want from me?"

"For openers," I said tersely, "an investigation into the circumstances of his death—which I understand is your job."

He didn't like that, but at least it got his attention. His jaw muscles tightened, and his light brown eyes glinted. "Where did you get that idea?"

"From people who claim it isn't their job—local cops, and presumably the state police, since they never showed up. I haven't checked with the FBI, CIA, or United Nations, but I'm sure they'd tell me the same thing—that whatever happens on the Hudson is your jurisdiction."

"You want to know what my job is, Frederickson? I'll tell you. This is the largest operational command in the Coast Guard. Six thousand ships a year pass through this harbor. I'm responsible for monitoring oil spills, polluters—"

"Aha," Garth said with quiet intensity.

"And a few other little things. It's our responsibility to enforce the laws of marine navigation; we're responsible for averting terrorist threats. I command three hundred and forty men and women, and thirty-two ships on the Hudson River all the way from this port up to the Canadian border. Now, gentlemen, we love the environment, the seas and rivers, as much as the next person—probably more, or we wouldn't have chosen to serve in the Coast Guard. But we're not an arm of the Environmental Protection Agency; we're armed forces. We're not pollution detectives. We don't have the manpower. One of Tom Blaine's problems was that he thought we should be pollution detectives, and that we should spend all our time helping him clean up his relatively small bailiwick up there around Cairn. If you've got a major oil spill from a tanker, we'll be on the scene in minutes; but if I had to cooperate with every environmentalist, every individual who brought in a lab report about some bad water and asked us to do something about it, there wouldn't be enough hours in the day to do that work, much less carry out our mandated responsibilities. Blaine wouldn't accept that position, and I finally had to bar him from this facility and stop our people from taking his phone calls—not because I wanted to, but because I had to. The reason your local police don't want to handle it is because they have to answer to the local politicians, and the politicians don't want to rattle the cages of the local industries that pay a lot in school and property taxes. In short, if you want something done about a minor pollution problem upriver, you're going to have to rattle the politicians' cages, not mine. I'm not saying that whatever's on those sheets doesn't represent a real problem; you're just going to have to take it someplace other than the Coast Guard."

"This may be more than just a minor pollution problem, Captain," Garth said quietly. "Tom Blaine was killed collecting samples like those. Maybe he was murdered."

"Murdered?" Marley said it as if the word itself had a bad taste.

I stepped closer to the edge of the desk. "Yes, Captain. Tom wasn't stupid enough to dive under a moving ship. There would be no reason for an oil tanker captain to power up the props while he was at anchor and flushing out his tanks."

"Who says Blaine was killed by an oil tanker, and who says a captain was flushing out his tanks in the river?"

"It's the conclusion the chemical analyses on those printouts points to—if you'd care to look at them." I paused, waiting to see what the Coast Guard commander would do. He glanced at the sheets, then looked back at me. I continued, "Garth and I think there's a good possibility that a captain of an oil tanker turned on the engines of his ship, knowing Tom would be killed, to stop Tom from collecting samples of what that captain was dumping in the river. If you'll look at those printouts, you'll see there was all kinds of toxic crap in the samples. I take it flushing out tanks in an inland waterway is illegal, right?"

Captain Richard Marley ran a hand through his thick brown hair, which immediately sprang back into place. "I think you're looking at the problem from the wrong end, Frederickson, and it's leading you to make unwarranted conclusions. A certain amount of leakage from bilge and ballast tanks is unavoidable— even though Tom Blaine would certainly have argued otherwise. There would be absolutely no reason for a tanker captain to risk a fine by flushing out his tanks in the river, because he'd have nothing to gain; he has nothing to transport back to the refinery in those flushed tanks. He delivers oil, then goes back to his shipping point in the Middle East, or wherever, to pick up another load. He has an entire ocean voyage to wash out all his tanks at his leisure."

Garth said, "Maybe he was taking a load of something out."

Marley extended his hands out over his desk, palms up. "What? The industries up the river are users of oil, not suppliers. You know how many millions of gallons those tankers can hold? They're not used for carrying seltzer. There aren't any chemical plants up there with either a capacity or product that requires tanker transport; barges, yes, but not tankers. That's what's wrong with your speculation. For the sake of argument, let's suppose a captain did flush his tanks in the river—maybe by accident, since I can't think of any reason for it. You think a captain is going to murder a man over what amounts to a relatively minor infraction? It would be like killing a traffic cop over a parking ticket. I find it highly unlikely."

"My brother and I would just like to make sure, Captain," Garth said in a flat tone.

"Look, I have no doubt that Tom Blaine was investigating something he considered important, and gathering evidence he hoped his employers could use in court. He was *always* investigating something; it was his job, and he loved it. But that doesn't mean there's a connection between what he was looking into and the fact that he was run over by a very big ship. You use the word 'murder,' but my guess is that the captain of whatever vessel killed him wasn't even aware of what had happened. He still isn't. And if he doesn't know what happened, then it's damned unlikely that you're ever going to be able to identify with any certainty the ship that was involved. That leaves you with whatever data you've got on these computer printouts you've brought me. I'm not unconcerned about whatever pollution violations may have occurred, gentlemen, but I can't set a precedent by doing for you what I wouldn't do for other people who came here with similar requests—as much as I personally might want to. I know who the two of you are, and your reputations truly precede you. It's why I agreed to meet with you personally. My recommendation is that you approach the appropriate New York State authorities with whatever you think the problem may be—pollution, or murder, or both."

So much for our visit to the Coast Guard. "Captain," I said, "I presume you keep a log of every commercial vessel that passes in and out of this harbor?"

He nodded curtly. "Each and every one."

I took a pad and pen out of my pocket, wrote down two weeks' worth of dates, put the paper down on the captain's desk, literally under his nose. "Sir, there's a time frame around the Tuesday night the medical examiner thinks Tom died. Would you be willing to give us the names and registration numbers of the oil tankers that were on the Hudson River on those dates?"

"No," he replied immediately, as he pushed the paper away from him.

"My brother and I are private investigators licensed by the state of New York, Captain. This is business, not a personal favor. Our licenses entitle us to certain privileges and courtesies from both state and federal agencies. You can check with any agency we've ever dealt with in the city, state, or federal government. You'll find that not everybody likes us, especially in this administration, but I think you'll also find that they all have respect for the way we deal with information, privileged or otherwise, that comes our way in the course of our business. We won't embarrass you."

"You mentioned privileges and courtesies, Frederickson, not rights. Again, if it were up to me personally, I'd just give you the information you want with my blessing. But I can't do that. It sets a precedent. If I hand Coast Guard data over to you, I'd have to honor the same request from every private investigator in the country, if it was made. It wouldn't be good policy."

"Nobody will know where we got the information."

"I'd know. Bring me a court order, and I'll give you the list— and buy you both a drink besides. But otherwise, no."

"You know we can't get a court order."

Marley looked uncomfortable. He averted his gaze, drummed his fingers on the desktop for a few moments, then looked at us out of the corner of his eye. "I really would like to help you gentlemen—maybe as a tip of my hat to Blaine, who pestered the hell out of me because he wanted a clean river. You want a list of oil tankers that were up the Hudson on certain dates, and I can't give it to you. There may be other organizations that compile such data. Have you considered other sources?"

Garth and I looked at each other. I didn't have the slightest idea what our coy Coast Guard captain was talking about, but Garth apparently did. "Thanks, Cap," he said, nodding to the man behind the desk. "Come on, Mongo. Let's go back to the brownstone and pick up a car."

• • •

I asked Garth, "You notice anything peculiar about these pictures?"

We were back at Jessica Blaine's home, in the basement. We had returned to ask the woman if we could borrow one of her husband's old ledgers, which we intended to show to a representative of the Cairn Fishermen's Association in the hope that he might be able to link the codes on the plastic jugs to past violators. Jessica Blaine had told us we could take whatever we wanted. I had forgotten about the photographs of tankers on the corkboard over Tom Blaine's battered desk, but now, as I stood staring at the display, I understood why the riverkeeper had taken them. They were evidence.

Garth looked up from the ledger he was studying, shrugged. "He liked to take pictures of tanker traffic going up and down the river. So what?"

"Up *and* down the river. That's the key. Look at the waterlines on those ships."

Garth stared at the photos for a few more moments, then clucked his tongue. "Aha. They're all just about the same."

"Thank you, Dr. Watson. You'd expect them to be riding low in the water going upriver, because they're carrying shipments of oil. They should be riding a lot higher going back downriver, but they're not—at least not as much as you'd expect. It means they damn well do fill up with something after they deliver their oil and flush out their tanks, and whatever they're carrying back displaces about the same amount of water as the oil."

Garth shook his head. "Marley told us there isn't even one industry upriver that ships out liquids in quantity, and yet here we have a dozen tankers, presumably coming from different locations, and all fully loaded as they head back downriver. The only cargo I can think of from around here that would fill that many tankers is . . . water."

"Right. River water. It may not be exactly fresh, but it's not totally saline either. It would be a lot easier to purify than seawater, a real bonus if you depend on desalinization for fresh water, and most of the capacity of your desalinization plants was recently knocked out by an invading army. I'll bet they're taking the stuff to Kuwait, and maybe a few other Middle Eastern countries."

"A goddamn slick trick, stealing millions of gallons of river water, and right under everyone's nose," Garth said, starting to take down the photographs, slipping them into the back of the ledger he held. "So now let's see if you and I can't find out who's gone into the sideline of selling the Hudson."

• • •

The Cairn Fishermen's Association rented office space in the basement of an Episcopal church in the center of town. We walked there, found the volunteer on duty to be an attractive red-haired woman in her early thirties who told us her name was Lonnie Allen. She had green eyes that went nicely with her red hair, and the kind of deep, even tan that comes from spending a lot of time on the water. She was wearing sandals, stonewashed jeans, and a *Clearwater* T-shirt.

We told the woman why we were there, then handed over the plastic jugs, computer printouts, photographs, and ledger for her to examine.

"That's oil tanker discharge," she said after only a cursory glance at the printouts.

"Right," Garth said. "We were hoping you might be able to provide us with a list of the tankers that were in this area around the time that Tom Blaine was killed."

Lonnie Allen nodded curtly. "We keep records of shipping traffic, but I don't have to look on the list to tell you where the samples in those jugs came from. The 'C' on the labels stands for Carver—Carver Shipping. In fact, all of the tankers in those photographs belong to Carver; they have red and yellow stripes running the length of the ship just above the waterline, although they're often too faded to see. What you have on the labels after the 'C' is the registration number of the tanker the sample was taken from. You can't see them in the photos, but the registration numbers are usually stenciled on both the bow and stern; from across the river, you can usually make them out with a decent pair of binoculars."

"Carver as in Bennett Carver?" Garth asked.

The woman nodded. "Our local Bennett Carver, yes. Carver, by the way, is by far the largest shipping line on the river. Bennett Carver founded it, but he retired a couple of years ago after taking the company public and cashing in for a hundred million or so. We were sorry to see him retire, because he was always pretty cooperative while he ran the company. And responsible. I guess things have changed. The analysis of the samples in those jugs tells us they've been flushing their tanks in the river. That's illegal."

I asked, "Who runs the company now?"

She shrugged. "The usual faceless board of directors, under some CEO whose name I can't recall right now. When we find somebody to replace Tom, which won't be easy, we'll put him or her to work on this tank-flushing business."

"Garth and I think there may be more to it, Lonnie. If you look closely at those photographs, you'll see that the tankers are fully loaded going back downriver. We think they may be carrying river water back to the Middle East to sell."

She picked up one of the photographs to look at it more closely, raised her eyebrows slightly. "You're right," she said, a hint of annoyance in her voice. "If it's river water they're carrying, that would be illegal too. The law says that the waters of the rivers and lakes in this country belong to all the people. In effect, these tankers would be shipping stolen goods."

"What would be the penalty if they were convicted of that?"

She put the photograph down, shook her head. "It's hard to say—maybe a couple of hundred thousand, probably less. Not enough, and not as much as they'd probably spend in legal fees to fight conviction. If they knew we had hard evidence, they'd probably simply stop. It's not the fines they worry about, it's the bad publicity. The fines don't usually mean that much to a company as big as Carver Shipping."

Garth said, "You have the evidence here."

Lonnie Allen again shook her head, ran her fingers through her long red hair. "No. What you have here are three plastic jugs containing what is essentially seawater, and some scenic photographs. To take it to court, Tom would have to be alive to testify himself where the samples had come from and under what

85

conditions. The same with the photographs, which the company might argue had been faked. And then you'd have to somehow prove that what was being done was company policy, and not just the unauthorized action of some captain; that would be their fallback position."

I pointed to the photos. "Those are all Carver tankers, and they're all different. It's not just one captain involved."

She nodded. "Yes. But again, you would need Tom to testify to the dates and times the photos were taken. Tom seems to have spent a lot of time carefully documenting the violations, because he didn't want the usual brush-off from the Coast Guard; it's very hard to get them to act on environmental matters, and you have to have an airtight case if you hope to win in court. A new riverkeeper will have to begin gathering fresh evidence."

"You might want to wait awhile before siccing anybody else on those people," Garth said quietly. "I'm sure what happened to Tom wasn't in his job description."

She frowned. "You think Tom was deliberately killed? Murdered?"

I said, "We think we'd like to talk to the captains of all the tankers who might have been in the area—running or at anchor—on the Tuesday evening when Tom was killed. His most recent log is missing, so we don't know what ship he was checking out. It wouldn't be the ones he labeled on those jugs, because he already had the goods on them. I found pieces of him here on Wednesday, across the river, so tide and current will have to be factored in when you're looking for the location of the tanker that might have killed him. I doubt if the company would be very cooperative, and even to ask them for information would tip our hand."

"I can give you the information you need," the woman said tersely as she rose, and walked to a filing cabinet set against the rear wall. She opened a drawer, took out a blue notebook, leafed through it until she found the page she wanted. She began to scan the page, then started slightly. "Oh, God," she said in a small voice.

"What is it, Lonnie?" Garth asked.

"I have the perfect candidate," she said, her tone now laced with disgust. "Except, according to our records, this ship was definitely at anchor. There would have been no—"

"Tell us about that ship, Lonnie."

The woman replaced the book in the file drawer where she had taken it from, then returned to her desk, slowly shaking her head. "Every three months we receive a listing of the command personnel assigned to tankers and barges; the companies themselves are usually pretty cooperative on this. On the night Tom was killed, there was an oil tanker at anchor almost directly across the river from here. High tide was around midnight, which means that if Tom was killed around that time, pieces of his body could have been carried upriver for a time, then caught in crosscurrents and swept over when the tide changed. There were five other big ships that came through that evening, but none of them fit as well into the framework of time, tide, and current you mentioned. It's an iffy proposition. Anyway, the registration number for that tanker is 82Q510. Its captain is a man by the name of Julian Jefferson. He's a drunk. Tankers he's captained have been involved in two oil spills and one running aground. We've been trying to get him off the river for years."

"Who does he work for?" Garth asked.

"Carver Shipping. But you have to understand that a ship at anchor would have no reason to start up its main engines."

Garth grunted as he wrote down the number in a notebook. "The company, state, and Coast Guard allow a drunk to pilot an oil tanker up and down the Hudson?"

She shrugged. "What can I tell you? His license has never been revoked. The rumors are that he has important family connections in the oil industry, and I guess that counts for a lot. According to the law, only foreign-registered vessels require a special pilot to take them up the Hudson; domestically registered ships can use just about anyone they want to. So Mr. Jefferson is still out there, another accident waiting to happen."

It looked like one had already happened, I thought as Lonnie Allen wrote down the registration numbers and owners of the other big ships that had been on the river that night, and handed me the paper. Except it might not have been an accident. I said, "Thanks for the information."

Garth asked, "When will you have a new riverkeeper?"

The woman with the red hair and green eyes sighed. "It's hard to say. The job doesn't pay much, after all, and you need a special kind of person to do it. A month, maybe more. Listen, may I ask just what it is you're trying to do?"

"Tom was a good friend of mine," Garth replied. "He was also a friend of the river I enjoy living on. From the way things look, he was working on an important case of pollution, and he felt he had to amass a mountain of evidence in order to get the authorities to pay attention. Now that he's dead, you say someone is going to have to start all over. Let's just say that Mongo and I are interested in keeping an eye on things until you can find somebody to take up where Tom left off."

Now the woman looked slightly embarrassed. "We can't afford to pay you."

I said, "This is on our own hook, Lonnie. We're doing it for our own reasons. But I'm sure Garth and I could develop a taste for shad, and I understand shad can be prepared in dozens of different ways."

Lonnie Allen's face brightened. "Well, shad is one thing our members have plenty of, at least when it's in season. If you'll agree to take deferred payment, I'll even throw in a batch of recipes for those dozens of dishes."

"Done," Garth said.

•   •   •

While it was true that Garth and I were interested in seeing that Tom Blaine's efforts to build a case against Carver Shipping not go to waste, we were even more interested in seeing that his death was properly investigated. That, it seemed, was not going to be so easy. The two matters were tied together. To get the state police or Coast Guard to investigate the circumstances of the man's death, it looked like we were going to have to prove that somebody had a motive for killing him, namely to prevent him from blowing the whistle on Carver Shipping for stealing Hudson River water, and in the process poisoning the well they were illegally stealing from. Proving the second part seemed a straightforward enough, if time-consuming, task, assuming

Carver Shipping hadn't stopped their practice of flushing tanks and taking on river water after Tom's death. We were just going to have to do the Coast Guard's job until the Coast Guard realized there was a job to do.

We set up a Minolta 35mm camera with a zoom lens on a tripod in a sheltered area on Garth's deck, focusing on an area of the deep channel between us and a tool and die factory complex across the river—presumably the facility Julian Jefferson's tanker had been servicing at the time of Tom Blaine's death. The proper business of Frederickson and Frederickson, namely making some money, could not be postponed forever, which meant I was going to have to go back to the city. However, between Garth and Mary, and maybe one or two college students home for the summer and looking for easy work, we could make sure that somebody was always at the camera during daylight hours to take photographs of incoming and outgoing Carver tankers, and then note the date and time in a log. If Carver Shipping was still transporting water, we would have our own photographs and witnesses. It was a first step. If we could get proof of a company policy to flout the law, a conspiracy first uncovered by a man killed by a vessel that most likely belonged to that company, then we would see what we could make happen next. There were always the newspapers, and Garth and I had plenty of contacts in the media.

Mary's strained voice came from the beach below the deck. "Garth? Mongo? Are you up there?"

Garth and I looked at each other, and Garth called, "Yes. What is it?"

"I think you two should come down here right away. There's something you should see."

Alarmed by the tone of Mary's voice, we hurried out of the house and down the path leading to the beach. We came to an abrupt halt when we rounded a corner of the boathouse, startled by the sight in front of us.

It was low tide, which meant that fifteen to twenty yards of beach were exposed. Left in the sand by the receding waters were what looked to be hundreds of hypodermic syringes littering the beach like some kind of malevolent glass and blue plastic sea creatures that had come ashore to spawn terror at the least, and maybe slow, agonizing death. Strewn among the needles like strands of poisonous afterbirth were long strips of bloody bandages. Mary, ashen-faced and with her arms wrapped around her, stood at the far end of the field of needles and bandages, which seemed to be confined pretty much to the area of beach around the boathouse.

"Mary, you didn't touch any of that, did you?" Garth asked tersely.

Mary slowly, almost solemnly, shook her head, then started walking toward us, giving the field of syringes and blood-soaked cloth a wide berth.

"I'm going up to the house to call the health department and the neighbors," Garth continued, turning to start back up the path. "From the looks of things, most of that shit ended up on our property, but the other people around here should be warned."

Garth hurried up to the house, and I took Mary's hand as she came up to me.

"I didn't exactly tell Garth the truth," she whispered hoarsely.

"What are you talking about?"

In reply, she lifted her left foot to show me the sole. It was stained with blood. "I was just walking along, thinking about this new song I'm working on, not watching where I was going. I stepped on one of the needles that was sticking up out of the sand. I . . . My first reaction was just not to frighten Garth." She paused, and the giggle that came out of her mouth was just a note or two short of hysteria. "Not telling him was certainly kind of silly, wasn't it? He's going to have to know sooner or later."

I ran up the beach and into the boathouse. With trembling hands I tore off a large strip from a roll of plastic sheeting we used to cover the catamaran in the winter. Then I hurried back out on the beach, carefully picked up three syringes and a strip of bloody bandage, rolled them up in the heavy plastic. "Come on, babe," I said, grabbing Mary's hand. "We're going to get Garth, and then we're taking you to the hospital."

She staggered after me up the path, looking back over her

shoulder at the ugly array of needles and bandages. "It's starting, just like I said it would," she said in a hollow voice. "Bad things; I told you Sacra makes bad things happen."

.   .   .

The nurse in the emergency room at Cairn Hospital wasn't much impressed by the small puncture wound in the sole of Mary's foot; he, and the doctors on duty, were, though, appropriately shaken by the bundle of syringes and stained bandage I had brought with me. Dr. Angelo Franconi, a friend of Garth's, immediately took the package, told us he would see what he could determine about the contents from examining the debris under a microscope. The nurse disinfected and bandaged the wound in Mary's foot, and he gave her a pair of paper slippers to wear. Then we went downstairs to the coffee shop in the basement and waited nervously.

Fifty-five minutes later Angelo Franconi, looking both relieved and puzzled, joined us. He pulled a chair up to our table, laid a hand gently on Mary's forearm, spoke to my brother. "We can't tell for certain that the needles are clean until we try to grow a culture, which I've already ordered done. But, from examining them under a microscope, I'd say the chances are ninety-nine out of a hundred that the needles were never used; one of them was still in its original plastic package. Somebody with a boat must have lost a lot of syringes overboard, and the carton broke up in the water somewhere very close to you. Wind and tide were just right to wash most of the stuff up on your beach. It certainly is a freakish kind of accident, but I don't think you have much to worry about."

Garth asked, "What about the bloody bandages?"

The dark-skinned doctor ran a hand back through his close-cropped black hair, shook his head. "Now, there's a real mystery. I can tell you the blood isn't infected with any pathogens you can see under a microscope. It isn't even human; it's chicken blood. I can't imagine where surgical bandages covered with chicken blood would come from, and it really is curious how that combination of garbage washed up on your property."

I didn't think it was curious at all, and I didn't consider it much of a mystery. When I looked at Garth, I could see he felt the same way.

"You said you wanted me to leave him to you, and I'm doing that," Garth whispered to me as we walked out of the hospital. "But you'd better be quick about it, because if I stumble across him before you do, I promise you his corpse will be the next piece of garbage that washes up on somebody's beach."

CHAPTER EIGHT

There were a number of messages waiting for me when I got back to New York, but there was one in which I was particularly interested. It was from Captain Perry Farmer of the NYPD, and he wanted me to get back to him as soon as possible. I picked up the phone, dialed his precinct station house, and asked for his extension.

"The prints you gave me matched up, Mongo," Perry said after some preliminary chitchat. "Your guy's name is Charles 'Chick' Carver."

Well, well. I cradled the receiver under my chin as I wrote it down, underlining the last name. "That's great news, Perry. What have you got on him?"

"He spent five years in Greenhaven for—now get this, Mongo—aggravated malicious mischief. He'd gotten fines and short jail sentences a few times before for similar things, so the judge in the last case decided to throw the book at him. It seems that when Mr. Carver takes a dislike to somebody, he just can't leave it alone. He served three and a half months in a halfway house rehab program and got out on parole nine months ago.

He also had an extensive juvenile record. Some of that is sealed, but from the kind of flag on the file, I'd say he may have been sent to a mental hospital, probably Rockland Children's Psychiatric Center up near where Garth lives now."

"You got an address for him?"

"Yeah; it's a walkup on the Lower East Side, but it's a phony. It's a real enough apartment, and the rent's paid up, but he hasn't been there in six months. I had one of my men talk to some of the neighbors. His probation officer isn't too happy about it, and he's going to have some explaining to do the next time he talks to her."

"You've spoken to his probation officer?"

"Yeah. I got kind of curious about what kind of guy can draw a five-year prison sentence for malicious mischief."

"A very malicious guy. Hey, Perry, you're a prince for taking the time you have."

"I haven't forgotten I owe you, Mongo."

"What did his probation officer have to say about him?"

"She says he can be a real charmer when he wants to be—like most sociopaths. He's pretty bright, but he has a real child's outlook on life. He wants to be a big man, but he doesn't have the patience or self-discipline needed to acquire the skills to become a big man. And so he's a schemer, a manipulator. He apparently has this witchcraft gig he likes to do on people he thinks will swallow it. Anyway, he may yet turn out to be a big man, because somebody arranged for him to get a job with the shipping company his family is connected with. It sounds to me like some strings were pulled."

"Indeed," I said, drawing a circle around the last name I had already underlined.

"Incidentally, when I say he's pretty bright, I'm talking fluorescent. He's a member of Mensa, for what that's worth. His probation officer thinks that he really could amount to something if he ever did get some discipline and learn to channel his intelligence and energy, but she's not optimistic. She thinks he's dangerous, says she wouldn't be surprised if he ends up killing somebody one day."

"Indeed."

"It's like having a Rolls-Royce engine under the hood of a Yugo. Anyway, that's what I've got for you. Any help?"

"Knowing who he is helps a lot. Now I want to find him."

"I never did ask you where you got those prints. What's Carver done that makes you so interested in him?"

"At the very least, more malicious mischief. But now I'm thinking it could be even more than that. I'll stay in touch. Thanks again, Perry."

"Anytime, Mongo."

I hung up, then got out my Manhattan directory and looked for Carver Shipping. There was no listing. There was also no listing in the Rockland directory, but I hit pay dirt when I checked the New Jersey directory. Carver Shipping's headquarters was in Jersey City. I dialed the number, and a pleasant woman's voice answered.

"Carver Shipping. May I help you, please?"

"I hope so. I'd like to speak with Mr. Carver."

"Mr. Carver is retired, sir."

It seemed Chick Carver had not quite yet achieved big-man status. "Not the founder. I mean the younger one, Charles."

"Oh, I'm sorry, sir. I just started this job yesterday. Just a moment, please. I'll look in the company directory." There was a pause for a few seconds, and then the woman came back on the line. "Sir?"

"I'm still here."

"There's a Charles Carver working in Security. I'll switch you over."

"Thanks—oh! Who's the head of that department?"

"Mr. Wellington, sir."

"Would that be Frank Wellington?"

"I believe his name is Roger, sir. Shall I switch you over?"

"Please."

There was some electronic whirring and clicking, and then another pleasant voice, this one a man's, said, "Mr. Wellington's office."

"Mr. Carver, please."

"Mr. Carver isn't at his desk at the moment."

That didn't surprise me; I was pretty certain he was in Cairn.

The big question was whether his business there was strictly personal or also corporate. "Can you tell me how I can reach him? This is the Esoteric Bookshop. Mr. Carver's order has come in. However, there seems to have been a mix-up concerning his current residential address and phone number. He did say he wanted the materials as soon as they came in. Could you give me his address and phone number, please?"

There was a short pause, then, "I'm afraid I can't give out that information over the phone, sir. Who did you say you represent?"

"The Esoteric Bookshop. Well, just tell him that the books he ordered on coprophilia, necrophilia, pedophilia, bestiality, and suicide by masturbation have arrived, and he can pick them up at his convenience. Have you got that, or would you like me to repeat it?"

"I will make sure he gets your message, sir," the young man replied after some hesitation. I thought I detected more than a hint of bewilderment, and I certainly hoped he would share this newly discovered information about Charles "Chick" Carver's reading habits with the rest of the office staff.

"Thanks. Have a nice day."

Next, I got my Rockland directory back out, called the Cairn Fishermen's Association. Lonnie Allen answered.

"Lonnie?"

"Yes. Who is this, please?"

"This is Mongo Frederickson, Lonnie. I was in the office with Garth the other day."

"Oh, Dr. Frederickson!" she said as if she were truly pleased to hear my voice. "I didn't know who you were when you were in here, but now I do. You're famous. I should have asked you for your autograph."

"Anytime, Lonnie. Listen, I'd like you to do me a favor."

"Of course, Dr. Frederickson. What can I do for you?"

"My friends and beautiful women like yourself call me Mongo. I need some information, and I'm not sure how to get it. I was hoping CFA might be able to help."

"What do you need, Mongo?"

"I'd like you to do some checking for me with the members of your association, and anybody else who's in tune with things that happen on the river. I'm looking for hard facts, but would also like to hear any gossip or rumors you might pick up. Specifically what I'm looking for are examples of bad luck, anything harmful, that may have happened to anyone who may have filed a pollution complaint against, or had any kind of run-in with, Carver Shipping."

There was a brief pause on the other end of the line, then Lonnie said, "Bad luck? I'm not sure I understand what you mean, Mongo."

"Well, take Tom Blaine as an example. He was almost certainly gathering evidence against Carver Shipping when he was sucked up into those propeller blades. Some people might call that bad luck. But I'm not necessarily talking about people dying; I'm looking for examples of anything unlucky happening to someone after they got on Carver Shipping's case in any way whatsoever. Does that make it clearer?"

"Yes, I think so. I'll make some calls."

"Good. But make sure you're discreet. Keep the conversations low-key, and just try to slide into the subject. Don't mention that you're making inquiries for me. I don't want any bad luck coming Lonnie Allen's way."

"I'll do it like you say, Mongo."

"Thanks, Lonnie. I appreciate it. I'll check back with you in a couple of days."

•   •   •

"Suicide by masturbation," Garth said drily. "Cute. But a bit sophomoric, don't you think?"

"It seemed like a good idea at the time. I'm not sure just what we're dealing with here, and I didn't want our boy Sacra Silver to know yet that I know who he really is. At the same time, it wouldn't bother me at all if he became the object of a little gossip and ridicule around the office. I was feeling a bit vicious."

"He dumps a boatload of needles and bloody bandages for my wife to walk on, and you pay him back by starting a gossip campaign. You call that vicious?"

"Cut me some slack, brother. I found out who he is, didn't I? Let him worry for a while about who made the call."

97

"He'll know it was you or me."

"Oh, I'm not so sure. I suspect our occultist bullshit artist has any number of enemies strewn over the countryside. That's why he's so leery of telling people his real name."

Garth grunted, sank back deeper into his canvas chair. We were sitting on his deck, drinking coffee and feasting our senses on the wide, sailboat-dotted expanse of river before us. After a week, we had ourselves quite a collection of photographs of Carver Shipping tankers going up and down the river. Every one of them rode as deep in the water heading seaward as they had been when they were heading upriver to make their deliveries; Carver Shipping certainly hadn't let Tom Blaine's death slow down their illicit sideline enterprise.

"So," Garth said, pointing to the stack of photographs on the glass-topped coffee table between us. "We've got lots of pretty pictures. Now what do we do?"

"I'm not sure."

"Turn these over to the Coast Guard? The CFA people? Or do we go diving now to get our own water samples?"

"Maybe, maybe, and maybe. But what would be the point? We've probably got the goods on them right now as far as taking on river water is concerned. We might even persuade the Coast Guard to make a call asking them to stop, assuming our friend Captain Marley was in a good mood. And they'd stop. If the Cairn Fishermen's Association decides they have enough evidence and witnesses now to take them to court, they'll stop. Then we'll be worse off than we are now, because we'll have tipped our hand. We didn't start this to prove Carver Shipping is polluting and stealing water; that's a sideshow. We want to find out if one of their captains is a killer."

"So what do we do next?"

"You must enjoy hearing me repeat myself. However, since you insist on probing the devious and resourceful mind of this master investigator, I might suggest we have another option besides turning over these photographs and putting everyone, including Julian Jefferson, on guard."

"What option would that be, O master investigator?"

"Work on our pal Chick Carver. He's a loose thread."

"Loose thread? He's a loose cannon."

"That too. But maybe we should pull on him for a while and see what unravels."

"You think he was involved in Tom's death?"

"I don't know. What we do know is that he works for Carver Shipping, as an assistant to the head of security. He sure as hell knows about the water-stealing scam; probably everyone in the company down to the shipping clerks knows. Whether he knows anything about Tom's death is something we may find out if we pull at him a bit."

"How?"

"Maybe he'll give us the answer to that question. He certainly is a persistent son-of-a-bitch, so I think it's safe to assume he'll make another pass at one or both of us. When he does, he may leave himself vulnerable in some way we can't know until he does it."

"It sounds to me like you want to keep playing with him, Mongo. The idea doesn't much appeal to me."

"I prefer my original metaphor of pulling on a loose thread," I replied a bit testily. "If you've got a better idea for forcing an investigation into your friend's death, please share it with me."

"I still say he's a fucking loose cannon."

"Then maybe he'll backfire."

"I want to be perfectly clear about something, Mongo," Garth said in a calm, casual tone of voice that, when combined with my brother's air of steely resolve, was always a powerful sign of danger. "I understand what you're saying. If it were only you and me Sacra Silver was playing with, your approach wouldn't bother me; I might even enjoy the game. But Silver sees Mary as the prize in this contest; he's playing with, and for, her. And that's where I have to draw the line. So you play with him; pull his chain all you want. But if I meet up with him face-to-face, I won't be playing any game."

I raised my coffee mug to him, nodded. "I think I get your drift, brother. Perchance you thought I'd forgotten the danger Carver poses to Mary?"

"I didn't say that, Mongo," Garth replied, uncharacteristically looking away. He picked up his binoculars from the coffee table and began scanning the river. "I just don't want you getting pissed off at me if your loose thread ends up with a broken back."

"We are in excellent communication, as usual."

"So we wait?"

"Wait, keep taking pictures, and see what happens with Mr. Chick Carver."

"Fine. Just so long as you remember what—" Garth suddenly stopped speaking, stiffened in his chair, then abruptly stood up and stepped to the railing of the deck. He was looking to the south through the binoculars.

"What is it, Garth?"

He motioned with his right hand for me to join him at the railing. I did, and he handed me the binoculars. Then he pointed downriver, toward an approaching tanker in the distance. "Check it out."

I peered through the binoculars, adjusting the focus. It was a big tanker, maybe seven hundred feet long, with a gray hull highlighted by red and yellow stripes along the waterline. As big as two football fields, the deck of the tanker was dotted with vent stacks, pallets of supplies, and large orange cranes on both its port and starboard sides. An enormous superstructure containing an elevated wheelhouse rose up into the sky at the stern end; painted white, the superstructure looked a bit like a three-tiered wedding cake. The tanker was negotiating its way between red and green buoys in an area where the deep channel crossed from one side of the river to the other, giving me a clear view of its length. The tanker's registration number was clearly visible on its stern end: 82Q510. Julian Jefferson was back in the neighborhood.

I said, "Son-of-a-bitch."

"Yeah," Garth replied softly. "That's what I was thinking."

I watched as the tanker made its turn, then continued to proceed north, toward us. Suddenly two medium-size tugs appeared in my field of vision, coming from the north. The water at the stern of the tanker began to churn even more as the captain reversed his engines. A half hour later, with the help of the two tugs, the tanker was securely anchored to a permanent mooring offshore from the tool and die manufacturing complex across the river, perhaps fifty yards from the end of the complex's steel and concrete dock. A half dozen crewmen appeared on deck, and we watched as the men went about their business opening valves and attaching enormous black hoses that would be connected to fittings on the dock.

"So near and yet so far," Garth continued quietly.

"Yeah."

"You want to go rent some diving equipment?"

"I didn't think our mother raised any stupid children. When was the last time you were scuba diving, brother?"

Garth shrugged. "Seven, maybe eight years ago—in the Virgin Islands."

"You think you can find the underwater venting ports on that hull in total darkness, with a four-or-five-knot current nudging you in the ass?"

"You're saying we're not qualified?"

"I'm saying Mom wouldn't approve, and you remember, I'm sure, Dad's lectures on the difference between courage and stupidity."

"I seem to recall him lecturing *you* on the difference between courage and stupidity. The fact remains that we have the ship that probably killed Tom sitting over there right under our noses. We don't know how long it's going to stay there, and we don't know when it will be back. We've got to go for it now."

"Go for what?"

"I don't know. Maybe call the Coast Guard again. *Something*."

"It would be a waste of time to call the Coast Guard. All they're doing right now is unloading a cargo of fuel oil."

"Mongo—"

"Okay, let's go," I said, hanging the binoculars on a peg on the railing.

"Where?"

"To see if we can't rattle the captain's cage, and see what transpires."

Garth obviously liked the idea. He grunted his approval, then quickly fell into step beside me as I walked out of the house and headed down toward the beach. "I thought the master investigator didn't think we should tip our hand."

"The master investigator has changed his mind; master investigators do that all the time, which is one reason why we're master investigators. I said we didn't want to tip our hand to the *company*."

"That's not what you said."

"This is—maybe—the captain who murdered Tom Blaine. If so, he may still be more than a bit edgy, and he might make a mistake. On the other hand, maybe what happened to Tom really was an accident, in which case Jefferson may not have any idea what happened. I just think it would be interesting to see how he reacts to us."

"You think he'll talk to us?"

"I guess we're about to find out, aren't we? It's risky, but we don't really know what we're going to do about Tom's death anyway, and we may never get another chance to get this close to the captain and ship that probably killed him."

"Agreed," Garth said, then slowed his pace. "I should probably leave a note for Mary."

"You do what you feel you need to do, but if the church meeting she's at lasts as long as usual, we'll probably be back before she is."

"You're right."

We went into the boathouse to retrieve a length of rope, as well as one of the green plastic jugs we had taken from Tom Blaine's basement office. We tied the jug to the lacing between the two halves of the catamaran's canvas trampoline, then dragged the cat down to the river's edge. Garth raised the sail, locked it into place. We pushed the cat into the water and hopped on, with Garth in the middle and me at the tiller, and we were off.

We were in no danger of being becalmed. It was, in fact, an ideal day for sailing, with white cream puffs of cloud high in an azure sky, a warm sun, and a steady twelve-to-fifteen knot wind from the southwest. The tide was going out, so I pointed a few degrees north of the tanker, on a starboard tack, and sheeted in the mainsail. The cat shot forward, its pontoons hissing, leaving nice rooster tails of surf in our wake. When I felt the pontoon beneath me begin to rise, I slipped both my feet beneath the hiking strap, let out the traveler to just past the three-quarters mark, and loosened the sheet a bit. It would have been great fun to fly a hull, but we were out on business, and I didn't want to take a chance on dumping. There was some swell, but Garth was expert at shifting his weight at the right moment to keep our center of gravity toward the rear to prevent us from accidentally pitchpoling.

Three quarters of the way across the river, and perhaps a quarter mile north of the tanker, I tacked, heading high into the wind, beating on a direct line toward the tanker's bow. A hundred yards away, I tacked again, heading directly into the wind and intentionally going into irons. I brought the traveler back to the center point and cinched down the boom to minimize luffing of the sail. While the wind was in our face and trying to push us back, our surface area was minimized; as I had hoped, the current caught us and carried us forward at one or two knots. Five minutes later we were drifting beneath the tanker's bow, looking up at two crewmen who had taken time off from their chores to watch us pass by. One of them, a dark-skinned man with a handle-bar moustache and a puffy, black birthmark on his cheek, looked downright hostile; the other, a sallow-faced crewman wearing a rumpled seaman's cap low on his forehead, merely seemed curious. I waved to the curious-looking one, who waved back.

"Ahoy, there," I called. "How's it going?"

"No hablamos inglés," the gloomy-faced man called back. Then he looked at the other man, and they both laughed.

Garth shouted, "We want to talk to the captain!"

"No hablamos inglés," the crewman with the cap replied, and they both laughed again.

I untied the jug from the trampoline lacing, held it aloft. "Try speaking this, *amigos*! We want to speak to your captain about what's in this jug! *Agua mala* from this ship! It's important! He's going to want to talk to us! Tell him we want to come aboard! Go get him!"

The two men conferred as we continued to drift down the length of the massive tanker. Then, somewhat to my surprise, the glum-looking one with the birthmark saluted us, then turned away from the railing and disappeared from sight. The second

103

crewman stayed where he was, staring after us with a somewhat amused expression on his face.

We came abreast of the stern. It was evident that the ship had already begun to unload its cargo, for the thick top of the great steel rudder was just visible above the waterline. It was time to turn around. I waited until we were about fifteen yards astern of the tanker, then nodded to Garth. I pushed the tiller as far as it would go to the starboard side while Garth unlocked the sheet and pushed the boom as far out as he could in the same direction, causing us to backwind. A catamaran is very fast when sailing in a straight line, especially on a beam reach, but it's a pig in water when coming about; locked in irons, the wind constantly tends to suck the craft back into a line parallel with, and facing, the wind's direction. However, after three near misses, we finally managed to get the stern kicked around to a degree where we had a proper angle to the wind and could make headway. I pointed north, at a forty-five-degree angle away from the tanker. I sailed us in a broad semicircle, then repeated my original maneuver, sending us into irons near the bow of the ship, cinching down the boom, and letting the current carry us along the port side of the ship. The two crewmen we had originally spoken to had been joined by a third at the railing. This crewman was thickset, with very large black eyes. He wore a red bandana around his head, and, despite the heat of the summer day, a heavy black wool sweater. His expression was somber as he stared down at us.

"Yo!" I called to the man in the black sweater. "You Captain Jefferson?"

"No," he replied in a deep, rich baritone that carried clearly down to us. He had a pronounced Greek accent. "What do you want?"

"We'd like permission to come aboard. There's a big police and Coast Guard investigation going on concerning the man who died under your ship a few weeks ago. He was taking samples of the bad water you people were flushing out of your tanks, and they think somebody on board may have purposely turned on your ship's engines while he was under there. That would make it murder. All we want to do is get Captain Jefferson's side of the story before the police, Coast Guard, and newspaper people begin swarming around here and he gets too busy to talk to us. How about it? You got a rope ladder we can tie up to? We don't have that many questions, and we won't take up much of the captain's time."

"Who the hell are you people?"

We were drifting out of earshot, and since the English-speaking Greek did not seem inclined to follow us down the railing, it meant we would have to come about once again.

"We're investigators working for your insurance company!" I shouted as I pushed the tiller hard to starboard to initiate the maneuver that would bring us around. "Just wait there! We'll be right back!"

"This is a waste of time, Mongo," Garth said evenly as he pushed on the boom, and I struggled to get us under sail. "Maybe worse than a waste of time."

"You could be right, but sitting around on your deck and watching the river flow was getting to be a waste of time too, wasn't it? You wanted to do something, remember? We're doing something. At the worst, we can always go to the Coast Guard with the photographs when we get back. The only way we can get a murder investigation started is to catch somebody else's interest. If we can't interest the police or Coast Guard, then we have to try to interest the captain—and hope he says or does something incriminating."

Garth merely shrugged. "I didn't say I disagreed with your reasoning, and I wanted to come out here even more than you did. We gave it a shot, but now I think we're wasting our time. I'd like to see Jefferson's reaction too, but we're not going to get on board."

"Ah, but we don't know yet how the powers that be on board that ship are reacting to my insurance investigator ploy. I say we make one more pass."

"Go for it."

We went around the horn again, with Garth making only an occasional disparaging remark about the believability of insurance investigators conducting official business on a fourteen-foot cata-maran. The sallow-faced crewman with the rumpled cap had been left alone at the rail to chart our progress. However, after we'd gone into irons and once again begun to drift with the current alongside the ship, the Greek suddenly appeared at the railing.

"Go away!" he bellowed in his resonant baritone, gesturing angrily. He paused, glanced toward the south, then looked back at us. "You're crazy! Get out of here!"

I once again held up the green plastic jug. It was time to let out all the stops. "This jug contains samples of water flushed from this tanker into the river. It proves you've been polluting. We can also prove that you've been taking on river water, in violation of the law, shipping it somewhere else and selling it. This sample was collected by the man who was killed under your ship. Now, we're trying to be fair about this. This is absolutely the last chance your captain is going to have to tell his side of the story before his picture and the Coast Guard's version of what happened get splashed all over the newspapers. It's in his interest to talk to us. We won't take up much of his time." I paused, waiting to see if my words would have some effect. They didn't. The two men remained where they were at the rail, but they were no longer paying any attention to us; both crewmen were now looking to the south. And we were once again almost out of earshot. "At least bring him up on deck to talk to us!" I shouted. "He's being accused of murder! Let us—!"

Suddenly both men turned and abruptly walked away from the railing.

"So much for rattling cages," Garth said in disgust. "Let's get out of here. We'll call the Coast Guard and the CFA, turn over what we've got, and be done with it. We've done everything we could, and we're at a dead end. Maybe we can leak some information to the papers, see what happens. There's no way we can do everybody's fucking job for them."

"When you're right, you're right," I said with a sigh, and pushed the tiller hard to starboard. "But Tom was your friend, and I had to hear you say we'd done enough."

From somewhere in the distance, from the south, the low rumble of a powerful engine could be heard. Garth shifted his weight toward the stern, uncinched the boom, pushed it out. I jiggled the tiller, trying to kick the stern around, but the wind had increased in velocity; we kept getting sucked back into irons, while at the same time being pushed ever closer to the tanker.

"Let's goose it out of here, Mongo," Garth said tersely, glancing back at the steel hull behind him at the same time as he pushed the boom even further to starboard.

"I'm trying, I'm trying."

The rumble of the powerboat's engines had become a roar; the boat was not only coming in our direction but sounded unusually close to shore, not out in the middle of the river where you would expect a large powerboat at full throttle to be. I turned, squinted, and could see a black shape on the surface with a large rooster tail of wake rising into the air behind it. The airplane-like sound the craft was producing indicated the boat was carrying an engine—maybe two—generating upwards of 350 horsepower; that would make it a cigarette boat, or an equivalent model. On its present course, it was heading right for the tanker—and us.

The breeze shifted slightly, and a puff of wind kicked our stern to port. I quickly sheeted in the mainsail and straightened the tiller. We began to slowly move away from the tanker as we stayed just on the edge of going back into irons. We were heading directly into the path of the approaching powerboat, but at the moment I was more concerned with avoiding being pinned against the hull of the tanker than with the powerboat and its cowboy driver. There was no way the man or woman at the helm of the black boat could avoid seeing our sail sticking up into the air; since anything under sail always has the right-of-way over powerboats, the driver would turn away. There was going to be some pretty powerful wake to contend with, but we'd been in rough waters before, and I was sure we could handle it. I eased the tiller over a bit, putting us on more of a port tack that would enable me to steer across the boat's wake at a forty-five-degree angle.

The problem was that the driver of the black boat wasn't bearing off; he was heading for us straight amidships.

"Son-of-a-bitch!" Garth said sharply. "The guy's crazy! He's coming right across our bow!"

I pushed the tiller hard to the right, trying to bring the bow of the catamaran to an angle that would enable me to head into the other boat's wake head-on—our only chance, under these circumstances, to keep from capsizing. I anchored my feet in the hiking straps, firmly gripped the handle of the tiller with one hand, and the steel frame behind me with the other.

"Hang on!" Garth shouted as he laid himself out flat across the trampoline, spreading his arms and legs out to his sides.

With a deafening scream of engines more familiar to an airport than a river, the thirty-foot-long, jet-black cigarette boat shot across in front of us, not more than six feet from our bow. In the quarter second before its bow wave hit us, I noticed that the name of the boat painted on the hull had been covered over with silver, water-resistant duct tape. The driver, only his head and shoulders visible from where he sat in the cockpit, was wearing a black ski mask.

Since it was a tad warm to be wearing a ski mask, my master investigator's instincts told me that the boat's close passage was no accident, and that the driver clearly intended to kill us.

That was all the time for thinking I had. The bow wave hit only a split second before the spray from the rooster-tail wake washed over the cat, blinding me. The bow wave rolled under the pontoons, lifting us high up in the air, then throwing us back toward the tanker. I leaned forward as much as possible, for at that moment the critical danger was of flipping over backward. In the next moment, the danger was the reverse as we shot down the face of the bow wave; if the tips of the pontoons nosed into the water at the bottom of the wave's trough, we were sure to pitchpole. Garth had rolled back toward the stern to bring the bow up. The nose of the cat did disappear into the water at the bottom of the trough, and for one sickening moment I thought we were going to be catapulted forward. But then the nose came out, and we rode up and over another wave.

In our situation, the cat's raised sail was worse than useless, for there was no way to harness the wind blowing at us in order to sail away; the Mylar sheet was flapping violently, causing the steel boom to bang back and forth over Garth's head and only inches from my face. The result was that we were turned ninety degrees, and the waves were coming at us broadside.

With the passage of the bow wave, and the next two or three

that rolled under us, the worst of the wake was spent, and we had not capsized. However, we were turned broadside, caught in irons, and the cigarette boat was making a very tight turn in order to make another pass at us. And we were no more than a few feet from the steel wall that was the hull of the tanker. There was no way of getting the cat under control before the powerboat came back at us, and I braced for the inevitable collision with the hull of the tanker as I looked out over the water, searching for other boats; there were two other sailboats in the area, but they were some distance away, across the river and to the south, and it was impossible to gauge if they could see what was happening—not that it would make any difference to the man in the cigarette boat; we were likely to be dead long before any kind of help could arrive. When we whapped up against the side of the tanker, we could either be knocked unconscious, and unceremoniously drown, or be forced underwater and carved up by barnacles on the hull that could slice like millions of tiny switchblades.

Without having any idea of just what I intended to do with a length of rope when I had it, I released the boom, grabbed hold of it, then untied the knot securing the sheet to the traveler's car. Garth saw what I was trying to do, rolled over on his back, reached up, and gripped the boom with both hands, holding it steady. I reached out for where the other end of the line was tied to a clew at the heel of the mainsail. I broke three fingernails, but finally managed to pull the line loose just as the powerboat, and its deafening wall of sound, roared past once again, this time only a yard or so from our starboard pontoon. The bow wave lifted us, hurled the cat back against the tanker's steel hull. The tip of the mast hit first, and there was a sound like a gunshot as one of the steel shrouds snapped, and the deadly end of the wire whipped through the air just inches from my face. The mast snapped at its base. The hull of the catamaran banged once more against the hull with a force that I could feel in every bone of my body, then flipped over, dumping us into the churning water.

I clawed my way to the surface, felt a moment of heart-freezing panic when my right hand touched Mylar; the sail was over us. With my heart pounding, terror consuming all the oxygen in my system, I jackknifed in the water, forcing myself to dive deeper, the only direction I could go if I hoped to survive. I flattened out, began desperately pulling with my arms and kicking with my legs, unable to see anything in the murky, silt-roiled water. With my lungs bursting, I shot up for what I hoped was the surface, knowing I would never have a second chance if I still came up under the death shroud of the sail. My head broke the surface only inches from the edge of the floating mass of Mylar. Pent-up breath exploded from my lungs, and I just managed to gulp some air before a wave washed over me, driving me back under the surface. The water carried a troubling new threshing, metallic sound that throbbed in my ears.

The ominous, deep growl was the tanker's engines rumbling to life, ripping the river with their giant talons of shaped steel.

I came back up, gulped more air, desperately looked around for Garth, and finally spotted him. One of the cat's pontoons had cracked open and sunk below the surface, but the other was still afloat, and Garth, blood from a gash on his forehead streaming down over his face, was draped over it, feebly moving his arms in an effort to hang on. But he was losing the battle, slipping. Fifteen feet beyond him, the water at the stern of the ship was frothing and churning from the thrust of the mighty engines far below the surface. That's where the current was carrying us both.

I clawed at the sail, pulling it into me, and it finally caught on the tip of the floating pontoon. I pulled myself hand over hand to the pontoon, heaved myself up on it, straddling the tiny island of fiberglass. Garth's head was slipping below the surface. I grabbed the back of his polo shirt, gave a mighty heave, and managed to pull him back up. His head lolled back, and I could see that his eyes were out of focus.

"Garth!" I screamed. "Garth, you've got to hang on! I can't haul you up! I can't do it alone, Garth! Hang on! Get your arms up!"

His right arm slowly came up out of the water, dropped over the pontoon. I gave his shirt another tug, then let go, quickly reached down, lifted up his left arm, draped it over the pontoon. The roar of the powerboat was rising, behind me and slightly to my left, as the driver came at us once again. The sail was now billowing in the water all around us, and the rope I had pulled loose from the rigging was floating on its surface. I grabbed it and pulled it in, gathering it in loose coils around my waist, looking for an end. I found one, and quickly formed a loop around Garth's chest, under his arms, and tied it off with a bowline.

The airplane-engine scream of the cigarette boat swept past behind me, and I braced for the thunderous wake and spray, gripping Garth's shirt collar tightly with one hand while holding a coil of rope in the other. I twisted around on the pontoon and stuck out both feet to fend off as we were swept up once more against the tanker's hull. I knew the shock might very well break my legs, but it was better that my legs be broken than Garth's back. Where there was life, there was . . . something, even if I couldn't quite recall at the moment what it was. I certainly preferred it to death.

The bow wave hit, lifting the catamaran, turning it, smashing its stern end into the steel hull, and saving my legs. The second wave turned us once again, and this time it was my head that smacked against the steel, barely a foot above a field of barnacles that would have scalped me. I felt the shock through my entire body, but, incredibly, there was no pain. For a moment everything went dark, but I managed to stay on the pontoon and maintain my grip on Garth's shirt collar. Knowing that to lose consciousness meant death for both of us, I screamed inwardly at myself, concentrating in the prickly, star-streaked darkness on the tactile feel of Garth's shirt, the fiberglass under me, the water pounding all around and over me; if those sensations went away, we went away.

Then my vision cleared, just in time for me to see that we were inside the frothing circle of water at the ship's stern, nudging up against the great steel rudder. I could feel us being sucked down.

As the shriek of the cigarette boat faded into the distance, heading back south, I looked around for something to grab hold of. There was nothing. With the water frothing all around us from the churning propeller blades below, I looked in a different direction—up. Throughout the attack by the powerboat, the tanker had apparently continued to off-load its cargo of oil, for the stern was now perhaps a foot higher in the water than it had

been, exposing even more of the squared-off top of the massive
rudder blade. It was the only angular surface in town, and it was
the one I was going to have to reach if we were to keep breathing
for more than another minute or two.

I checked to make certain that the loop around Garth's chest
was secure. I had no idea where the other end of the line was,
nor time to find it. What I did have was a coil of rope in my left
hand, with the rest of the line floating in the white water around
me. I stood up on the pontoon, flexing my knees for balance,
then gathered in more rope and flung the coil over my head,
trying to catch the edge of the rudder blade. I missed by an inch,
and the rope fell back into the water. Swaying unsteadily on the
slippery fiberglass surface of the sinking pontoon, I gathered up
the rope, flung it aloft once again. This time a loop caught on
the edge of the rudder. I began to draw in the slack, hoping with
some fervor that I wasn't simply pulling up the loose end. Then,
suddenly, the rope went taut. I pulled even harder, and Garth's
torso rose a few inches out of the water. It would have to be
enough, for I was running out of time and in imminent danger
of losing consciousness. I tied off the rope in the loop I had
already knotted around Garth's chest. As the ruined catamaran
was sucked under the boiling water, I leaped onto Garth's back,
wrapping one arm tightly around his neck below his windpipe
and using my free hand to cup his chin and tilt it back in order
to keep his head above water.

If we could just survive for another five or ten minutes, if the
rope held, I thought there was a chance we could make it. The
tanker was continuing to unload, and rising ever higher in the
water as it did so, lifting us with it. The crew and captain of the
tanker couldn't see us, but two men dangling on a rope off the
rudder of their ship should certainly attract some attention from
the crew of any other boat that passed close enough to see us.

I thought I felt the rope slip a little. I looked up to try to
determine if the line was slipping over the edge of the rudder,
and was amazed to find that I couldn't see that far. My field of
vision was filled with sparkling red, blue, and green dots sur-
rounded by a shiny black border that kept growing, swallowing
up the dancing points of light. I tasted blood, but wasn't sure

whether it was mine or Garth's, since I had my cheek pressed against his.

I tightened my grip around Garth's neck, closed my eyes. The rope was going to hold, I thought; I just had to make sure that I held. We weren't going to drown, we were going to be lifted clear of the water, I was going to be able to maintain my grip, somebody was going to see us dangling, and we were going to be rescued. I kept repeating those thoughts in my mind like a mantra, and I was a third of the way through the third rerun when I passed out.

CHAPTER NINE

It must have been a pretty decent mantra, because, sure enough, I woke up in a hospital bed; I had a blinding headache and a taste in my mouth like rotting fruit, but the evidence seemed incontrovertible that I was alive. Garth was in the bed next to me, his eyes closed and his head swathed in bandages. Mary, her chalky pallor accentuated by the dark rings around her eyes, was sitting between us in a straight-backed chair. She smiled wanly when she saw I was awake, leaned over, and kissed me on the cheek.

"Hello, Mongo," she said.

"Garth?" I asked anxiously.

Mary nodded. "He has a severe concussion, and he may not be awake for another day or two, but the doctors think he's going to be all right." She paused, shook her head. "Somebody on a sailboat saw the two of you hanging on a rope off the rudder of a tanker across the river, and they radioed the ship. A couple of crewmen went over the side on a rope ladder, rigged up a sling, and hauled you aboard. The Sheriff's Patrol brought you to the hospital. You saved Garth's life, didn't you, Mongo?"

"That's our hobby, saving each other's life." I sat up, groaned when a searing pain shot down through my skull, pushed Mary's hand away when she tried to get me to lie back down. "How long have we been here?"

"In the hospital? Two or three hours. What on earth *happened,* Mongo?" She paused, laughed nervously. "I can't leave the two of you alone together. When I do, you either end up becalmed miles from home, or unconscious and hanging off the rudder of a ship."

"Yeah, well, we played pretty hard even as kids. Mary, Tom Blaine was murdered."

The tentative smile on her face vanished. "Murdered? You're sure?"

"I'm sure. He was murdered by the captain and crew of that particular tanker. They tried to do the same thing to us."

"But they helped rescue you."

"They didn't have any choice. We'd been spotted by another boat, and the captain of that boat probably radioed the tanker on channel eight, which all the barges and tankers monitor for emergency communications. Any other big ship in the area would have heard the call, and there was no telling who else the captain of the sailboat might have contacted. There were witnesses, and so they had to act. But the fact remains that they were in on the attempt to kill us. That's the ship Tom was trying to take samples from when he was killed. Garth and I sailed over to see if we could make a little eyeball-to-eyeball contact with the captain. While we were drifting around over there, somebody on board—probably the captain—made a radio call to somebody. A few minutes later a guy driving a cigarette boat and wearing a ski mask tried to mash us into the hull of the tanker. Then—"

I stopped speaking when I heard somebody else in the room clear his throat. I looked to my right as Harry Tanner emerged from behind a curtain. The Cairn policeman with the handlebar moustache and soulful hazel eyes looked properly concerned, but also uneasy, perhaps even embarrassed. I wondered why. "Hi, Mongo," he said. "Glad to see you're back with us."

"Well, Harry, I'm certainly glad to see you," I replied, watching him carefully. "I have a few things I'd very much like to share with you."

The policeman looked down at the foot of the bed. "I was on the phone down the hall talking to the dispatcher when you woke up, but I got back in time to hear most of what you were just saying."

"You heard me say that the captain and crew of that tanker killed Tom Blaine and tried to do the same to Garth and me?"

Now Harry Tanner looked even more embarrassed. "Yeah, I heard that."

"You know, Harry, damned if it doesn't sound like you don't believe me."

"It's not that I don't believe what you're saying, Mongo—although I can't see how whatever happened to you proves anything about what happened to Tom. You may even be right. But the fact remains that it *was* the captain and crew of that tanker who saved your bacon by hauling the two of you aboard and then calling the Sheriff's Patrol to bring you to the hospital."

"Only after somebody on a sailboat radioed them, and they knew there were witnesses."

"The first mate says you were warned to get away, that you were too close."

"What about the black cigarette boat?"

"There was a boat like the one you describe stolen from the Haverstraw Marina. They figure it was some kid wanting to take a joyride."

"Wearing a ski mask?"

"You're the only one who saw the driver, Mongo. They found the boat smashed up on a piling at the Tappan Zee Bridge."

"Abandoned, just like Tom Blaine's boat. Harry, I'm telling you an attempt was made to kill us, and the men on board that tanker were in on it. They tried to murder us because we're on to the fact that they murdered Tom Blaine. The engines of that tanker came on after we were dumped into the water."

The policeman shifted his weight slightly, pulled at the ends of his handlebar moustache, shrugged. "Mongo, I'm here because I'm a friend of you and your brother, but also because I was asked by the Coast Guard to get your statement, since you're in the hospital here in Cairn. What else do you want me to do? If you say the props were turning, then they were turning—or you thought they were. I'll put it down. But you know the captain of the tanker is going to deny it."

"Harry, somehow I get the feeling that even if I do tell you what else I want you to do, you're going to inform me that the matter is out of the Cairn Police Department's jurisdiction. Right?"

He flushed slightly. "The tanker's moored across the river, Mongo, servicing a factory in Westchester. We're not even in the same county. Nobody over there is likely to want to make waves—if you'll pardon the expression. The powerboat was stolen from the Haverstraw Marina and ended up in Nyack, so those two departments will look into that. But they're not going to involve themselves with what happens on the river."

"You make the river sound like Dodge City when the marshal's out of town."

"It's not a bad analogy, Mongo. Not a bad analogy at all. The only certain jurisdiction is the Coast Guard's, and they're literally out of town most of the time. But that's who you have to go to if you want to file a complaint with an agency that has unquestioned jurisdiction. I'm not trying to put you off, Mongo; I'm just telling you the way it is."

I wasn't too happy about it, but I knew Harry was right. In fact, we'd already learned a lesson or two about the jurisdiction politics of the river in connection with Tom Blaine's death, so I had no reason to be shocked at what the Cairn policeman was telling me. Garth and I could have saved ourselves the sailboat ride, and unpleasant dumping, because it had gotten us nowhere. The only option we had left was the same one we'd had before going out on the river: give the photos to the newspapers and Cairn Fishermen's Association, and trust that bad publicity and a threatened court action would force Carver Shipping to stop flushing out its tanks in the Hudson and taking on river water. They would undoubtedly mend their ways—at least for a while, until they were no longer in the spotlight. Captain Julian Jefferson and a few other people might even be fired, but they would most likely only be reprimanded, since they had obviously only been carrying out company policy.

And somebody was going to get away with murder and attempted murder.

For all our time and trouble, all we'd received was insult and injury: Garth in a coma, the Coast Guard and police telling us they didn't have jurisdiction, or were too busy preparing for the possibility of terrorists on the river to deal with the terror that was already there. If our clients had been anybody but ourselves, I would probably have advised them to cut their losses and stop wasting our time, and I'd probably have given them back their retainer.

"I gotta go, Mongo," Harry said quietly, reaching over the foot of the bed and gripping my ankle. "The doctors say Garth should be all right, and I'm damned happy the two of you made it through this thing okay. I'm sorry there's nothing I can do for you; I really wish there was. I love the river; that's why I live in Cairn. I don't like these rich hypocrites who live upstream and piss in our water any more than you do, but I'm just a Cairn cop, and Cairn cops don't handle pollution complaints—which is all you've got. I really am sorry."

"It's all right, Harry. I understand."

"I'm going to pass on what you told me to the state police and Coast Guard, Mongo. I'm also going to give the Westchester cops a call, tell them what you say happened, and ask them to keep an eye on that tanker while it's moored over there."

"That's great, Harry," I replied, barely managing to keep my tone free of the anger, bitterness, and frustration I felt.

Harry nodded, then turned and walked out of the room. I turned toward Mary, who was slumped in her chair, holding my brother's hand. Tears were running down her cheeks, and she looked every bit as dispirited as I felt. She whispered, "I told you, Mongo."

"You told me what?"

"Everything that's happened started after Sacra came to Cairn. Now maybe you can understand why I acted the way I did. He's bad luck; I don't know how or why, but he can make bad things happen, just like I told you."

Well, that was all I needed to hear. Up until my beautiful and talented sister-in-law had decided to resume what I considered to be her inexplicable indulgence in nincompoopism, I had been lying there with my splitting headache feeling sorry for myself and raging inwardly at the injustice of it all. Now I was just raging. My fury galvanized me, and I swung my legs over the side of the bed. The reward for this minor exertion was a renewed assault on the nerve endings in my head and a sudden attack of nausea and dizziness. I closed my eyes, took deep breaths. When I felt I could stand without throwing up or falling down, I hopped down on the floor.

"Mongo! What are you doing?"

I wobbled over to the wardrobe in a corner of the room, opened it, and was pleased to find my clothes—which is to say the swimming trunks, T-shirt, and tennis sneakers I'd been wearing. It would be just enough to get me back to the house without fear of being arrested for indecent exposure.

"Mongo—?"

"Listen to me, Mary!" I snapped, wheeling on her. Fury lent strength to my legs, my voice. "Your old boyfriend, Sacra Silver, isn't bad luck, he's bad news. That magic act of his is as phony as his name. Did it ever occur to you to ask yourself why he just happened to pop up in Cairn at this particular time? Why now? Haven't you ever wondered what his real name is?"

She frowned slightly, slowly shook her head. "To me, he was always just Sacra Silver."

"His real name is Charles Carver, and he's the son of your fellow churchgoer, pillar of the community, and former shipping magnate, Bennett Carver. He works for the company his father founded, my dear, and my guess is that his job is to act as some kind of enforcer. I think he originally came to Cairn because word had gotten to company headquarters that Tom Blaine was about to cause them grief, and it was Charles 'Chick' Carver's job to run interference, to stop Tom. After he got here, he found out that you lived in the neighborhood, and he thought it might be fun to pass the time by visiting an old girlfriend and playing one of his little games, just to see what would happen. You're rich now, and more famous than you ever were. You would be quite a prize for him, and he had nothing to lose—or so he thought, at least—by making a play for you. But I think his real reason for coming here in the first place was to deal with Tom Blaine."

Again, Mary slowly shook her head. She seemed confused, doubting. "You're saying you think Sacra had something to do with Tom's death?"

"It's a working hypothesis. I'm not saying he activated the engines himself, but he may have ordered it—or approved it. Either way, it would make him an accomplice to the murder. He's the troubleshooter, the one who gets the call when Carver Shipping's interests are threatened. Well, he got a call earlier today, from the captain of that tanker across the river where Garth and I were nosing around. I'm willing to bet a lot of money that it was Chick Carver who stole that boat and then tried to ram us into the ship. For all we know, that cigarette boat may not have been stolen at all; maybe it belongs to somebody employed by Carver Shipping. I'll check that out when I get the time; there can't be that many black cigarette boats with slips at Haverstraw Marina."

"Mongo, I don't think you should just leave like this," Mary said, rising and clasping her hands together nervously. "The doctors say you suffered a concussion too."

"If I have a concussion, it's a mild one—and it's not my first. It'll pass. I've got myself a beauty of a headache, but I can walk, and my vision is clear. I don't know how long that tanker is going to hang around, and I can't afford to waste time lying around here. I'm going to check myself out. I'll be back as soon as I can."

I stepped behind a screen, slipped out of my hospital pajamas, pulled on my trunks, T-shirt, and sneakers. Then I stepped back out. Mary had sat down again, but her hands were still clasped tightly together. She looked very uncertain and worried.

"I'm afraid I'm not dressed too well for travel. I'd like to go back to the house to change, if you don't mind."

"Of course, Mongo. But—"

120

"And maybe you'd be so kind as to loan me money for a cab. I don't quite feel up to jogging."

Mary picked up her purse and rummaged through it, while I went over to Garth's side and looked down at his still form. The anger in me was deep, surging and rising like a high tide. Mary found a ten-dollar bill, handed it to me. I started for the door.

"Mongo," she called after me, "where are you going?"

"To look for a tall, ugly thread to yank."

•   •   •

It was six-thirty when I arrived back at the house. The tanker was still at its mooring across the river; its cargo of fuel oil had been delivered, and it was riding high in the water, a broad band of rusted orange undercoating indicating that it hadn't flushed out its tanks and started to take on river water—yet. I went into the house, out onto the deck, and took a photograph of the tanker, just for the record. It was overcast, with dark thunderheads rolling low in the sky, and I took two more photographs at different exposures. Then I took a long, hot shower, dressed in dark slacks, shirt and tie, and a sports coat. I seriously wanted a drink, but suspected that alcohol wasn't the best thing in the world for my persistent, throbbing headache. I opted for three aspirin and a glass of seltzer water, then picked up the telephone.

•   •   •

The man who came to the door of the soaring Victorian mansion on the banks of the Hudson in Upper Cairn had to be in his mid-eighties, but he obviously took good care of himself, and looked fit. He had a full head of wavy silver hair, and a somewhat cherubic face fit for a Macy's Santa Claus, except for the pale green eyes which were bright, suspicious, and which would not be reassuring to children who had misbehaved during the year; he looked like the kind of Santa who, while fair and willing to listen, would not hesitate to leave coal in the stocking of any miscreant. He was about six feet tall, and his body had the kind of gaunt look displayed by people who have recently lost a lot of weight in a short time. There was a definite air of authority about him.

121

"I'm Robert Frederickson, Mr. Carver," I said, extending my hand. "I very much appreciate your agreeing to see me on such short notice."

He shook my hand. "I've heard of you, Frederickson. I believe your brother is married to Mary Tree, who's a member of my church. It's why I agreed to see you. You don't live in Cairn, do you?"

"No, sir. New York City. I'm just visiting."

"Well, Mary is a member of my church, and she and Garth are my neighbors, and so I'm happy to extend you this courtesy." He paused, narrowed his eyes slightly. "You're not here to talk about that American flag business, are you?"

"No, sir. It's something else entirely."

"Come in."

I followed him through a foyer of dark wood brightened by fluorescent lights, down a corridor, then through a door into a richly furnished library that smelled of old leather. There was a walk-in fireplace, and Impressionist oils on all four walls. The bookcases were decorated with models of sailing ships, and hanging above one was a framed captain's license. Bennett Carver, it seemed, was more than just a man who'd made a lot of money with big ships; he obviously loved ships themselves, and the sea, and knew the challenges of both firsthand. I thought it reflected well on him.

"Would you like a drink, Frederickson?" he continued, motioning for me to sit down in one of two leather armchairs set in front of the fireplace, which was currently serving as the summer home for an enormous, flowering cactus.

Would I ever. "Maybe a club soda, please."

He produced a glass and some ice from a small wet bar to the right of the fireplace, poured some club soda into the glass, brought it over to me. "Let's get down to business, Frederickson," he said, sitting down in the armchair across from me. "I don't mean to be rude, but I recently had some minor surgery, and I tire easily. I usually go to bed quite early. Just what is this important matter that you wish to discuss with me?"

"Carver Shipping."

122

"You may have come to the wrong person, Frederickson. I'm retired. I took the company public a while back, sold it. I retain a substantial portion of stock, but I have nothing to do with the day-to-day operations of the company. It's run by a board of directors. I have no duties. Aside from the rights due any stockholder, I have no power, no say."

"I understand, sir, but I suspect that you have a continuing interest in the company you founded, and that interest is more than purely financial. You seem to be a man who takes pride in the things he creates, and would be concerned with how something he had created was being managed by its current caretakers."

"That's true. What's your point, Frederickson?"

"Carver Shipping's tankers are illegally washing out their bilge, ballast, and storage tanks in the river after they unload their shipments of oil. Then they're refilling those tanks with river water, which they're probably selling in the Middle East—most likely to Kuwait. I can't prove if, or where, they're selling it, but I can show that the tankers are loading up on water. In fact, there's one across the river doing it right now—or about to do it. If you care to check it out, all you have to do is watch out your window for a few minutes, while there's still light." I paused, reached into my jacket pocket, withdrew the packet of photographs I had brought with me, handed it to him. "Those are before and after pictures of Carver Shipping tankers—heading upriver to deliver their oil cargoes, heading downriver after. As you can see, they're all riding just as low in the water going as coming. They're carrying something back with them, and the only thing it could be is river water."

Bennett Carver looked through the photographs, then set them down on a glass-topped coffee table to his left. Then he looked back at me. He definitely did not seem impressed. "Water? The important thing you wanted to talk to me about is tankers carrying river water?"

"You don't seem to take it very seriously."

"I'm not sure just what there is to be taken seriously. River water? Do you anticipate a shortage?"

"The water isn't theirs to take and sell, Mr. Carver. It belongs to all of us. And they pollute the river when they flush their tanks to take it on."

"Have you notified the Coast Guard?"

"They don't take it seriously either—or they don't take it seriously enough. I got the impression they feel they have more important things to worry about."

The silver-haired man with the pale green eyes thought about it awhile, then said, "Assuming they are shipping the water to Kuwait, or some other Middle Eastern nation that needs it, some people might call it a worthwhile endeavor. It may even be legal."

"I doubt very much that selling a public resource for private profit is legal, Mr. Carver. It's easy enough to check out. But washing out their tanks in the river is definitely illegal. You live on the river, and I'm frankly surprised you aren't offended that somebody's dumping toxic chemicals in your backyard."

The old man flushed, and anger gleamed in his bright eyes. "You're out of line, Frederickson. I was living in Cairn, on this river, before you were born. My father and grandfather were fishermen, and our family lived in a shack that stood on this very property. So don't tell me I don't care about environmental matters. Ask the local fishermen who contributed large sums to their association, to the *Clearwater,* and just about every other environmental group you can name that's been set up to protect this river. I have lent support to legislation that adversely affected my own company's operations and profits."

"But you're not running things any longer, Mr. Carver, and it looks to me like the people who are in charge now aren't following the same enlightened policies you did. I'm here speaking to you because I thought you might still care about the image of the company, and might still have enough influence to get them to stop what they're doing."

"Will you take these photographs to the press?"

"The thought had crossed my mind."

"What makes you think anybody would be interested?"

"I'm not sure anybody will be. But a thing like this can sometimes create quite a stir of bad publicity for a company, and this company still bears your family name."

He grunted, nodded curtly. "I'll make a deal with you. I'll place a couple of calls to look into this matter, see what the story is. When I have the information, I'll get back to you. Is that good enough for you?"

"I'm afraid not, Mr. Carver. I think you're going to be unpleasantly surprised at how difficult it's going to be to get answers out of those people. They're going to be downright upset when you bring up the subject."

"What are you talking about?"

"There's more to it."

"What?"

"Tom Blaine, the riverkeeper. He—"

"I knew Tom well, Frederickson. He was a deacon in our church. That was a terrible thing, the accident that happened to him."

"I don't think it was an accident, Mr. Carver. At the time he died, Tom was working hard to gather enough evidence against Carver Shipping to force the Coast Guard and other authorities to take action. Some of the ships must wash out and refill their tanks at night, so Tom was diving at night. He was underneath a tanker, taking samples as the pollutants were being flushed, before they could be diluted in the river. I believe somebody on board that tanker, probably the captain, knew or was tipped off that Tom was diving that night, and he started up the main engines while Tom was under the ship. That's called murder."

"That's utterly absurd, Frederickson. Do you believe anybody, much less a licensed captain, would kill a man over a boatload of river water?"

"People have killed other people over a lot less. And we're talking about lots of boatloads of river water over an unspecified period of time, profits earned that may not be recorded on the company's books, maybe unpaid taxes. The federal government may not give a damn about them heisting water, but tax evasion is a whole different matter. Besides, the captain of this particular tanker—the one that's parked across the river right now—has a lot to hide. He's a drunk. My brother checked with Motor Vehicles, and it turns out he lost his driver's license in Connecticut, where he happens to live. He's been involved in oil spills, and he

125

just might have been afraid that, if he got caught, he'd be made the fall guy for the whole illegal operation. Maybe he panicked; maybe somebody intimidated him. I don't know. But I do intend to find out exactly what happened."

"Have you gone to the police or Coast Guard about this particular . . . theory?"

"When it comes to things floating, sailing, and motoring on that river out there, it's very difficult to get the police in any one section to say, 'Oh, yeah, we'll look into that.' It seems that whatever happens on the river is someone else's responsibility. The Coast Guard is the one agency with undisputed jurisdiction on the entire length of the Hudson, but right now they're acting like they don't want to be bothered."

"Obviously because they don't believe anybody's been murdered."

"Yeah, well, the fact that the particular tanker that probably killed Tom is moored across the river right now lends the matter a certain sense of urgency, Mr. Carver. I have reason to believe that the captain who was in command of that ship on the night Tom was killed is on board now. I'd very much like to interview him before he leaves."

"Do you actually believe he would admit to starting up his engines while there was a diver under his ship?"

"I don't know what he'll admit to before I talk to him, Mr. Carver. I just want to hear what he has to say about the whole affair. Once he leaves, I assume it will be another month or more before he comes back again. I'd like to talk to him now, before any of this other information becomes public, before you talk to any of his superiors."

"You intend to just walk up to the man and ask him if he's guilty of murder?"

"I'm not sure what I'm going to say to him. I just want to talk to him about the matter face-to-face, and get his reaction."

The silver-haired old man gazed at me steadily for a few moments, then squinted slightly and asked, "Just what is your interest in this business, Frederickson? Is someone paying you and your brother to investigate Tom's death?"

"You said Tom was a member of your congregation, and I

know from talking to my sister-in-law that you're a devout man. What's your interest in going to church?"

He seemed taken aback by my question. He considered it for a while, said, "To pay homage to the God of the universe, Dr. Frederickson."

"But God would still be God whether or not you went to church to worship. What you're saying is that attention must be paid."

"Yes."

"Tom Blaine was a man who spent all his adult life trying to clean up and keep clean what must surely be one of God's greatest creations, that river outside your window, for all of us. As a result of that work he died alone, horribly, in the cold and dark under that river. Maybe it was an accident; but then again, maybe it wasn't. Attention must be paid. If nobody else is going to pay attention, then I guess it's up to Garth and me to do it. If Tom was murdered, that's sacrilege in the place where I worship. It has to do with responsibility. If someone murdered Tom Blaine, I want to fix the blame. It's my way of paying attention, and my brother's."

"I don't understand your answer."

"Then I guess I didn't really understand your question. It doesn't make any difference. I'm here to ask you to use your influence to get me an appointment to talk with the captain of the tanker moored across the river."

He considered my request as he studied the cactus in the fireplace, then looked back at me and shook his head. "I don't know, Frederickson. I can certainly alert board members that Carver Shipping may be inadvertently violating environmental regulations, but for me to do what you want is another matter entirely. The captain of any ship is an important and powerful person. I find it highly unlikely that any captain would agree to meet with you, or that the company would pressure him to do so, just so that you can accuse him of murder."

"I simply want to ask Captain Julian Jefferson a few questions. I have a suggestion as to how you might approach whoever is in a position to get me a talk with Jefferson."

"What would that be?"

"If I can get a meeting with Jefferson, then I won't be interested in pursuing the matter of their little water-shipping sideline, and the pollution that goes with it. Other people are working on that, and I'm satisfied that the work Tom started will be finished. There probably will be minimal publicity, if any. I'm less discreet. I'm interested in investigating the circumstances of Tom's death, and if Carver Shipping won't cooperate with me, I am going to use certain contacts that I have in the media to try to assure that Carver Shipping gets very bad notices, complete with photographs, on what they've been up to. What I'm talking about has nothing to do with petty fines, Mr. Carver. It's not guaranteed, but it's possible that a lot of people are going to be upset when they learn that Carver Shipping has been sucking up free water, *our* water, to sell overseas, and dirtying up the Hudson River in the process. Nasty things could be said and written. Tell that to the board of directors."

Bennett Carver stiffened, gripped the edges of his armchair, and glared at me. "That's blackmail pure and simple, Frederickson."

"You call it what you want. To my way of thinking, *they* should have demanded an investigation, or started one of their own, when it was learned that one of their tankers could have killed Tom—accidentally or otherwise."

"I'll tell my contacts on the board of directors what you said, Frederickson," the old man replied coldly. "I assume you can be reached at your brother's home?"

"I can be reached right here. Make the call now, ask that the meeting be set up for the morning. I don't know how much longer that tanker is going to be around. It's already unloaded its cargo and will probably be filling up with water once it gets dark. Jefferson may be getting ready to take off."

"How long has the ship been at its mooring?"

"Since late morning."

"Then you have time. The normal turnaround time at a port of call is a minimum of seventy-two hours, to run routine maintenance checks and give the crew shore leave. If you say this captain's home is in Connecticut, that's probably where he is right now. It's past nine o'clock, and I'm not going to intrude on anyone at this hour. I will call one or more board members sometime tomorrow, during normal business hours. I assume you have copies of these photos, so I will keep them, if I may, in case the people I call want to look at them. It will be up to the CEO or members of the board to decide if they want to give you permission to speak to one of their employees. I will tell them what you have told me, and give you their answer. That's all I can do." He abruptly stood up. "Good night, Dr. Frederickson."

I remained sitting. "There's still more, Mr. Carver."

"No, sir. There will be no more."

"I need to get in touch with your son. I'd like you to tell me where I can find him. In fact, it occurred to me that he might be staying here. Is he?"

For a moment I thought Bennett Carver was suffering a heart attack. He uttered a small gasp as his hostile look quickly changed to one of astonishment, and the blood drained from his face. He staggered slightly, then virtually collapsed back into his chair. "What are you talking about?" he asked in a voice that had suddenly grown weak and hoarse.

"Are you all right, Mr. Carver?"

He made an angry, dismissive gesture with a right hand that trembled slightly. "I asked what you are *talking* about!"

"Your son, Charles. Chick. I need to talk to him in regard to his health, and he gave his probation officer a phony address. Where is he?"

The movement of Bennett Carver's head when he moved it back and forth was slow and deliberate, almost lethargic, unlike his words, which came fast and clipped. "I haven't seen or spoken to my son in twenty years, Frederickson. I have no idea where he is or what he's doing. Most people don't even know I have a son. How did you find out? And what gives you the right to pry into my private affairs?"

His face and tone of voice indicated to me that he was telling the truth, and I found it quite astonishing. "I have an update for you, Mr. Carver," I said quietly. "One Charles 'Chick' Carver is working for the shipping company you founded, and he's no deckhand. He works out of the main office for a man by the name of Roger Wellington, who's in charge of security. I'm beginning

129

to strongly suspect that one of that department's responsibilities is to make sure that nobody objects too strenuously to Carver Shipping's little sideline of selling Hudson River water to some country in the Mideast. Earlier today, somebody driving a cigarette boat tried very hard to kill my brother and me. Garth's still in the hospital, in a coma. The boat was stolen, and the cops think it was some kid or kids joyriding. I think otherwise; I find it highly unlikely that a kid would boatnap something that big from the Haverstraw Marina in broad daylight. I have a very strong suspicion it was your son driving that boat, and it's going to be interesting to see what individual or company holds the registration on the boat. The captain of that tanker across the river called security to let the company know Garth and I were snooping around on our catamaran, and security ordered your son to take care of business. He's been hanging around the county, you know. Incidentally, I also wouldn't be surprised if he had a hand, literally, in the fall that broke your assistant pastor's back, but that's another matter."

"You're insane."

"I may be wrong about a few details, but I'm not insane. One reason I want to talk to your son is to find out just what he's been up to. I can assure you that he has been hanging around and that he does work for Carver Shipping."

Bennett Carver's face darkened, and his pale green eyes glittered with anger. "I can't believe they would hire my son and put him in such an important position without at least extending me the small courtesy of informing me."

"Believe it, Mr. Carver. Check it out. Incidentally, I can't help but note the fact that you haven't objected to the notion that your son might be capable of trying to kill somebody."

His face darkened even more, but I somehow sensed that his anger was no longer directed at me. "How do you know Charles is in Rockland County?"

"He tried to insinuate himself into the lives of Garth and Mary, come between them. But now I think he was only doing that to pass the time after he learned that Mary, an old girlfriend, lived in Cairn. He was already here on business. He's calling himself Sacra Silver, and he seems to fancy himself some kind of master of the occult who can cast evil spells. It appears to be an old *schtick* with him, an act he puts on to intimidate and control foolish and impressionable people." Like my sister-in-law, I thought, but didn't say so.

"If this man is calling himself by another name, how do you know he's . . . Charles?"

"He forced the issue, and I took steps to find out who he really was. I managed to get a set of his fingerprints. He has a police record, he's spent time in prison. He may also have done a stint as a juvenile in a mental hospital. But I'm sure you're aware of that."

"Charles always wanted to be a chief before learning how to be an Indian," Carver said softly, slowly shaking his head back and forth as if he were suffering from some neurological disorder. Suddenly his lips compressed, and he shot out of his chair. "I'll be goddamned if somebody is going to make him a chief in the company I started without at least extending me the courtesy of telling me about it! I'm going to find out what's going on here!"

It sounded good to me. I rose from my chair, then stepped back out of his way as he stormed past me to a telephone on a desk set against the opposite wall. He snatched up the receiver, punched at the buttons.

"Enough!"

I jumped, thoroughly startled, and turned around to see the stooped figure of a woman, presumably Mrs. Carver, standing between the open, louvered French doors leading to what appeared to be, now that the lights in the room had been turned on, a small study off the library. Mrs. Carver had obviously been sitting in the room, in the dark, listening to everything that had been said. She was a slight woman, frail-looking, leaning now with both hands on a silver-tipped cane. Age had bent her body, wrinkled her flesh, and thinned out her white hair, but I could see that she had once been beautiful, with high cheekbones, full lips, fine features. She wore a hearing aid, a kind of mechanical redundancy at the moment, for she had obviously heard enough already and didn't intend to do any more listening. There was nothing frail about her regal bearing, or her voice.

"Hang up the phone, Bennett!"

After a few moments' shocked hesitation, Bennett Carver—multimillionaire, church official, pillar of the community, and general all-around big-time mover and shaker—did what he was told. I'd have done the same thing. Having supervised this, the woman made her slow but majestic way across the room to the small, glass-topped coffee table next to the chair in which her husband had been sitting. She picked up the photographs Carver had placed there, threw them at me. It was a physically feeble gesture, and the photos only made it half the distance to where I was standing before fluttering to the floor, but her fury and strength of will were an almost palpable force, and I felt as if I'd been slapped in the face.

"Get out of here, you nasty little man!" she screamed at me in a hoarse voice that cracked at the top of its range. "And take your stupid pictures with you! Do your worst with them! But know that if you do anything to hurt my boy, you will regret it for the rest of your life!"

I stayed where I was, considering it a very real possibility that she would start beating me over the head with her cane the moment I walked forward and bent down to retrieve the photographs. I had no training whatsoever in how to defend myself from assaults by enraged octogenarian women.

"You," Bennett Carver said in a shocked, breathy voice as he stared at his wife. He sounded a little like an owl. Both his tone and face amply demonstrated his surprise and disbelief. "Carla, you've been in touch with Charles? *You* got him this job?"

"*Yes,* I got Charles this job, you old fool! *Somebody* in this family has to act like a parent, and you gave up on that responsibility twenty years ago! Did you think I was going to disown my own son the way you did?"

"Carla—"

"Don't you 'Carla' me!" the stooped woman shrieked at her husband, her voice rising even higher. "If you'd been a decent father, none of the things Charles has suffered would have happened! He loved and admired you so much! All he ever wanted was to be like you, and you turned your back on him!"

Bennett Carver extended his arms imploringly toward his wife, but he stayed where he was. "Carla, don't you remember the things he would do? Don't you remember all the money we spent for doctors and hospitals? None of it made any difference. He wouldn't change. He was never happy unless he was making somebody else unhappy. He couldn't stay out of trouble."

"I don't care what he did! I don't care what people say he's done now! He's my son! I want—!"

I'd been trying to make myself even smaller than usual, but now Carla Carver once again took cognizance of my presence at this little family *tête-à-tête,* and exception to it. "I told you to take your filthy pictures and get out!" she keened in a high-pitched, breathy scream, and came toward me, brandishing her cane in the air.

I got out, fast. Since I did have copies of the photos I had brought to show Bennett Carver, as well as the negatives, I thought it a wise decision to leave the ones on the floor behind.

·   ·   ·

It was raining hard when I came out.

I drove back along the river, just to make sure that the tanker that had almost certainly killed Tom Blaine was where I had left it. It was, although it took some heavy-duty squinting to make out the dark shape across the river in the wind and rain of the summer storm. I had brought no raincoat, so I ducked inside the house to get one of Garth's umbrellas before going back to the hospital.

Garth was still unconscious. The doctors were at once happy to see me back and a bit miffed that I had left without their permission. I told them I was all right, that I had survived worse knocks on my head, and that I would rest and take aspirin for my headache, which had become so persistent I had almost, if not quite, gotten used to it. I was going home. The doctors didn't like that idea. We negotiated, and I agreed to let them take some X rays. They did, confirming their initial diagnosis of a mild concussion, and agreed it would be permissible for me to go home as long as I didn't engage in any strenuous activity for two or three weeks; I was to come back if the headache persisted for more than twenty-four hours. I signed a release form, then went back to Garth's room to sit with Mary for a while. I checked with the nurse on duty to make certain Garth's condition was stable, then went back to the room once more to say good night to Mary. The day's doings had caught up with me, and I was thoroughly exhausted; I badly needed the rest I had promised to take, and if the information Bennett Carver had given me was accurate, I still had better than twenty-four hours to decide how to attack the problem of the tanker and its killer captain before the ship set out for the sea.

Wrong. When I got back to the house and used Garth's binoculars to check once more on the tanker, it was gone from its mooring.

CHAPTER TEN

The disappearance of the tanker disturbed the nasty little man very much, and I kept peering out into the driving rain, looking for some dark shape, the glint of anchor lights, unable to believe that Julian Jefferson not only would have weighed anchor two days before his scheduled departure but would be getting under way with both a thirty-knot wind and the tide against him. Stunned, thinking that maybe the blow to my head had affected my vision, I kept adjusting the focus of the binoculars as I scanned the river. But there was nothing wrong with my eyes, or the binoculars; the tanker was definitely gone.

Obviously, Mother Carver had called Sonny to warn him that trouble was brewing, and Sonny had gotten on the horn to tell Julian Jefferson to haul ass immediately for the open sea, where he would be immune to the further attentions of the nasty little man, and virtually anyone else for that matter.

I hurried to Garth's office, picked up his New York directory, and looked up the number of the Coast Guard Command on Governors Island. I started to dial the number, then slammed down the receiver in disgust and frustration. I knew exactly what the Coast Guard was going to do—nothing. Richard Marley had already rejected my request that his agency investigate Tom Blaine's death, dismissing the idea that it could have been murder, and there was no way they were going to stop a seven-hundred-foot-long, multi-ton tanker—which, considering the haste of its departure, might not even be carrying purloined water—just because a certain private investigator wanted to talk to its captain.

I glared at the phone, thinking of my brother lying in a coma in the hospital, of Tom Blaine's horrible, lonely death, and the fact that the tanker and captain that were an integral part of the affair were getting closer to the open sea with every second that went by. Once the ship got out into the Atlantic, I suspected there was little likelihood it would ever again enter the territorial waters of the United States, or that I would ever be able to find Julian Jefferson. Not that it would make any difference if I did. I had no proof of anything but water theft, absolutely nothing else to go on but suspicions and a loose thread who called himself Sacra Silver.

Checkmate. Carver Shipping and Julian Jefferson might or might not eventually be called to account for pollution and water theft, but it was looking more and more likely that the whole cast was going to get away with murder and attempted murder. Black magic indeed.

Without the slightest notion of just what it was I intended to do, knowing only that I had to do *something* and do it *now* or forget about it, I slammed out of the house, got into my car. I jammed the gears into reverse, spinning my tires on the gravel driveway as I shot out into the street. At a decidedly unsafe speed, I headed toward 9W, the narrow, twisting, and dangerous highway that ran roughly parallel to the river. I glanced at my watch. I had been at the hospital a little more than two hours, and the tanker had been at its mooring when I'd gone back. I had no idea how long it took to get something that size under way, but I presumed at least a half hour—maybe more, if it had begun taking on water after dark. So 82Q510 had been under way for ninety minutes or less. With the tide and wind against it, I didn't think it could have gotten all that far.

I caught up with the ship, faintly backlit by lights from towns on the opposite side of the river, at Haverstraw Bay just below Croton Point, six miles or so from the Tappan Zee Bridge. I couldn't be absolutely certain that the dark hulk, dimly outlined by the white points of its running lights, was the tanker I was after, but I was certain enough; I had seen no other traffic on the river, and the chances that Jefferson had continued north toward the narrow section of the river at Bear Mountain were nil. Although it might have been wishful thinking, considering the poor visibility, it looked to me like the tanker was ploughing heavily through the water, riding low, as if it might have greedily taken on one last load of illegal cargo before trying to scamper away. That was potential good news, if I could find anybody in authority who cared one way or another.

It would be hours before the massive tanker chugged into the choppy waters and swirling tides of New York Harbor on its way to the sea. I had plenty of time to get to Governors Island to rant and rave at Captain Richard Marley, or whoever else was on duty; if the Coast Guard still refused to stop the tanker pending an investigation of whatever it was I could get them to investigate, then I would start placing calls to every influential person I knew, looking for one soul who might be able to persuade the Coast Guard to intervene, to stop the ship just for an hour or so to inspect its illicit cargo, and then maybe . . .

Right. All my ranting and raving was going to get me, along with a buck and change, was a ride on the New York subway, along with a loss of credibility and influence with anybody I asked to intervene to stop a ship I claimed was carrying a great big load of . . . water. I had zip. The lumbering tanker I was now leaving behind me might as well be on another planet for all the good my chasing after it was going to do; by midmorning it would be out of sight of land, beyond the reach of any United States authority. I was just wasting my time, gas, and bridge tolls.

I found all of this highly aggravating, which undoubtedly explains why I abruptly cut off 9W onto the access ramp to the Tappan Zee Bridge when I saw the flashing yellow lights in the middle of the great span, indicating construction in progress. The problem of the tanker and its rogue captain was, I thought, going to require a much more personal, hands-on approach than I could ever hope to persuade the Coast Guard to take; I suspected that among the construction equipment I hoped to find on the bridge would be something I could use to try to facilitate just such a direct approach.

I was certainly angry—but not so angry as to be blind to the possible consequences of what it was I planned to do. The least of these consequences would be a parking ticket and tow charge, and so I simply pulled into the far right-hand lane of the bridge, on the wrong side of a string of reflective cones and flashing warning lights, and parked right behind a bright yellow New York State Thruway Authority electrical generator truck. I shut off the engine, leaving the keys in the ignition, and got out, leaning into the wind and driving rain. I'd left the umbrella behind at the house, but it wouldn't have done me much good on the bridge anyway. Although I was thoroughly soaked, rage and the adrenaline being pumped at the thought of what I was about to do were warding off the chills I had begun to suffer. I thought I might be running a slight fever, but I had no time to worry about it at the moment.

There was a considerable amount of scaffolding and other rigging around the area where they were replacing the roadbed, and it didn't take me long to find a suitable length of rope, two hundred or so feet of it, that wasn't serving any critical function. I snaked out the entire coil of rope to remove any kinks, then tied a bowline on a bight at one end to serve as an impromptu bosun's chair. Next, I jury-rigged a pulley system around a section of railing directly over the middle of the wide central span. I set up the bosun's chair and rope in the pulley the way I wanted it, then crossed the road to the opposite, upriver side of the bridge. I climbed over the railing and squatted down behind one of the great support beams, where I would not be seen by passing motorists.

Forty-five minutes later the tanker loomed out of the night, rain, and mist about a half mile away, near the lighthouse in front of the General Motors plant in Tarrytown. I trotted back across the roadway, slipped the loops of the bosun's chair around my legs, snug against my thighs. I climbed over the railing, grabbed the length of rope on the opposite side of the pulley, and stepped back into the wet night, slowly lowering myself hand over hand down through the rain and windswept darkness.

As I had learned from sailing on the catamaran, the Tappan Zee Bridge acts as a great disrupter of wind, tide, and current, sometimes focusing the natural elements, at other times causing them to clock and swirl around at varying speeds. I had intended to lower myself to the appropriate height, then simply slip out of the bosun's chair as the ship passed under me. I'd lowered myself no more than fifteen feet when I realized it wasn't going to be all that easy, and that what I was about was very dangerous business indeed. Gusts of wind lashed raindrops that felt as big as marbles across my face, while at the same time swinging me back and forth and spinning me around, first in one direction and then another, like some battered pendulum. If I was not careful—or even if I was careful—there was a good chance I was going to smash into one of the loading cranes or other equipment on deck, or even miss the deck altogether and end up in the water. With no life jacket, my chances for survival next to a moving tanker in the foaming, roiled river below were not good, to say the least.

I was hanging onto my control rope with both hands as the wind spun me around and swept me back and forth in great arcs across the central span of the bridge. With no way to wipe the water from my eyes, or shield them with a hand, I was effectively flying blind. I judged that I had descended approximately half the distance to the water. I lowered myself some more, arching my back and trying to shield my face in my left armpit at the same time as I tried to look down, behind, all around, on the watch for anything that might be moving.

My little impromptu journey had temporarily cured my headache, and it had also dampened, as it were, my rage; sheer terror is a most powerful distraction from whatever else it is that's ailing you.

The wind continued to spin me around and swing me. I squinted against the rain, looked down between my legs, and when I saw a yellow glow below me that had to be one of the ship's running lights, I knew I had seriously misjudged my position, and distance left to go; I was at least forty feet above the great foredeck, which was rapidly passing beneath me, and there was a good chance now I would smash into a crane or the tall superstructure at the stern end containing the wheelhouse—that is, if I didn't miss the tanker altogether and have the ship chug merrily along on its way without me. That could leave me in a most unpleasant situation, since I doubted I had the strength and stamina to pull myself back up to the bridge. There was no time left to gauge wind, distance, or anything else. I loosened my grip on the control rope and felt the nylon filament burn my palms as I plummeted in what I hoped was a controlled drop calculated to land me on the deck at a velocity just slightly short of that which would break my back or neck.

I landed hard, the wind and my momentum driving me due north on the foredeck of the tanker, which was heading due south. I immediately released the control rope as I was thrown forward, rolling like a lumpy bowling ball down the length of the foredeck. There had been no time to get my legs out of the loops of the improvised bosun's chair, and after my third bounce and roll I was hopelessly entangled in the line. I had not tied a knot at the end of the rope, and with luck the line would simply pass freely through the pulley up on the bridge railing, drop into the water, and trail behind the tanker. Then again, there were all manner of sharp metal angles on the bridge and construction equipment above to snag a flailing rope, or a trailing rope might be sucked down and become entangled in the ship's great props. If either of these unfortunate events occurred, I would either be unceremoniously dragged off the tanker to drown or pulled along the deck until I got caught in some equipment or rigging, and I would end up a bloody skin bag full of broken bones and crushed organs long before the rope broke.

These were the happy thoughts that flashed through my mind as I caromed off something that was rounded and hard, bounced and rolled some more, and finally banged to a stop against a wooden pallet loaded with diesel-oil drums. Impossibly entangled from head to toe in the rope, there was nothing I could do but wince and wait for a tug on the rope that would signal the beginning of a second, brief and ignominious journey. But the tug didn't come. The line had passed through the pulley and was—for the moment, at least—trailing freely alongside of or behind the tanker.

Suddenly two oilskin-clad crewmen loomed out of the darkness and bent down over me. They looked at each other, then began to speak rapidly in Spanish. I wriggled a little bit, found that despite the fact that I felt like one great bruise, there didn't seem to be anything broken. I wriggled harder, trying to free myself, but finally gave up. I looked up at the two crewmen, grinned. "So?" I said. "What's the problem? Take me to your leader."

CHAPTER ELEVEN

I couldn't tell if they were amused, because I couldn't even be certain they understood me, but it did seem certain that they considered the unauthorized presence of a hog-tied dwarf on board their vessel a sufficient reason to seek the counsel of higher authority. They proceeded to untangle the line from around me—no easy proposition, and done none too gently—and then perfunctorily grabbed me under the armpits and hauled me to my feet. Then, keeping a tight grip on my arms, they hustled me around the oil drums, across a section of the foredeck, then down a sloping companionway into what appeared to be the crew's quarters of the ship, which looked like an outtake from a cheap submarine movie and smelled of engine oil and cooking grease.

As I was half marched, half dragged along I became aware of a new problem, one that not only was causing considerable discomfort but also posed a real danger. Hypothermia. It was early August; the night was quite warm, despite the wind and rain. However, I'd been walking, waiting, dropping, swinging, bouncing, and rolling in that wind and rain for nigh unto two hours, and my body had decided to register a protest; it was saying that I had been knocked seriously unconscious earlier in the day and that I was supposed to be resting; it was saying that if I was so stupid as to flagrantly ignore the doctors' orders, then it was going to take matters into its own hands, as it were, and shut me down until such time as I got more sense into my head— or died, whichever came first. My body was going to lower its core temperature and see how I liked them apples. I was suddenly very cold and began to shiver uncontrollably. I didn't know the Spanish word for towel, but I asked for one anyway. Due to the language barrier or indifference, or both, I didn't even get a response, much less a towel. We just kept marching along.

We marched down one long, narrow corridor, then turned right and marched down another one, which ended at a scarred wooden door with a slatted portal. The man on my right, who had pushed back his hood and whom I now recognized as the sallow-faced crewman I had seen at the railing earlier in the day, used his free hand to knock on the door. Without waiting for a response, he opened the door, and I was pushed through it.

The captain's cabin was spacious, somewhat baroque with its walls of dark oak, matching rolltop desk, and large chart table set up in the middle of the floor. To my immediate left was a bunk bed bolted to the wall. Indeed, with its four quaint, barred portholes to provide a scenic view, the cabin would have seemed to me a most pleasant floating studio apartment, were it not for the smell: a mixture of disgusting odors that served to amplify my already screaming headache into something even louder, and made me nauseous. Underlying the stink of rotting food, an unwashed body, and spilled liquor was the even more acrid odor of vomit. This was no seagoing *pied-à-terre* but a sickroom; the man swaying unsteadily in his chair at the chart table, which was littered with half-empty liquor bottles, unwashed dishes, and greasy papers, was obviously sick, and had been for a long time. He wasn't likely to get any better as long as Carver Shipping, incredibly, kept him on the payroll and afloat in what had become for him nothing more than a steel tomb.

Although this man had, presumably, initiated plans to kill Garth and me not too many hours before, he gave no sign of recognition as he stared at me. One of the crewmen said something to him, and then both turned and walked out of the cabin, closing the door behind them, leaving me alone with the balding, bloated, pasty-faced drunk. He kept staring at me, bleary-eyed and swaying back and forth, then spoke to me in a hopelessly slurred mumble. Not having brought along my jiffy Universal Translator, I suspected we were going to have some difficulties communicating. But then he repeated it, and I thought I got the general drift.

What the fuck are you?

What the fuck was I, indeed? I was damn cold was what I was, and without further ado I stripped off the shirt that was pasted to my skin, grabbed a blanket off the unmade bunk bed, and wrapped it around me. The blanket felt greasy, and smelled as foul as everything else in the room, but at least it would help to preserve my rapidly diminishing body heat. Captain Julian Jefferson didn't protest and was in no position to do anything about it if he did; I doubted he could stand. I pulled up a wobbly wooden chair and sat down across from him at the wobbly chart table *cum* bar. The other man's dark brown eyes were glassy and occasionally rolled in his head as he tried to fix his gaze on me. There seemed no easy way to slide into the topic I wished to discuss, so I decided to dispense with any talk about the wretched weather, get right to the subject at hand, and see what happened.

"My name's Frederickson," I said through chattering teeth. "I'm investigating the death of a man by the name of Tom Blaine, who got chopped up by some very big propeller blades not too many weeks ago. I believe it was this tanker that killed him. Uh, the state police and Coast Guard are following right behind me, but they don't like working in the rain. I want to know why you started up your engines while the ship was moored and you were washing out your holding tanks. Now, I know you're shipping—"

I stopped speaking when I saw his lips moving. He was mumbling something in his drunken slur, and I leaned forward, trying to decipher it. "What?" I asked.

He repeated it, or mumbled something else, and this time I thought I understood him.

He was saying that the guy who was killed should have minded his own business.

Well. For a moment I forgot about both my headache and the bone-deep cold that was racking my body as I stared at the man in stunned silence. It certainly sounded like a confession of sorts to me. I had hoped to initially shock him into at least a denial of the accusation, which I had then hoped to use to pressure him into saying something, anything, incriminating, which I had then hoped to use to goad him into saying something even more incriminating. But he had apparently been impatient for me to get on with my masterly interrogation, since he had interrupted my opening gambit to effectively admit he had known there was a diver under his ship when he'd activated the engines. Or so it seemed.

"You're saying you *knew* there was a diver under your tanker when you started those props spinning around?"

He drained off the bourbon in his glass, poured himself some more from a bottle of Wild Turkey, then mumbled something to the dark liquid in front of him.

Sure he'd known, the drink was informed. It wasn't the first time this troublemaker had visited them, diving around and under the ship. He'd started the first night they were moored, and he'd been nosing around the last time they came upriver. He was on to the company's trick of flushing out tanks in the river and taking on water, and he was getting ready to make big trouble for the captains of the tankers, and the company.

"You've been selling the water in the Middle East?"

Yes. Kuwait.

"Whose idea was it?"

Company policy. Wanted to increase profits.

"Were your orders in writing?"

He shook his head.

"Who gave you the orders?"

The devil.

"Fuck the devil," I said with disgust. "Jesus Christ, Captain, do you really think a tankerful of water is worth a man's life?"

He slowly, determinedly, shook his head back and forth, then again spoke to his tumbler of bourbon.

The devil made him do it.

At his first mention of the devil, I'd assumed that, in his stupor, he'd been trying to be funny. Now I wasn't so sure. There was certainly nothing funny about the look of horror and anguish in his eyes. The captain, it seemed, had not only imagination but a conscience as well. And all his drinking had failed to erase his visions of what happens to a man when he's sucked up into the whirling props of an oceangoing tanker.

"What devil, Captain? Who told the captains to start taking on river water? Who ordered you to turn on your engines while there was a diver under your ship?"

He said the name, enunciating it clearly, with no need for straining to understand. "Mr. Carver."

"Charles Carver?"

He nodded.

"Mr. Charles Carver ordered you to kill a man."

"Start up engines."

"It's the same goddamn thing. He was on board this ship the night that man was killed?"

The question elicited a response, but Julian Jefferson's speech had reverted to slurred mumbles. However, by now I'd gotten somewhat used to the alcoholic garble, and I didn't think I missed much.

In regard to the illegal water-hauling operation, Roger Wellington was the administrator all the captains reported to and received their orders from—but all communications to and from Roger Wellington went through Charles Carver, a man most of the shipping personnel considered very strange, and whom many feared. He was rumored to be the son of the founder and to have more power and influence in the company than his title would suggest. A number of the captains had warned Mr. Carver that there was a man who seemed to be on to what they were doing and who was actually diving under their ships while they were flushing their tanks in order to gather evidence of pollution. They had been ordered to continue the practice, since the fines involved if they were ever brought to court were likely to be considerably less than the profits they were realizing from the operation. Then Mr. Carver had unexpectedly shown up one night, driving the company's black cigarette boat, and come aboard to wait for the diver to show up. The man had come and had made a dive under the ship as the tanks were being flushed out. Then Mr. Carver had ordered the captain to activate the main engines. At first the horrified captain had refused, but Mr. Carver had reminded him of his drinking problem and of the accidents in which he had been involved. The captain had been told that his family connections would not prevent him from being fired this time if he did not comply with the order to start up the engines. He had done so.

It had been Mr. Carver, followed by a crewman in one of the tanker's motorized dinghies, who had driven off the diver's boat and wrecked it, after throwing everything on board into the water.

Now the captain couldn't sleep, didn't want to sleep, because he was tormented by a vivid, recurring nightmare of how the diver under the boat must have felt in the cold and dark when he heard the engines come on, and the terror he must have experienced in the seconds before he was torn apart. Even awake, the captain couldn't stop thinking about it, seeing the images, and no amount of liquor seemed to help. He stayed in his cabin all the time now and let the crew handle the ship. He was terribly sorry for what he'd done, but felt he'd had no choice.

When the captain had finished, he drained off the tumbler of bourbon.

My heart was beating very rapidly, sending adrenaline-laced blood through my system, temporarily warming me. Never in the history of the world, I thought, had a complete confession been so easy to obtain. The problem, of course, was that it was worthless in the form it had been given, with me as the only witness. I had to find somebody else to listen to it.

I cleared my throat, half rose to reach out and touch his shoulder, then thought better of it and sank back down into my chair. "You've done the right thing, Captain Jefferson," I said carefully, watching him. "You're going to start feeling a whole lot better about things now that you've gotten this off your chest. Now we're going to get the man who's really responsible, the man who ordered and pressured you into doing this thing. But you're

147

going to have to repeat what you just told me in front of another witness. Where can I find your second-in-command?"

The glassy-eyed captain hiccupped, mumbled some more.

There was no second-in-command; he was the only one in command. But he wasn't interested in commanding anything. The crew ran things, and shared the bonus money, and just carried him along. Everybody seemed to prefer things that way, and he really had no place to go anyway. He wasn't even sure he would be allowed to leave the ship if he wanted to. He didn't care just so long as they kept bringing him liquor, which they did.

I thought about going up on deck to try to coax one of the crewmen, perhaps the English-speaking Greek, down to listen to the captain's confession, then decided that wasn't such a great idea; the Greek, indeed all of the crew, might take serious exception to any plans of mine that would upset the status quo, attract the unwelcome attention of the Coast Guard, and possibly implicate them all in a murder. That meant exposing myself in an attempt to get to their radio. I just wanted to obtain Julian Jefferson's confession in some usable form, then get off this damned tanker as quickly as possible, notify the Coast Guard of what I had, then sit down under a hot shower and do some serious drinking of my own, concussion or no.

"Okay," I said, "then do you have something to write with? Paper and pen or pencil? I'll write down everything you said to me, and you can sign it. Just tell me where the stuff is. I'll get it."

I'd been wrong about him not being able to stand; he knocked his chair over and not only managed to stand but proceeded to stumble and sway his way across the garbage-strewn cabin to a chest of drawers at the foot of the bunk bed. He opened the top drawer, began rummaging around, strewing clothes over the floor at his feet. It seemed an odd place to keep writing materials, but a perfectly logical place to keep a revolver, which was what he was holding when he removed his hand from the drawer. He raised the gun, aimed at me, and pulled the trigger at almost the precise moment that I rolled out of my chair to my right and onto the floor. Moving turned out to be a dangerous mistake;

his aim was off by about four feet, which meant that the bullet pierced the front edge of the chart table and thudded into the floor about an inch from my nose. The report of the large gun in the relatively small, closed space was not only deafening but had a most unpleasant, amplifying effect on my headache, and for a moment it felt like my head was literally going to explode.

He fired again, and this time the bullet missed by a good six feet, smacking into a framed picture on the wall to my right. So far, so good, but sooner or later this very drunk man was going to get lucky with one of his shots—or simply walk around the overturned table and put the gun to my head, where, smashed as he was, he would still be hard put to miss.

To make matters worse, if that was possible, I was all tangled up in the greasy blanket I had wrapped around me. However, after some shrugging and kicking, I managed to free myself. On my hands and knees behind the totally inadequate barrier of the chart table, which had been turned on its side by the force of the bullet smashing into it, I glanced behind me at the door. It was twenty feet away, and closed; it also opened inward, which was to my distinct disadvantage. The captain might keep missing if I simply stood up, ran to the door, and pulled it open—but then again, he might not. But then again, again, I obviously couldn't stay where I was.

I raised myself to a crouch, gripped the bottom edge of the chart table, came up with it. The oak table was a good deal heavier than I'd anticipated, but I heaved it as far as I could in the general direction of Julian Jefferson, then ran to the door, turned the knob, and pulled. The door was stuck.

The gun exploded again behind me. For a split second I thought I was hit, but it was only another matching explosion of pain inside my head from the noise of the revolver. I waited nanoseconds for a bullet to rip into my back, through my heart and lungs, but instead it whacked through the louvers on the door about two feet above my head. As I yanked on the doorknob, a rather unusual theory formed in my mind, that maybe the smartest move I could make was no move at all, to simply stand still and wait for Julian Jefferson to run out of ammunition.

Perhaps another time. I yanked once more on the knob, and

the door flew open. I headed out of the cabin, sprinting down the narrow outside corridor as the revolver fired again and a bullet whistled through the air an inch or two from my left ear. I skidded around the corner into the second corridor that led up to the deck, and found myself less than three feet from the dark-skinned crewman with the black, puffy birthmark on his cheek who had been at the railing that afternoon watching Garth and me float by on the catamaran. He grunted with surprise, crouched, and put his arms out to his sides to block the corridor. I didn't even slow down. I lowered my very sore head and rammed him hard in his exposed midsection. The air whooshed out of his lungs and he went back and down. I skipped over him, using his face for a stepping-stone, trying to ignore the spikes of pain flashing through my skull.

I could hear the captain shouting something unintelligible behind me. I raced down the corridor and up the companionway at the end. At the top of the companionway I ducked under the outstretched arms of two more crewmen, darted between two pallets loaded with crates of supplies, turned right and ran half the length of the vast foredeck until I saw the dark shape of a loading crane looming before me in the rainswept darkness. I ducked under the crane's huge counterweight and crouched, huddling and shivering in the night, holding my throbbing head with both hands as I tried to figure out just what it was I was going to do for my next trick.

From where I was crouched under the crane, it certainly looked like nothing less than, well, a very dark and stormy night indeed. Bare-chested, without the blanket that had for a time helped to restore my body heat, my core temperature was dropping again, and my shivering was threatening to turn into uncontrolled spasms. I was going to have to find a way to get warm soon, or I was going to lose control of my movements, probably pass out, and certainly die.

Of course, on this night there was no shortage of ways to depart this very wet veil of tears. The captain, against all odds, had somehow managed to ambulate up on deck, and above the wind and through the drumbeat patter of the rain hitting on the steel all around me I could hear him shouting what I presumed

were orders in his drunken slur. The revolver he had drawn held seven rounds, and he had already fired four of them. Of course, he could have reloaded or brought more rounds with him, but considering his condition I doubted he had done either. Then again, whether he managed to put a bullet in me or even simply stay on his feet was largely irrelevant in light of the fact that he had any number of crewmen to help search for me. If and when they did find me, the captain would no doubt order me knocked unconscious and thrown overboard, and the crew would no doubt do it.

I took off my shoes and socks, since they were thoroughly soaked anyway and of absolutely no use to me. A great shudder convulsed my body, passed, and then I resumed my garden-variety shivering. My teeth were chattering so hard I was afraid I was going to start chipping them. I looked east, toward the Westchester side of the river, which would be closest, but could see nothing. I estimated the shore would be a half to three quarters of a mile from our present position in the deep channel, and even if I weren't half frozen to death and suffering the effects of a concussion, it would have been a very risky proposition, if not downright suicidal, to try to swim to shore without a life jacket in the six-foot waves crashing against the hull. I could always dive overboard and take my chances if I ended up cornered, but that would be a last—probably literally—resort.

What I really wanted was to be picked up—preferably by the Coast Guard, but any old Sheriff's Patrol along the river would do nicely. That meant I was going to have to find a way to signal, and a large fire on board would make a dandy emergency flare. The problem, of course, was finding a way to start such a fire. There were pallets loaded with diesel oil on the deck, but diesel fuel won't burn if you drop a match in it—assuming I had a match to drop, which I didn't. I needed gasoline and a means to light it.

There was a large tool box bolted to the deck on the starboard side of the crane. I could hear snatches of voices carried by the wind, but at the moment nobody seemed to be too close to me. I ducked out from beneath the counterweight, tried the lid of the steel box. It wasn't locked. I opened the lid, fumbled around inside. I had desperately hoped to find a supply of emergency flares, but there weren't any. What I did find was a crowbar, which would make a very effective weapon at close range. I closed the lid and, crowbar in hand and trying very hard not to think of how very cold I was, set off, keeping close to the railing on the starboard side, in search of gasoline and a life jacket. Not necessarily in that order.

The wheelhouse at the top of the soaring superstructure that separated the massive foredeck from the stern was visible now as a pale yellow glow in the driving rain. I thought it might be worthwhile to take a look at what might be on the stern section of the ship, but that meant negotiating a very narrow section of deck on either the port or starboard side of the tanker, where I would be completely exposed and vulnerable if anybody should happen to be glancing in that direction. I crouched down next to the pallet loaded with barrels of diesel fuel and looked around, watching and listening. Men shouted to each other in the darkness, and once I heard the captain's voice rise in a bellow of rage, but as far as I could tell all of the voices were coming from the foredeck. The barrels of diesel fuel were fitted with petcocks, and I opened every one I could reach. Oil began to lap out on the deck. Diesel fuel might not burn if you dropped a match in it, but it will certainly explode if the right combination of heat and pressure is applied. At the moment I didn't even know how I was going to start a fire, much less cause an explosion, but I wanted to create as many options for myself as possible.

A crewman appeared at the opposite end of the narrow section of deck to starboard. I lay down flat on the wet, oily, ice-cold deck as he came toward me, then walked past. It was time to make my move. When I could no longer hear the man's footsteps, I got to my feet and sprinted to the stern area, holding the crowbar at the ready in a position to whack anybody who might suddenly appear in front of me. But when I reached the stern section, there was nobody there. And there in front of me, vaguely illuminated by the stern running lights, I saw what I wanted.

The tanker carried two large wooden lifeboats on mechanical hoists. Next to the lifeboat on the starboard side was an inflatable

Zodiac dinghy with a wooden rib designed to hold an outboard motor. The motor was secured to the deck beneath the dinghy, and next to the motor, nestled in protective netting to keep them from sliding overboard, were two red plastic five-gallon containers of what had to be gasoline.

Pressing close to the railing so as to avoid the lighted area as much as possible, I inched along the deck. The tanker was designed as an oceangoing vessel, so the relatively puny six-to-seven-foot waves now roiling the Hudson didn't even cause the great ship to roll. However, the noise and spray generated by the waves crashing against the hull were considerable, and the wet deck was treacherously slippery. I reached the containers, stripped off the safety netting. One container was full, too heavy to throw any distance, but the gasoline in the second container sloshed around; I estimated it was about half full, which I thought should be just about right for my purposes. I picked up the container, scampered back along the railing, and ducked into the partial shelter provided by one of the lifeboats on its hoist. I was so cold that for a moment I was tempted to climb up into the boat and cover myself with canvas, but I knew that was too passive; sooner or later somebody was going to look there, and I would be trapped.

Shouts and the sound of running footsteps rose over the furious noise of the storm, and the footsteps were coming right at me. I moved back as far as I could, pressed hard against the railing, and tensed, ready to lash out with the crowbar at the first unlucky soul who stooped down to peer into the shadow under the lifeboat. But the sailor ran past me. I looked out, watched as the man made a quick survey of the stern area, then ran back along the narrow deck on the port side of the superstructure.

My hands had nearly lost all feeling. I set down the crowbar, wrung my hands and slapped them against my thighs until some sensation came back. Then I picked up the bar again and used the sharp, notched end to tear at my right pants leg until it was shredded. I tore off a length of fabric, wrung as much water out of it as I could, then twirled it around to form a kind of wick. Then I unscrewed the top of the container, soaked both ends of the makeshift wick in the gasoline inside. Next, I wadded one end into the top of the container, leaving a two-foot strip hanging out.

I was trucking right along, so far, and now all I needed was to get lucky. There was, to say the least, lots of room for error in what I was about to try; it was possible I was going to succeed only in making a lot of noise, alerting the murderous captain and his crew to my position; or I could be too successful, getting myself real warm in a hurry, only to cool off permanently. However, short of stopping some crew member and asking him for a light, I had no other options.

I set down the container at the very edge of the deck, draped the end of my gasoline-soaked wick over the bottom rung of the railing, then hauled back with the crowbar and struck a glancing blow at the steel, just in front of the fabric. What I managed to produce in the partially enclosed space was a loud, melodious *bong* worthy of the percussion section of the New York Philharmonic, and a shower of sparks, but nothing else. I glanced out from beneath the lifeboat when I heard shouts, but nobody appeared on the narrow section of deck. I swung again, with the same result—or lack of it; sparks shot out over the end of the wick, but it didn't catch fire.

Shaking violently, I snatched the twisted rag from the container, used my forearms to raise the container and splash gasoline over the railing. I replaced the wick, once again draped the end over the rail, willed my fingers to close around the crowbar, and once again banged steel against steel. And again.

That did it. There was a different percussive sound, a loud *poof* as the rag lit, and suddenly I was crouched next to a live bomb, the mother of all Molotov cocktails, and reflecting, quite insanely, on how very good the flame's warmth felt on my gelid flesh.

Now I had to deliver my bomb to the diesel fuel dump, and be damn quick about it. There was no time to waste worrying about who was going to see me doing my Captain Flash number, which would include just about everyone on the foredeck, and I could only hope that the captain with his revolver wasn't too close by. I grabbed the jug of gasoline by its handle, darted out from beneath the lifeboat, and ran as best I could on my cold-numbed legs alongside the superstructure toward the foredeck.

154

A crewman suddenly appeared out of the darkness, running toward me, but when he saw the flaming package in my hand he promptly skidded to a halt on the slippery deck, his arms windmilling, managed to get himself turned around and running in the opposite direction.

When I came to the end of the superstructure, I slowed, then used what was left of my momentum to spin around twice, holding the handle of the blazing gasoline container with both hands, and then released the container like a hammer thrower, letting it fly up and away into the darkness in the general direction of the pallet of diesel fuel where I had opened the barrels' petcocks. The missile created a flaming arc, cutting through the cloak of night, descending.

There was the sharp report of a gun, and a bullet thwacked into the wooden frame of the superstructure, just above my head. The captain's aim was improving. There was a disappointingly small explosion off in the direction of where I had thrown the container. I turned around, began stumbling back toward the stern. I had gone only a few steps when there was a second, thoroughly satisfying, very large and loud explosion that made the deck beneath my feet shudder.

Now *that,* I thought, should manage to get somebody's attention. My only remaining job was to stay alive and out of sight, virtually the same thing, long enough to be able to enthusiastically greet the first visitors. In the meantime, I assumed the little conflagration I had started would keep the crew, if not the captain, occupied for the time being.

But the fact remained that I was trapped on the open stern deck, and that did not seem a good place to be. There was only one direction left in which to go, and that was up—so up I would go. I ran back to the lifeboat, retrieved the crowbar, then went to the door at the rear of the superstructure that I hoped opened on stairs leading up to the wheelhouse. I opened the door, saw stairs—but they suddenly looked very steep, and they only led to another closed door at the top. If that door was locked, and the captain made an appearance soon, he was going to find killing me as easy as shooting a dwarf in a stairwell.

But there was no place else to go. I stepped inside, closed the door behind me. There was no lock. I stumbled on the first step, pulled myself to my feet, started up. But now my vision was blurring, and I was having a great deal of difficulty making my trembling legs and knocking knees work properly. I'd climbed mountains—but none that seemed so steep and insurmountable as these steps seemed to me at the moment. I could no longer breathe properly, and the constant trembling of my body was starting to cause my muscles to spasm and seize up. I wanted nothing more than to curl up where I was and go to sleep. But I had to get up the stairs.

Using the crowbar as a kind of staff, levering myself up step by step, I struggled toward the top of the stairs. Twice I thought I was going to pass out, and I paused, leaning back against a wall and taking deep, shuddering breaths until my vision cleared.

And then, finally, I was at the top. I turned the knob, pushed the door open. There was a crewman standing at a large control panel, legs spread wide apart, leaning forward as he tried to see out through a wraparound window that was smeared with oil. The noise of the inferno below rose above the insistent tattoo of the driving rain.

I tapped on the wooden floor with the crowbar to get his attention. He whirled around, and his pale brown eyes opened wide with surprise when he saw me. He cried out and started toward me, then stopped when I raised the crowbar. I moved away from the door, giving him plenty of room to get by me, then motioned with the length of steel to indicate he should leave. He stayed where he was, staring hard at me, thinking about it. I had no idea what I looked like, but suspected that I didn't present too daunting a figure. But then, I was holding a crowbar, and that must have been daunting enough, because after another fifteen seconds or so of hesitation, he darted past me through the door and clambered down the stairs. I closed the door. The bolt-type lock on the door looked pretty frail, but it was better than nothing. I threw the bolt across, braced the crowbar under the knob, then staggered across the small wheelhouse to the control console.

My intent was to steer the tanker toward the relatively unpopulated east shore, where a railroad bed served as a buffer between the river and any houses. This would not only avoid a collision with any ships traveling up the deep channel, but should also enable me to make a hasty exit, since the momentum and mass of the tanker would drive its nose right into the riverbank.

But steering the tanker anywhere wasn't going to be easy, what with my blurred vision, trembling hands and knees, and nary a clue as to what the various controls on the panel under my chin did, or how they operated. At least a dozen red lights were flashing, and the feel of the ship under me was different, somehow draggy, as if the helmsman had reversed engines in an attempt to stop, or at least slow, the ship; that would be the logical action to take under the circumstances, but I couldn't be sure what had been done, or how to undo it. There was no wheel, but there was a stubby steel joystick on a track in the very center of the console, and I assumed this was a steering device. I moved it up and down, back and forth; the joystick moved without any resistance, which didn't feel quite right to me. I blinked, trying to focus my vision on the various lights on the console. There was a bright amber light to the right of the stick; by going up on my toes and virtually putting my nose to the light, I could just make out a switch below it, and a blurry sign that read AUTOMATIC PILOT. I flipped the switch and the light went off. When I moved the joystick again, there was some resistance. I pushed it all the way to the left, held it there.

I had no idea how long it would take for a vessel this size to change course, especially if its engines were reversed; but the tanker was still making headway, which meant it could still be steered. With the window totally smeared with oil and smoke residue, it was impossible to tell what was happening.

There didn't seem to be much more I could do, even if I was capable of doing it. And there was nowhere to go. It seemed as good a time as any to take a nap, particularly in view of the fact that I no longer felt cold; indeed, I no longer felt much of anything at all. The floor seemed very far away, so instead of trying to ease myself down on it, I just fell forward on my face. The noise level all around, over, and under me was increasing. Somebody was pounding on the door. Then the whole ship shuddered, and a very deep, grinding sound came up through the steel hull, through the superstructure, and vibrated inside my throbbing skull. I didn't care. I was warm all over, very sleepy, and filled with the most wondrous sense of well-being; I couldn't remember what it was I had been so excited about.

The last thing I heard, piercing through all the roaring, grinding, banging, and pounding around me, was a single gunshot, loud and seemingly very close, a sonic exclamation point to a jumbled paragraph of chaos that weighed down on me and pushed me into unconsciousness.

CHAPTER TWELVE

I dreamt, wildly and at length, in vivid color and full stereo sound. The same drama over and over again.

I was on a cruise ship. It was sometime in the past, when April Marlowe and I had been in love; but instead of running away from her as I had done, I'd married her, which was what I had desperately wanted to do. We were on our honeymoon. April was somewhere below deck in our honeymoon suite, but at the moment I couldn't quite remember where that was, or how to get there. I was standing at a railing on one of three foredecks, dressed in a green tuxedo. Although the dozen or so scantily-clad bathers cavorting in the purple pool on the deck below appeared comfortable enough, I was cold. The brown sun was going down, and the couples below were starting to go inside to dress for dinner. April, I knew, was already dressed and waiting for me, but, try as I might, I couldn't remember how to get to our cabin. I couldn't remember how I had gotten out on this particular foredeck, and when I turned around I saw there was no door for me to go through, no way off the deck. When I turned back, I found I was alone in dirty twilight. And I was suddenly terribly lonely. I opened my mouth to call for help, but I could make no sound. The front part of the ship, so noisy only a few moments before, was now completely cloaked in silence, and I was unable to break it.

The waves on the brown-black sea had suddenly disappeared, and the surface was as smooth as glass. The ship seemed to be speeding up, heading straight toward the black hole in the sky where the sun had disappeared. I desperately wanted to find my way below, back to where my wife waited, where there was light and warmth and food and music and where I would not feel so terribly lonely. We would eat, and dance late into the night on the stained-glass floor of the ballroom, and then we would go back to our cabin and make love.

I looked down, found that my green tuxedo had inexplicably disappeared, and I was naked. I couldn't wander around the ship naked, especially when I didn't know where to go, but my tuxedo was nowhere in sight. I would have to look for it, but I couldn't move. I was growing colder, freezing.

The glass surface of the water around me abruptly began to buckle, crack, and crinkle, becoming ever uglier, a crusted black and brown expanse that heaved and collapsed and heaved again, spewing a foul-smelling gas. I had to get away. I spun around, found that the entire section of the ship behind me had disappeared. I was in the middle of a vast, open sewer that stretched to the horizon in all directions. I turned back, found that the rest of the ship was gone from before and beneath me. I was all alone, ankle-deep in the poisonous, black-brown sludge, and slowly sinking. There was nothing to do, no place to swim to even if I could make my way through the thick, fetid ooze. The bubbling mud came up to my waist, then my chin. I threw my head back, struggling for one last gasp of air before I went under. And then, suddenly, it began all over again.

I was on a cruise ship . . .

That's how it went, on and on, over and over, for what seemed like years. When I woke up, I felt so bad that I was almost willing to go back to the world of my recurring nightmare, which was terrifying, but pain-free. I felt about as strong as a sponge with a hangover and couldn't even lift my arms off the bed in which I was lying. There were needles stuck in both my arms and a tube up my nose. I felt the urge to gag, but couldn't even work up the strength to do that. Garth and Mary were at my bedside, and when I opened my eyes, my brother got up from his chair and leaned over me.

"Mongo?"

"Grrrrmph," I said, and promptly went back to sleep.

I was on a cruise ship . . .

When I awoke again, the needles were out of my arms, and the tube gone from my nose, but I didn't feel any better. Garth, wearing different clothes, was still at my bedside. He was unshaven and looked like he had a three- or four-day growth of beard.

"You look like shit," I said in a croaking whisper. Just the act of speaking brought up a foul, green and black taste of grease, medicine, and smoke, but it felt so good to be off my nightmare cruise ship in the savage ocean that I kept talking anyway. "You smell too. Do you know how depressing it is to wake up in a sickbed to find a man who hasn't bothered to shave, with body odor and bags under his eyes, standing next to you?"

My little speech finished, I proceeded to have a coughing fit, which brought up more vile tastes, bile, and thick phlegm. Garth supported me with his arm, gently patted me on the back. When the spasm of coughing finally passed, he poured me a glass of water, steadied my head while I drank it down. I drank another, then lay back.

"Some of the doctors here thought you were going to die, Mongo," Garth said simply. "I told them they were wrong."

"What did they think I was going to die of?"

"Oh, the combined effects of a dozen or so maladies. Let's see if I can't recall the highlights of the doctors' diagnosis. How about double pneumonia aggravated by smoke inhalation, severe exposure, and brain inflammation? There were a few other minor items."

"Brain inflammation?"

"I told them you didn't have a brain to be inflamed, but they insisted. You walked out of here with a mild concussion, right?

Well, it's not so mild anymore. All that time you were running around doing whatever it was you thought you were doing, you could have had a stroke at any time. The swelling is down now, but if you look like Mr. America when you get out of here, it's because of all the steroids they've been pumping you full of. The way you've been bouncing around on your head, it's a wonder you've got any uncracked brain cells left. But you never put that organ to much use anyway, do you?"

"Tee-hee. You've got a great bedside manner, Garth. How long have I been . . . away?"

"Not quite a week."

"Not quite a fucking *week?*"

"Take it easy, Mongo," Garth said quickly, putting his hand on my chest and pressing me back down on the bed as I tried to rise. "You're out of danger, but you're going to have to stay here another week at least, and probably longer. I was told not to talk to you for longer than fifteen minutes if you came around. The doctors said you'd probably want to go back to sleep by that time."

"Well, they're wrong again. I don't want to go back to sleep. I have nightmares. What the hell's been happening?"

Garth smiled wryly, chuckled, and rolled his eyes toward the ceiling—a flamboyant display of reckless emotion from my taciturn brother. "I'll bring you your reviews in a day or two. You've made two out of three of the network broadcasts, and I can tell you that you're selling a lot of newspapers. That's the good news, if you're a newspaper publisher."

"Aha. Since I'm not a newspaper publisher, my surviving brain cells interpret that to mean there's plenty of bad news for me."

"We'll talk about it tomorrow or the next day. Really, Mongo, I don't think I—"

"Damn it, Garth, I've been sleeping for a week. I promise I'll rest. Just tell me what's been going on. I absolutely guarantee I'm going to get better, because I'm going to find Julian Jefferson and separate his head from his shoulders. That's twice the son-of-a-bitch tried to kill me."

Garth sighed, propped me up with some pillows behind my back, then sat down again in the chair next to my bed. "Too late for that. Jefferson already separated his head from his shoulders for you—at least most of it. He shot himself on the deck of his tanker, presumably with the gun he was using to try to kill you."

"Well, well," I said. I thought about it for a few moments, waiting for some sense of satisfaction that refused to come. "It doesn't make any difference. He was just a drunk doing what he was told, and the person who ordered him to rev up those engines was none other than Chick Carver, our friendly neighborhood sorcerer. Carver was on the tanker that night, because Jefferson called him to report that the local troublemaker was back. He also seriously trashed Tom's boat, then drove it himself down to the salt marshes."

"The captain told you that?"

"Yep."

"You got it on tape?"

"Gee, Garth, I don't. I plumb forgot to pick up my recording engineer before I went chasing after that ship."

"So you haven't got it on tape. Too bad."

"Anybody else aboard the tanker killed?"

Garth shook his head.

"Jefferson was just something broken that Carver used as a murder weapon. But Chick Carver's kind of broken too. I want to nail him, but I want even more to nail the gray suit or suits responsible for hiring a freak like Carver in the first place, and then giving him free rein to act as an enforcer to cover up their illegal water-transport business. Maybe that's Roger Wellington, but I suspect it's somebody even higher up, somebody Mama Carver could pressure. Damn it, Garth, this whole thing is about responsibility, and I want to nail the people responsible for making policy."

Garth grunted, then stared at me for some time with an enigmatic expression on his face. Finally he asked quietly, "Just what the hell did you think you were doing, Mongo?"

"Uh . . . bringing things to a head?"

"You mean onto a head; your head. I can't understand what you hoped to accomplish, aside from almost killing yourself, by playing Tarzan off the Tappan Zee Bridge, and then trying to hijack a tanker."

163

"*Hijack* a tanker? I wasn't trying to hijack that thing, I was trying to *park* it, for Christ's sake! And don't give me any more of this 'what did you think you were doing' crap. I was pretty pissed off when I left the hospital, because you were where I am right now. I went to have a little chat with Bennett Carver, to show him the photos and ask what the hell his company and son were up to. He was pretty shocked by the whole thing, especially since he disowned his shithead son years ago. But Mama wasn't shocked; she wasn't even surprised."

"She got him the job?"

"Right. She's a tough one. The lady as much as told me to go to hell, because there wasn't a damn thing I could do about any of it. That kind of annoyed me. I got even more annoyed when I got back and found the tanker gone; obviously Mama had called somebody, probably her boy, to tell him the tanker should get out of there fast. I took off after it in the car, because I knew if it ever got out of New York Harbor, we'd never see it or Julian Jefferson around here again. I was intending to make a last-ditch effort to get the Coast Guard to stop them, but while I was on the road I realized that was a waste of time. I saw the construction equipment on the TZ, and I just went for a head-to-head with the captain; I knew it was probably the last chance I'd ever have. If you'd been in my place, you'd have done the same damn thing."

"Yeah," Garth said mildly. "You're probably right. These goddamn people and their attitudes, and the attitude of the authorities toward these people with attitudes, is enough to give you an attitude. Well, you certainly stopped that ship, brother, and you sure as hell made sure the situation would get a public airing. But we're left with a few problems."

"Like what? Everything you've told me so far sounds like good news."

"Care to guess where you are?"

"Uh, Cairn Hospital?"

"Try the hospital ward on Rikers Island."

"Oh-oh."

"Even as we speak, the state and federal authorities are arguing over who gets to beat on you first. Since Carver Shipping claims you caused three million dollars' worth of damage to their tanker, they want at you first in a state court so they can sue you for everything we've got. But the feds' position is that what you did was an act of terrorism, and they want to make an example of you by first trying you on charges of attempted hijacking of a ship and then putting you away for twenty-five or thirty years. Naturally there's politics involved. We don't have anything but enemies in this administration, and this is probably their way of punishing both of us for what they believe to be our close ties to our dear ex-President."

"Who's winning? State or federal?"

"Your lawyers, I hope."

"Who are my lawyers?"

"Benson, Quadratti, Kratz, and Pringle."

"Hoo-boy," I said, raising my eyebrows. "Ira's on the case, is he? Talk about heavy hitters."

"Yep. He's working *pro bono*, no less. Any number of the firms we've done business with over the years volunteered to represent you. I thought it best to let Ira handle it."

"Why pick a Washington firm?"

"Because that's where the real pressure in this case is coming from, and Ira *does* have friends in this administration. Even more important, he has friends in high corporate places, and, to my thinking, it's in the boardroom that this little drama you've produced is going to play itself out."

"*Your* thinking? What about *my* thinking? *I'm* the one they're trying to brand and try as a terrorist!"

Garth grunted. "I'm taking over as quarterback. You worry about resting and getting your strength back. You're going to need it. Right now you're being held without bail, so there's no place you can go, and nothing you can do if you could go someplace. Your P.I. license has been suspended."

"I don't need a goddamn license to hunt Chick Carver."

"Ah. But you're not going to do anything unless Ira or I tell you." Garth's tone, as usual, was mild, but I knew he was deadly serious. He continued, "When Mary and I couldn't think clearly, you did our thinking for us. I appreciated it, and I *cooperated*. Now the situations are reversed, and *you're* going to cooperate. Sacra Silver isn't our main concern right now; he's not even a secondary concern. These are worthy opponents you're up against now, Mongo, and if we're not very careful, they're going to blow you right into prison. Now that you've come around, there'll be a formal arraignment. Ira and I haven't made a decision yet whether or not to even ask for bail."

"Give me a break, Garth. You'd let me sit in the can because you're afraid of what I might do if I get out?"

"Frankly . . . maybe. But the main point in keeping you locked up is so reporters can't get to you."

"I would think we'd want reporters to get to me."

"At a time and place of our choosing. When I bring you the papers, you'll see that the situation is getting plenty of ink, and what makes it more than just another corporate scandal story, frankly, is the involvement of Mongo the Magnificent. For some reason, there seem to be a lot of people who find you a colorful figure."

"It sounds to me like you've been orchestrating the media campaign."

"To the extent that I can, sure. The photographs of the tankers went to all the right people in the press, and I've emphasized that Mongo the Magnificent was working on the same matter that killed a heroic, small-town riverkeeper."

"Have you told anybody the whole story about what happened to Tom?"

"Two people—Henry at the *Times* and Beverly over at the *Post*. But nobody's going to print any of that, because they'd be sued for libel, but it should guarantee that now we've got investigative reporters looking deeper into the story. We need all the help we can get. But what's keeping this story hot at the moment, dear brother, is the image of the aforementioned colorful figure lying forlorn and alone, near death, in a hospital bed here on Rikers Island."

"It brings tears to my eyes."

"There are a lot of people who don't believe that a man of your reputation would trash a multi-ton tanker over a minor environmental infraction and water-hauling scheme, and they're waiting to hear the whole story—from you. But it will do absolutely no good to just talk to reporters; what's introduced and

166

said at your trial is going to be what counts. In order to explain your motivation for going aboard that tanker, we have to at least strongly hint that Carver Shipping is guilty of corporate murder, not just corporate skulduggery. Ira says that won't be easy. He's thinking that we should let you sit tight here for a while and let the investigative reporters keep digging. There's no sense in tipping our hand, and it could backfire if you make allegations we can't prove."

"For Christ's sake, Garth, I delivered up a whole tanker filled with Hudson River water that was illegally being hauled. That's no allegation, it's a fact. Are you going to tell me the hull cracked open and all that water leaked out?"

"Nope. But it's virtually irrelevant. I told you I got the pollution and water-shipping stories out. I also told you these people we're up against are worthy opponents. They haven't exactly been sitting still; Carver Shipping has squads of lawyers and public relations people, and they have their own sympathetic reporters to talk to. Within an hour after this story hit the street, their CEO held a press conference to announce that the company itself had uncovered a plot by Julian Jefferson and a few other so-called rogue captains to line their own pockets. The company categorically denies knowing anything about it, and they officially deplore what was happening. At the same time, they are agreeing to take responsibility, to pay all appropriate fines, and even donate half a million to various environmental groups—including a hundred thousand to the Cairn Fishermen's Association, in Tom Blaine's name. Now, *that's* public relations, brother."

"Now you really are bringing tears to my eyes."

"But wait; there's more. The very next day, our beloved Secretary of the Interior, the same one who's giving away all the timber, coal, and marshlands, held a press conference in Washington to praise—and these are his words—'Carver Shipping's exemplary record of good citizenship and corporate responsibility.' He also took the opportunity to deplore the actions of a 'well-known vigilante type.' Anybody who knows us realizes that I'm the vigilante type in the family, but I believe he was referring to you. He also used the word 'terrorist' a few times. So, for what amounts to pocket money for the company, probably only a fraction of what they've already made selling water to Kuwait, Carver Shipping is looking to come out of this not only with their profits secured, or most of them, but with a new and burnished image as a kind of New Age corporation that really cares about the environment. You get a thirty-year prison sentence. The CEO's even called for a full shareholders' meeting in six weeks to ask for a vote of confidence in himself and the board of directors."

"I love it."

"I knew you would. Get the picture? Make a peep about murder now, and they'll just say it's the self-serving rantings of that well-known vigilante type and soon-to-be-convicted felon. So you just sit tight. We're going to save our ammunition, if we can find any, for the trial."

I looked away. Now I wished I'd just gone back to sleep when Garth had suggested it. The nightmare I'd been dreaming suddenly seemed pale in comparison to the one I'd awakened to, and at least that had only been a bad dream. "What about the other captains involved?" I asked quietly. "Maybe one of them will come forward and tell the truth."

"You think so, huh? Maybe a few captains really have been fired, like the company claims, but it's more likely they've been transferred to cushy jobs somewhere else in the world, where we won't be able to subpoena them, in exchange for keeping their mouths shut. And you'll never get a member of any crew to testify; half of them are probably illegal aliens."

"What about Carver and Roger Wellington?"

Garth shrugged. "What about them? Nothing's going to happen to them, and they'd certainly lie on the stand. They're in administration, remember? And for the company to can anybody in administration would be to acknowledge that higher-ups might have been involved, and they won't risk that. No, the official line is that it was a conspiracy of captains only, to earn extra money. Carver and Wellington will stay at their desks."

"And so Chick Carver, and the men responsible for him, get away with murder."

"Hey, I hope I don't have to tell you that I'm no happier about that than you are. But right now, you're up to your ass in alligators, and that's what we have to focus on. For now, we let things simmer. Lots of people have seen the photographs of those loaded tankers, and some people—except for the Secretary of the Interior, of course—are already beginning to wonder out loud how a half dozen ships could cart millions of tons of water, month after month, without somebody at the corporate head-quarters being aware of it. When the current publicity dies down, then we spring you to tell at least part of your side of the story. Who knows? By that time, we may be able to make a deal."

"Maybe I don't want to make any deal."

"That's easy for you to say; you're not the one who'll have to spend all that time commuting to a federal prison for thirty years to visit his brother. You'll do what this quarterback says, Mongo. I'll call you off the bench when Ira and I think the time is right. Just sit tight; catch up on your reading. Now go back to sleep."

.   .   .

I went back to sleep, allowed my body to heal, read the newspa-pers, watched television, and otherwise sat tight.

Ten days later Bennett Carver demonstrated his political influ-ence by managing to get in to see me. I could have refused to talk to him, but I was curious as to what he had to say. Although I was still in the hospital ward, on narrow-spectrum antibiotics and a blood thinner, I actually felt much better. I didn't think Bennett Carver could say the same. The silver-haired man's walk was unsteady, and he was using his wife's cane, which was too short for him. His pale green eyes had lost their brightness, and were watery. I was sitting up in bed, reading, when he was admitted to my cell. He nodded curtly, then pulled up a chair next to the bed and eased himself down on it.

"I came to cut a deal with you, Frederickson," he announced with his characteristic bluntness. "I hope you're going to be happy with the terms; but even if you're not, I hope you'll have the good sense not to reject the offer."

"If I had good sense I wouldn't be in this pleasure palace, now would I, Mr. Carver? I hope you have other business in the city, because otherwise you've come all the way down here for nothing."

"The company will drop all charges and lawsuits against you. If that happens, the chances are good that, with a little prodding— which I guarantee will be provided—the Justice Department can be persuaded to drop its charges; if Carver Shipping denies that its ship was hijacked, it's difficult to see how the government can claim otherwise. In exchange, you promise not to discuss the matter with the media. When asked questions, you'll reply, 'No comment.' All this publicity is bad for the company."

"I thought Carver Shipping had the glowing imprimatur and praise of the Secretary of the Interior."

Carver made a sound of disgust. "Those fools on the board of directors think that's worth something; it isn't. I didn't found that company to have its reputation depend on the praise of a man who's a hypocrite and bullshit artist. There are people I respect, and friends of mine, who believe Carver Shipping is guilty of something precisely because that man said the things he did."

"I'm glad to hear you say that, Mr. Carver, because the company you founded is damn well guilty of a lot of things. You know it, and I know it. But I'm still not sure what you're worried about. Those people you're referring to are a distinct minority. I read the papers, watch television. Their public relations people, it seems to me, have done a pretty good job of turning things around and making Carver Shipping look like a paragon of an environmentally concerned corporation. It's already old news."

"It won't be when you get out of here. I don't know what you're going to say, or how you plan to prove any of the allegations I'm sure you're going to make, but none of it can be good for the company. With your reputation, you could have been out of here on bail; since you're not, I have to assume that keeping you secluded in here is a ploy by your lawyer to eventually mount a second publicity assault on Carver Shipping. You're a dangerous man, Frederickson."

"Thank you. Have a nice day, Mr. Carver."

"You're facing a thirty-year prison sentence, Frederickson!"

"So I've been told. Look, Mr. Carver, this isn't about pollution, or illegal water hauling, both of which we know Carver Shipping is guilty of. And it's not about which side can mount the best public relations campaign. As far as I'm concerned, this is all about responsibility. Specifically, it's about your son's responsibility for causing a man's death, and the responsibility the company you founded bears for, in effect, giving him the license to do it."

"You don't know—"

"Yes, I do know. Before he stuck a gun barrel in his mouth and pulled the trigger, Julian Jefferson told me exactly what happened the night your fellow church member was killed. Jefferson called your son to report that Tom was poking around the ship, and your son came on board that night to put a stop to it. He ordered the captain to start up the engines while Tom was under the tanker, and he personally stripped and trashed Tom's boat."

I expected him to deny it, or at least to point out the obvious—that my version of something I claimed a chronic drunk had told me before he killed himself was totally worthless in court, and libelous if I repeated it in public. But he did neither. Instead, he winced and turned away slightly, as if I had struck him a physical blow. It seemed proof of what Chick Carver had done, or the bizarre circumstances under which I had obtained the captain's confession were irrelevant to this man, for Bennett Carver seemed to know—had always known—that his son was capable of doing the things I had described.

"Charles no longer works for the company, Frederickson," he said in a very low, weak voice. "He's been sent off to a . . . place very far away, where he will stay until the day he dies if he ever hopes to see another penny of the trust fund he's been living on for twenty years, or of his final inheritance. Neither you nor I will ever see him again."

"At the risk of sounding insensitive, I have to point out that his mother isn't going to care much for that arrangement."

"Well, she's going to have to learn to live with it," he said in a stronger voice, lips pulled back from his teeth. "I carry much blame for what Charles has become, Frederickson, but I consider his mother responsible for what's happened here. Charles should *never* have been put in a position of power or responsibility over other people. And Roger Wellington is gone too. He'll never work in the shipping business again."

171

"You seem to have a lot more say about what goes on in that company than you let on in our previous conversation."

"What I have is a very large block of stock."

"It's not enough, Mr. Carver."

"You can't expect me to help in the destruction of my own son, Frederickson! I've sent him away! He'll never bother anyone from around here again!"

"We'll see how far away he goes, and how long he stays. But I'm not talking just about what Charles did, nor about the immediate superior who let him loose. I'm talking about the company itself; it was company policy, finally, that was responsible for everything that happened. But companies can only be fined. The *people* who created or checked off on that policy must be held accountable, which in this case means a CEO and a board of directors. You and I both know there was no cabal of captains; they were following what they understood to be official orders. There are enough killer companies in the United States, and under this administration they're going to multiply like rabbits. I'd like to see the men responsible for turning Carver Shipping into a killer company buried; I want them exposed, removed from power, and punished."

"You're crazy, Frederickson."

"So I've been told on more than one occasion."

"You can't touch them."

"You're probably right."

"You're willing to throw away your freedom to fight in a battle you can't possibly win? Why, for God's sake?"

"Because the cost of agreeing to keep my mouth shut is too high. These are bad guys, Mr. Carver; they're a pack of gray-suited thieves and murderers who hide behind corporate bylaws. They're the same kind of bad guys as the gray suits who looted the savings and loan industry, the kinds of people who are the root cause of so much that's wrong with this country that you feel so strongly about. To you, it's important that the United States be honored by having its flag displayed on the altar of your church. I try to honor my country—and myself—in my own way, by making sure that a bunch of rich, greedy, corporate pricks don't get away with complicity in the murder of a very fine man who was working for all of us, and then be hailed as heroes by a spokesman for this administration. At least I try. It turns everything I believe in on its head. I know what makes you mad, Mr. Carver—somebody trying to remove the U.S. flag from your church altar. And now you know what makes me mad. So you go back to your people on the board and tell them to stick their deal up their collective corporate ass. Also, tell them I'll see them in court."

Bennett Carver seemed stunned. He stared at me, blinking slowly and with his mouth slightly open, for some time. Finally he rose from the chair and, leaning heavily on his wife's cane, walked unsteadily to the door. But he did not signal for the guard.

"Perhaps I was wrong for trying to bargain with you, Frederickson," he said in a thick voice, without turning around. "I think I knew—or should have known—what your reaction was going to be. I understand why you had to go on that ship, and I admire your courage. I know what you did next you did because you were fighting for your life. Perhaps it's true that Tom Blaine's life was taken from him, but I can't do anything about that beyond what I've already done. If I cooperate in the prosecution of my son, I will lose my wife. I *do* bear much blame for what Charles has become; I was not a good father. But you have also been wronged, and you're in danger of being ground up and spat out by the part of the system that you so reasonably deplore, and that I *can* do something about, and have. It was done before I came in here. Carver Shipping has agreed to drop all charges and suits against you, and influential people I know are, at this moment, pressing the Justice Department to do the same. I believe they'll succeed. I will be very much surprised if you're not a free man again before this day is out, Dr. Frederickson. I told you I admire you for your courage, but courage can only take a man so far. You've dodged a very big bullet. My advice to you is to put this matter behind you and get on with your work and your life."

"Just a minute!" I said sharply as the old man raised his hand to knock at the door. He hesitated, then slowly lowered his hand and turned to look at me. I swung my legs over the side of the

173

bed, stood up, and walked across the room to stand in front of him. "There is more that you can do."

"I've told you I can do nothing more regarding Charles."

"I'm not talking about Charles. I want to get the men who wrote the stage directions. I'm thinking maybe you do too. I understand the CEO and the board have called for a shareholders' meeting in a few weeks to call for a vote of confidence. You be there. Use that big block of stock you own, and your influence, to at least get rid of those people. Take back control of the company they screwed up, for at least as long as it takes to get decent people to run it."

Bennett Carver slowly shook his head. "Even assuming I had the power to do that, and the physical strength to wage such a battle, I would still need some proof of serious malfeasance, or a criminal charge, to use against them. Pollution and illegal water hauling? That was a conspiracy of captains, remember? If they weren't already out from under that one, you wouldn't be walking out of here."

"Then think of some other way."

Again he shook his head, then turned back and knocked on the door to signal for the guard. "This business is finished, Frederickson. Get on with your life."

CHAPTER THIRTEEN

Damned if it didn't look like he was right.

Just as a very wily and powerful Bennett Carver had predicted, all civil and criminal charges at both the state and federal levels were dropped, and before dinnertime I walked off Rikers Island a free man. I spent the next week and a half wasting a lot of time trying to track down Chick Carver and Roger Wellington, all to no avail. It appeared that Chick Carver had left the country, undoubtedly with a large amount of money his family had given him. Roger Wellington had been rewarded for past services with a solid-gold parachute as severance pay, and was rumored to be sailing somewhere off Tahiti. Carver tankers were delivering their shipments of oil, then obediently cruising back down the Hudson empty of everything but the bilge water and residual pollutants they had previously been flushing into the river. The Cairn Fishermen's Association was making plans for how to spend the hundred thousand dollars Carver Shipping had donated to them in memory of Tom Blaine.

Neither Garth nor I had forgotten the murder, but there

seemed to be nothing whatsoever we could do about it. With the suicide of Julian Jefferson, there seemed to be no way to pin anything on anyone, and with the disappearance of Chick Carver and Roger Wellington, there wasn't even anyone to pursue; the ruling echelon of the company appeared to be totally insulated. It would be a waste of time, not to mention a threat to my credibility, to prattle on about a murder I couldn't prove to reporter friends who couldn't print anything I said, even if they wanted to, without having their newspaper sued for libel.

And so, despite my best intentions, I found myself, by default, following Bennett Carver's advice, going back to my work and life. The burning rage that had propelled me onto a tanker in the middle of a storm was now only a memory, and even the smoldering outrage that had replaced it had gradually cooled to a kind of residual anger that came and went like a mild case of malaria. I had become resigned to the fact that I would probably never be able to avenge the riverkeeper's death or the assault on Garth and me. I tried to console myself with the thought that at least my work, now that I was back in the good graces of the state, consisted of something other than the equivalent of stamping out license plates.

That was my general state of mind when Garth called me at six o'clock on a Thursday evening. I'd almost missed the call, as I was on my way out the door to pick up a gift for Harper, who was due back home from the Amazon in the morning; after some hesitation, I went back and picked up the receiver.

"Frederickson and Frederickson."

"Robby?"

"Yeah."

"It's Garth."

"I know who it is. I'm listening."

"Mary and I want you to come up for dinner. We miss you."

"When?"

"Right now."

"I assume you want me to bring along some friends who might be feeling blue and need cheering up?"

"No. Just bring yourself."

"You sure? The company might do you both good."

"No."

I glanced out the window at the clotted traffic on West Fifty-sixth Street and gnawed at my lower lip, trying to think. It wouldn't be dark for almost three hours. "I'm with a client. I probably won't be out of here for another hour or so, and traffic looks bad. It could be two or three hours."

"We'd really like you to come up right now, Robby."

"I told you I can't. If you and Mary get hungry, go ahead and eat without me."

"We'll wait. Get here as soon as you can."

I hung up, walked quickly to the stairway leading up to my apartment on the fourth floor. Robby, indeed. Nobody but our mother and Harper ever called me Robby; that, along with the fact that Garth had not called on my private line, formed a clear warning signal.

Upstairs, I took my Beretta and its shoulder holster out of the safe where I kept it these days, checked to make sure that it was clean, oiled, and loaded, and strapped it on; it had been some time since I'd carried a gun, and it felt odd. For added measure, I took out my small Seecamp with its ankle holster, strapped that on. I went down to Garth's apartment on the third floor to pick up a souvenir from a case we'd handled many years before—a German-made sniper's rifle and a specially calibrated scope that went with it. Then I went down to the garage to get my car.

·   ·   ·

There was a tie-up on the George Washington Bridge, and I didn't arrive in Cairn until eight-fifteen, a half hour or so before sundown. I parked in the municipal lot beside the river to check out conditions on the water, center myself, and wait for dark. There was no wind, and the river was about as calm as it ever gets, virtually glassy. That was all to the good. I kept going over the brief conversation with Garth in my mind; I had clearly asked him if he wanted me to notify the police, or bring them along, and his answer had clearly been no. It meant not only that Sacra Silver was in complete control of the situation but that he was, in Garth's judgment, desperate enough to start killing people if he found himself trapped. I was on my own.

177

The good news, if it could be called that, was that Chick Carver hadn't left the country after all; the definite bad news was that he was back in the faces of Garth and Mary, and was now presumably relying on more than his mouth to do harm. The self-styled ceremonial magician was going to require some smoking out, and I thought I had just the right smoker for the job.

I needed a large, stable rowboat, and I thought I knew where to get one. As the sun dropped below the horizon, I started up the car. I drove north through town, cut west for two blocks to avoid driving in front of Garth and Mary's house, then headed back down toward the river and the huge mansion housing the Fellowship of Conciliation, the pacifist organization to which Mary had once belonged. The Fellowship had been an integral part of an investigation I'd conducted three years before, a case of murder and political intrigue that had brought me to Cairn in the first place and led to my brother meeting and marrying Mary Tree, the love of his life. The people in the mansion knew me; borrowing their rowboat would presumably present no problem. However, I was feeling increasing time pressure, and I didn't want to stand around in their lighted entranceway chatting them up or answering questions while holding a sniper's rifle in my hand. Consequently I parked out on the road, took the rifle and scope out of the trunk, and pushed my way through the hedge surrounding their property.

I made my way through the moon shadows, around the mansion, and down a long, sloping lawn to the river. The Fellowship's sloop was moored out in the river. There was a rack holding the group's three canoes and a kayak, and there was a steel Grumman rowboat tied to the dock. I looked up toward the mansion to see if anyone might be at the window; there wasn't. I untied the Grumman, hopped in. I put the rifle and scope down on the floor, fitted the hickory oars into the oarlocks, and began rowing out onto the river. I went out a hundred yards or so, then pointed the bow south. The tide was going out, carrying me along with it. I rested the oars on the gunwales and allowed the boat to drift, using the time to fit the sniper scope to the barrel of the rifle.

It took less than fifteen minutes to cover the distance to Garth and Mary's home, and from my position I had a partial view into the glass-enclosed music room that looked out over the river. I recognized the tall, slim figure of Chick Carver, backlit by the fluorescent lighting in the room. He had his back to me and was leaning against the windowsill. I couldn't see anyone else.

I trained the rifle on him, then adjusted the scope until I had the back of his head in the cross hairs. But I didn't pull the trigger. I was going to need a very good excuse—not only for the police but for myself—before I blew off a man's head, and Chick Carver aka Sacra Silver, intellectual thug and accessory to murder, taking his leisure in my brother's home, wasn't it. He didn't appear to be holding a gun on anyone, and in fact seemed to have his long arms folded across his chest.

Half a minute later, the tide and current had carried me out of viewing range. I put the rifle down, placed the oars back in the water, and rowed back upriver to a point where I could once again drift abreast of the house and try to appraise the situation further. A tug pulling a barge out in the deep channel would help some, since I knew that when the wake generated by the tug reached me, the rowboat would be raised two or three feet, giving me a better angle to see what was going on in the music room. I unscrewed the scope from its fitting on the rifle barrel, waited.

The tug's bow wave arrived just as I was drifting in line with the house. As the rowboat rode up on the swell, I put the scope to my eye, sighted—and what I saw in the second or two before the boat dipped down in the wave's trough disturbed me very much indeed. Mary was sitting at her piano over by the recording console, and appeared to be playing. Garth was sitting very stiffly in a chair near the center of the room, the bright overhead lights glinting off what appeared to be a bare wire wrapped around his neck.

While trying to decide whether Garth with a wire around his neck was sufficient reason to execute Carver, a second swell raised the rowboat back up. I sighted through the scope again as another person, a slight woman with silver-streaked, wheat-colored hair like my brother's, entered the room. I put the scope down. I would be doing no shooting from ambush. First of all, I could miss, and there would be no second chance; then there was no telling what Chick Carver would do with his hostages, including the littlest one. Even if I didn't miss, the last thing in the world the littlest hostage needed to see was the image of a high-velocity, soft-nosed bullet exploding a man's skull. April Marlowe's presence in the house almost certainly meant that Vicky was there too. I might gamble with the lives of Garth and Mary, in an effort to save them, but not the child's; too many people she loved and had once trusted had already tried a similar trick, and had twisted her mind, and almost killed her, in the process.

I had no Plan B, but it was time to put it into effect anyway. Whatever Plan B might turn out to be, it had to unfold inside the house, where I could further appraise and try to control the situation, minimizing any physical or further psychological harm to Vicky.

I rowed the boat to shore, worried now that my tardiness in arriving at the house could suddenly trigger Chick Carver into a killing frenzy. I landed a hundred and fifty yards downriver, where the scraping of the boat as I pulled it up on the shore couldn't be heard in the house. I wrapped the painter attached to the bow around a rock, then hurried along the shoreline to the house. As I went up the path beneath the overhang, I inspected the underside of the house, near its foundation, on the off chance that Carver might have planted explosives. There didn't seem to be any—which didn't mean that explosives might not be planted at the front or sides, but I didn't have time to check out the entire structure.

I took off my jacket, unstrapped my shoulder holster, and removed the Beretta. I shoved the gun into the waistband of my slacks, against my spine, then tossed the shoulder holster and harness off to the side. Then I took a deep breath, worked my face up into something I hoped resembled a smile, and pushed through the screen door. Mary was still playing the piano, and the decidedly incongruous music of Chopin drifted through the house.

"Hello?" I called loudly in my best faux-cheery voice. "Anybody home? How come I don't smell anything cooking? I'm hungry."

The music stopped. "In here, Mongo." It was Garth's voice, flat, with no trace of emotion.

180

I walked through the living room, and when I saw that Chick Carver wasn't standing in the doorway to greet me, I whipped the Beretta out of my waistband and placed it on the shelf of a bookcase that stood adjacent to the entrance to the music room. It was a snap decision; leaving the gun behind was a calculated risk, since I might never have a chance to get at it again, but I still had the Seecamp in my ankle holster, and it would have to be enough. If Carver saw or sensed that I'd known he was waiting for me, and that I had come armed, it would lessen any chance I might have of getting the drop on him.

I walked into the room, stopped just inside the door, and affected shock at seeing Chick Carver—at the same time quickly glancing around the room to see what the situation was.

Vicky was not in the room, which was at once both a relief and a worry. Mary was at her piano, staring at me with a strange expression on her face that I found impossible to read. April was sitting very straight in a chair a few feet in front of the piano, her feet flat on the floor, and her delicate hands folded in her lap. My witch friend and ex-lover looked pale but composed, as I would have expected. Garth was strapped into a metal chair in the center of the room, his pants legs rolled up and his bound bare feet in a tub of water. The wire around his neck was the stripped end of a cable, which snaked down from his body and across the floor to an amplifier with a glowing green light that indicated it was turned on. An auxiliary cable connected the amplifier to a foot pedal that was used for electric guitar special effects. The pedal, with its glowing purple, red, and amber lights, was only inches from Carver's right foot. If he stepped on the pedal, my brother, sitting in the improvised electric chair, would die instantly and noisily as his flesh burned and his brain boiled.

The tall, gaunt director of this little melodrama was still leaning against the windowsill, looking quite pleased with himself. In his right hand he held a cheap, nickel-plated Saturday Night Special, and it was pointed at my chest. I looked at Garth. His expression, as usual, was impassive, but I thought I detected more than a trace of curiosity and concern in his soulful brown eyes— understandable, under the circumstances, since he had been depending on me to pull off a rescue. Now we were both wondering what I was going to do next.

"You just keep turning up like a bad penny, don't you, Chick?" I said to the man across the room.

His self-satisfied expression instantly changed to one of rage. When he spoke, his raspy, nasal voice was even more high-pitched than usual, sharp and almost petulant, like a child's. I didn't like the sound of it at all. "Don't call me Chick! My name is Sacra Silver!"

"All right, Sacra Silver, what's the story here? You trying to graduate from accessory to mass murderer? As far as I know, you have yet to manage to kill anyone on your own. I'd think you'd want to keep it that way, quit while you're ahead."

"Shut up! Come in the room!"

"I am in the room."

"Come further into the room! Do as I say, you dwarf fuck, or I step on this pedal and turn your brother into a French fry!"

I walked to the center of the room, stopped beside Garth, looked over at April. "Are you all right?" I asked quietly.

"Shut up!" Carver barked as my witch friend nodded slowly. "Raise your arms to your sides and turn around very slowly!"

I did so—and was very happy I'd left the Beretta behind.

Carver continued in his angry child's voice, "Now open your shirt. Pull it all the way up."

"What's your problem, Sacra?" I asked as I began to unbutton my shirt.

"You're late!"

"I had business with a client, and I said so over the phone. Weren't you listening?"

"I didn't hear your car pull into the driveway."

"I just got a new muffler."

"Open your shirt and pull it up. Turn around."

"Listen, Sacra," I said, holding my shirt open and slowly turning, "if I'd known you were here, taping our conversation wouldn't exactly be high on my list of priorities of the things I'd like to do with you. Now, I asked you what was going on. Why all these other people? I thought this was between you and me."

"Who are you to talk?" he screamed at me, spittle flying from his thin lips. His face had suddenly gone crimson, and he was leaning so far forward that I was afraid he was going to lose his balance and fall, killing Garth by accident, or shooting me, or both.

"Just take it easy, Sacra," I said very quietly. "Calm down, and we'll talk about what it is you want."

Suddenly, in a sea change of emotion that both astounded and terrified me, his features wrinkled up, and he burst into tears. "You thought this was between you and me?" he sobbed. "*You* brought my family into this! You went to see my mom and dad, and you talked about me behind my back. You had no right to do that! You made me lose my job! Now I'm supposed to go to Europe and never come back, or I'll lose my inheritance. I don't even *know* anybody in Europe. Now even my *mom* doesn't want to see me anymore, and it's all because of *you*. It isn't *fair!*"

So that was that, I thought with a decidedly sinking feeling. Chick Carver aka Sacra Silver had skidded right around the bend. Garth had been absolutely right in insisting that I not invite the police to the party; this man was now more than ready to start doing his own killing, at the slightest provocation, and his first victim was only a footstep, or a twitch of his trigger finger, away.

"Where's the girl, Sacra?" I asked softly.

"Vicky's safe."

"She's not safe," April interjected in a low, dignified tone laced with anger and defiance. "She's unconscious in the trunk of this man's car. He made her drink some milk on the way down here, and it must have been drugged. She could suffocate in there. At the very least, she's going to be terrified out of her mind when she wakes up and finds herself locked up in a small, dark space."

"We're not going to be here that much longer," Carver said. He had stopped blubbering, and had undergone another mercurial shift in mood, this time to gloating.

"Sacra got April's name and address out of my address book when he was here before," Mary said in a curiously mild, wooden tone that made me wonder if she might not also be drugged. I looked over to where she was sitting behind the white piano, and found her staring off into space at a spot somewhere above my head. "Vicky was here then, and I told Sacra about her situation."

183

I sighed. "What do you want with Vicky and April, Sacra? They have nothing to do with any of this."

"You stuck your nose into that girl's family business too, didn't you, you little shit? After Mary told me about Vicky, I did some reading in the library. I know all about what happened. *That's* why I brought Vicky here, along with the woman who's been helping you to turn the girl against *her* parents. If I knew where your parents lived, Frederickson, they'd be here too. I'm going to teach you a lesson you'll never forget about sticking your nose into other people's private, family business and involving their parents. Now let's see how *you* like it!"

"You've already taught me a lesson I'll never forget, Sacra. And if I hadn't interfered in Vicky's family business, as you put it, she'd be dead. What do you plan to do with her?"

"She can't go back to her parents; thanks to you, they're both in the loony bin, and probably will be for the rest of their lives. So I'm going to be her father, and Mary will be her mother. If I have to go away, I'm not going to be alone. I'm tired of being alone, with nobody to love me. It's time I started my own family anyway."

There was no telling precisely what was going on in Chick Carver's decidedly deranged mind at the moment, the same as there was no telling what he was going to do from moment to moment, but the prospect of at least two lives being saved was infinitely better than a zero score, and so there was no way I was going to pose the unasked question.

Mary answered it anyway, speaking in the same wooden tone. "I've agreed to go with him, Mongo. Sacra's been right all along. He's the only man who's ever really understood me, and the only man I've ever really loved. Now that I realize that, I don't want to die."

Looking at Mary's face, listening to her voice, I didn't believe her at all—except, naturally, for the part about not wanting to die. I didn't think Garth believed her either, and I was surprised Chick Carver did. But the fact that the man had apparently bought her story could only be good news, of a sort; her ploy, if that's what it was, had at least gained her freedom of movement, even if at the moment I couldn't see what good it was going to do. She couldn't very well attack Carver with her piano. If I could get close enough to her to whisper, I'd tell her about the gun on the bookshelf outside the door, but I doubted whether Carver was going to let me do too much moving around. I had to find a way to stall and look for some kind of opening before killing time began, and the only weapon I had close at hand, in a manner of speaking, was my mouth. Sooner or later, Carver was going to tire of whatever game he was playing, and I had to make my move before then.

"Sacra," I said evenly, "take your family's money and split. If you kill us, the police are going to be after you no matter what country you try to hide out in. Considering the fact that you've already killed one man, some people would say that you're getting off easy."

"I didn't kill anybody!"

"You caused a man to be killed; you ordered his death. It's the same thing."

"Sacra," Mary said in a more animated tone, one that had become companionable and soothing, "tell Mongo what happened the same way you told us before. Explain why what's been done to you is so unfair."

Carver turned his head slightly to look at Mary, but the barrel of his pistol didn't move away from its dead aim on my chest. Mary gave him a reassuring smile, and he looked back at me.

"The whole business of using empty tankers to haul water to the Middle East was *my* idea," he said in a whiny voice that was laced with both rage and self-pity. "I put it in the office suggestion box. They loved it! The chairman himself took me to dinner to tell me what a wonderful idea it was. I got a five-thousand-dollar bonus, and they told Wellington to put me in complete charge of making sure that the plan was carried out."

"Do you know why they did that, Sacra?" I asked quietly, my gaze fastened on his trigger finger.

"To make me the fall guy if something went wrong!"

"Good thinking, Sacra. You'd be the fall guy if things went wrong—if charges started to go up the ladder. So far, that hasn't happened; everybody seems to have bought the story about the rogue captains. But things could change. That's another reason why you should leave now without doing something very stupid that's sure to draw attention to you, and make people start asking questions again."

I thought it was pretty good advice, but Chick Carver wasn't listening to anything but the twisted, emotionally stunted voices in his own head. He said, "Everything would have been fine if that son-of-a-bitch Blaine hadn't started messing around! He *deserved* to die! The company was making millions of dollars in extra profits on that water. Nobody else *cared!* Kuwait needed the water after all the fires, the company was happy to provide it for them, and I know I was due for a big promotion. And then it was all threatened because some jerk from some jerkwater river town was ready to make trouble just because the ships were dribbling a little oil in his precious river! What kind of sense does that make?!"

"It didn't make sense to you, so you gave the order to kill him. Tom Blaine was taking samples from all the ships, but you waited until he got to that particular tanker, because you knew you could bully its sorry liquor bottle of a captain into doing what he did. In the eyes of the law, that makes you equally guilty. Like I said, you should quit while you're ahead."

"He got what was coming to him, the same as you're going to get what's coming to you! Nobody gave a thought to that man's death until you and your brother started nosing around. And then you turned my parents against me. Now I don't have *any-thing,* and you're going to *pay* for what you did!"

Chick Carver was getting himself really worked up. Killing time was getting nearer, but I didn't have the slightest idea what to do to stop it. With my quickness, I was pretty certain I could dart to one side and start rolling. The chances were good that he'd miss me with his first shot, and by the time he tracked me and got off another I would have pulled the Seecamp from my ankle holster and put a bullet in his head. But Garth would die. I had to wait, keep hoping that something would happen that would give me at least a slim chance of saving my brother's life, along with April's and my own.

"You've already got me in your sights, Sacra," I said, suppressing a sigh. "You're taking Mary and Vicky with you. Why threaten April and Garth? What more do you want?"

"I want to hear you say you're sorry for turning my parents against me, and I want to hear you beg for your life!"

"Okay. I'm sorry I turned your parents against you, and I'm begging you for my life. Can we go now?"

It was obvious I should have chosen my words, or tone of voice, more carefully, for now blood rushed to the other man's face, and spittle appeared at the corners of his mouth. I certainly didn't want to play games with Chick Carver, but statistics showed that sincere pleading can just as easily trigger a psychotic episode as passive defiance, which can delay execution because it denies gratification. But the fact of the matter was that, with Garth's death only a footstep away, I just didn't know what to say to the other man, nor how to act. I could only play percentages and hope that Carver would stand still and talk instead of walk.

"Say it like you mean it!" he shrieked.

"I can't, Sacra. You're making me too nervous."

"Then let me hear you beg for your brother's life!"

Garth, who had seemed almost bored throughout my exchange with Chick Carver, now spoke for the first time since calling me into the music room. "If you beg for my life to this skinny bag of shit, Mongo," my brother, who'd always had a way with words, said, "I swear I'll come back from the dead to break your scrawny neck."

"You heard him," I said to Carver, watching him, again thinking of the gun strapped to my ankle. Now I was trying to gauge how long it would take me, without ducking away, to simply reach down for the gun and snap off a shot. That would still take too long. He might or might not miss the stationary target I would present, but he certainly wouldn't miss the pedal with his foot; even if I managed to bore him right between the eyes, he would still fall on the pedal, and Garth would die. "He won't let me."

"We know you're going to kill us anyway, Mr. Silver," April said, her tone calm, quiet, and dignified. "It won't make any difference what Mongo, Garth, or I say to you. But it also doesn't make any difference if we die. Everybody dies." She paused, looked at Garth, then at me. She smiled warmly, and her limpid gray eyes glowed with affection. "I'm happy to die with friends I love and respect. As for you, Mr. Silver, your life is miserable now, and will only become more miserable after you kill us. You will only become more twisted and bent, and that is the only kind of love you will ever be capable of giving or receiving. It's 'rebound,' Mr. Silver, and I'm frankly surprised that a student of the occult like yourself shouldn't have perceived the dangers of the path you chose to take."

"I can see that I have to get your attention!" Chick Carver screamed as he lifted his right knee to an exaggerated height, almost to his chest, and then proceeded to stomp on the foot pedal in front of him.

Despite the fact that I'd been anticipating, dreading, just such an action, Carver's movement was still so sudden and unexpected—so *unthinkable*—that I didn't even have time to cry out. Now I screwed my eyes shut and screamed inside myself, expecting to hear the crackle of electricity over my brother's brief scream, then smell the burning of his flesh. But nothing happened. I opened my eyes, looked at Garth—and found him looking back at me. I glanced across the room at Chick Carver, who was staring at Garth in astonishment. And then we both looked down at the foot pedal under the sole of his boot. The lights on the pedal were out, as was the light on the amplifier.

Mary, sitting at her piano—which incidentally happened to be flush to the master console that controlled every piece of equipment in the music room and recording studio—had shut everything off at precisely the right moment.

Chick Carver started to swing his pistol around in my direction, then stiffened in shock as his own voice boomed throughout the room, at ear-splitting volume, from two huge floor speakers on either side of him.

WHO ARE YOU TO TALK?

It seemed Mary had been doing even more than keeping her right hand close to the off switch on the master console while she played her piano; she had also been taping the entire proceed-

188

ings. This time I hadn't had to bring my own recording engineer with me; she'd been here all along, waiting for me to show up so that the show could begin. I wondered if Garth had known, or suspected.

YOU BROUGHT MY FAMILY INTO THIS!

The high-decibel assault, combined with the realization of what had been done to him, momentarily froze Chick Carver. I dove to one side, snatched the Seecamp from my ankle holster, rolled over, and came up on my feet with the gun aimed at Carver's head, ready to fire. But Mary had already beaten me to the punch, in a manner of speaking.

There had been a twelve-string guitar resting on a high stool between Mary and Carver, and as her tormentor had started to turn toward me, she had jumped up from the piano, grabbed the guitar by the neck with both hands, and smashed its face into Carver's face.

EVERYTHING WOULD HAVE BEEN FINE IF THAT SON-OF-A-BITCH BLAINE HADN'T STARTED MESSING AROUND! HE DESERVED TO DIE!

Six of the twelve strings on the guitar were steel wire, strung under high tension, and they acted something like a cheese cutter on Mary's hapless target. The first blow flayed the skin from Carver's nose and left cheek, sending blood spraying in all directions. The second blow to his face broke the neck of the guitar and sent the man crashing back through the plate-glass window behind him onto the outside deck.

"I'll kill him!" Mary screamed, and, still holding the broken guitar with its tangled, bloody strings by the neck, leaped head-first through the broken window after her intended victim.

"Uh, I'll be right back," I said to Garth and April as I quickly headed for the open space in the wall of glass.

"Take your time, brother," Garth said drily. "I think Mary has the situation under control."

That was a matter of opinion, I thought as I hopped over the sill with its necklace of broken glass onto the deck and found Mary kneeling behind the blood-soaked and wildly flailing Chick Carver. She had one of the steel wire guitar strings wrapped around his neck and was tugging on it with both hands. Blood was welling from her palms, where the wire was cutting into them, and from Chick Carver's fingers as he desperately pulled at the wire that was threatening to choke the life out of him if it didn't sever the carotid artery first. His face, or what I could see of it behind a shimmering mask of blood, looked like something a very large cat had been playing with. His gun was lying beside him on the deck, and I kicked it away.

"I'll kill him," Mary said in a very low, purposeful tone as she pulled even harder on the wire. She kept repeating it, like a mantra. "I'll kill him. I'll kill him."

A neutral observer would have to say that whatever spell Sacra Silver had cast over Mary had been broken. Apparently unhappy with her lack of progress, she shifted her position, sat down, and put both her feet in the space between Carver's shoulder blades for added leverage. She was just getting ready to give the wire another, really serious tug when I stepped between Carver's flailing legs, reached forward, and grabbed her wrists.

"Whoa, sweetheart," I said. "You've got him reined in nicely here. Take it easy. Nice job, incidentally—what you did in there."

But Mary wasn't going to be mollified by any of my sweet talk. She was still tugging on the wire, at the same time pushing on Carver's back with her feet, and threatening to pull me off balance. "I'll kill him, Mongo," she said through bloodless, trembling lips. "I swear I'll kill him."

It was April who, having freed Garth and mercifully turned off the blaring tape recorder, now saved the day, along with Carver's life and my dignity. She and Garth had come out on the deck, and now April quickly stepped behind Mary and put her hands gently on Mary's shoulders, while Garth gripped my forearms to help steady me. "Let go, Mary," April said softly. "It's over now. Let go. Let Mongo and Garth handle him."

Mary gradually relaxed her grip on the wire, although her face remained clenched in rage. Carver fell over on his side, both hands covering his bloody face, and I eased myself down on the deck next to him. April helped the trembling Mary to her feet, and then Garth went to his wife and took her in his arms.

"I have to get Vicky," April continued, gently easing Mary away from Garth, cradling the other woman's bleeding hands.

"Then I'll clean up Mary's cuts. Do you want me to call the police?"

"In about ten minutes," I replied. "After you take care of Vicky and Mary. Tell them to bring a doctor. And, if you will, you can bring our friend here a wet towel."

April nodded, then led Mary, now spent and slumped, into the house. Carver had curled himself up into a fetal position. He was staring at me with his right eye through a slit in his blood-soaked fingers. There was no hatred now in the eye, not even rage. It looked shiny but empty, like a doll's button eye.

"The man looks like he could use a drink, brother," I said to Garth. "Me too. Would you do the honors?"

Garth looked at me curiously for a few moments, then said, "Somebody call you in off the bench?"

"You did. And you'll like this play."

He shrugged slightly, then turned and walked back into the house.

"I was the one who first warned you about rebound, wasn't I?" I said to the empty, button eye. "Now you're up to your eyeballs in shit, and there's no way you're going to wade out of it. We now have your taped confession admitting complicity in the murder of Tom Blaine, and you'll be facing additional charges of kidnapping and attempted murder. So, can we talk?"

After a long hesitation, Chick Carver nodded his head slightly. Garth appeared with two glass tumblers filled with Scotch and ice. I helped Carver up to a sitting position, then eased him back against the wall behind him. He took his hands away from his face, and it was all I could do not to avert my gaze. Blood continued to ooze from the lacerations on his face. His nose was broken, and it looked like his left eye was gone. Mary had played quite a tune on him. I handed him the generous tumbler of Scotch, which he downed in three long swallows. Garth squatted down beside me, stared at Carver.

"The police are going to be here in a few minutes, Sacra, so listen up," I continued quickly. "Now, I imagine you can try to cut some kind of deal with the cops by offering to tell all you know about Carver Shipping—about how all the executives approved of the idea you put in the suggestion box, how you were taken out to dinner, paid a cash bonus, and all that. Naturally the company will deny it. You tell me if I'm wrong, but I'll bet you don't have anything in writing, and any other bonuses you received were in cash. They're just going to claim you were in league with their mythical rogue captains all along. You're overboard, Sacra, and the sharks are circling. Your ex-bosses get away with the money they made off your idea, and they'll be laughing at you while you go away to prison. There's no way in hell you can escape a long term, and I'm not going to insult your intelligence by telling you there is. But Garth and I may be in a position to help you get something that I think means a great deal to you, and that's the respect of your father. Assuming we can convince the authorities to cooperate, which shouldn't be a problem, we can help you win back that respect, while at the same time getting in some licks at the boys in the gray suits who used you. Are you interested?"

There was another long pause. Then, in a thick voice, Carver said, "Yes."

"Me too," Garth said drily.

I picked up my tumbler of Scotch, handed it to Carver. "Then drink up while you have the chance, and keep listening. I've got a proposition for you. We're going to make Sacra Silver a star."

EPILOGUE

I stood on a chair and watched through a square viewing portal in the projection booth as the five hundred people who had shown up for the luncheon and shareholders' meeting of Carver Shipping milled about in the grand ballroom of the Times Square hotel, waiting for the gathering to be called to order. There were an unusual number of media representatives, due not only to the notoriety of recent events involving Carver Shipping but also to the presence of the United States Secretary of the Interior—the guest of honor, main speaker, and pompous village idiot who could always be counted on to put his foot in his mouth in any speech lasting more than sixty seconds. The good Secretary was expected to rain praise on this "great American company" and then endorse what was expected to be a routine vote of confidence in the board of directors and a celebration of the company's policies.

At the moment, the Secretary was seated at the center of a flower-bedecked table set up on a stage beneath a theater-size screen. A specially produced promotional film with the title *We Love the River* was scheduled to be screened in, according to my

193

watch, five minutes. The Secretary, a tall, stooped man, was engaged in animated conversation with Barry Russell, a short, rotund man with a pencil moustache who was the chairman of the board. The Secretary of the Interior was not an impressive-looking man, nor was the chairman of the board, nor, indeed, were any of the directors, men who seemed almost swallowed up in their thousand-dollar suits. I was struck once again by how much the lives of every citizen of the United States were controlled, finally, not by the Sacra Silvers of the world, but by faceless, unimpressive white men in gray suits. I thought they all looked like third-string Godfathers—but then, I was decidedly prejudiced.

At precisely twelve-thirty the chairman pounded a gavel on a lectern set up to the left of the table, and the crowd obediently quieted as people sat down in their seats. Russell motioned for the Secretary and other members of the board schmoozing at the table to take their places in a special section in the front row of seats that had been partitioned off with a thick velvet rope strung between gleaming brass stanchions. They did so, and then the chairman looked up at the booth to signal for the film to begin. As his eyes met mine, he frowned, then cocked his head to one side and squinted, as if there might be some hint of recognition. I gave him a salute and a grin, then turned and signaled Garth to start the projector as I dimmed the auditorium lights on the master control console to my right. Then I turned back to watch the show. The projector began to whir, and Garth stepped up to the viewing portal on the opposite side of the booth.

There were no opening credits at the beginning of the film, and no music—just a stark close-up of Chick Carver's ruined, stitched face. There was a sharp, collective intake of breath from the audience below, which obviously did not find this a suitable image to open a corporate promotional film.

"My name is Charles Carver," the man who had once described himself as a sorcerer and insisted on being called Sacra Silver said directly to the camera. "Until recently, I worked as an assistant to Roger Wellington, the chief of security for the Carver Shipping Company. I am the son of Bennett Carver, the founder of this company you now all collectively own, but my father is in no way responsible for the criminal actions I am about to describe to you. My father has avoided contact with me for twenty years, and with good reason."

I considered the picture quality of the 35mm film to be quite good, considering the fact that it had been transferred from quarter-inch videotape—a little grainy, but I thought that appropriate to the subject matter. The sound was too loud, even for the large auditorium, but it never even occurred to me to turn down the volume. Even above the booming sound of Chick Carver's voice, I could still hear shouts of protest and the loud buzz of excited conversation from below.

Chairman Barry Russell rushed up on stage, shielded his eyes with one hand, and squinted as he repeatedly made cutting motions across his throat with the other hand to indicate to the projection booth that the film should be stopped. Although I knew it was unlikely he could see me against the glare of the projection lamp, I made a series of cutting motions of my own back at him, and grinned. Then he started shouting orders and making frantic motions toward both sides of the auditorium. Security guards began running up the aisles, heading toward the stairwell leading up to the projection booth. I wasn't worried; careful preparations had been made for this special screening. In the lobby their security guards would meet our security guards, off-duty NYPD and transit cops hired for the occasion, and there was no doubt in my mind that our security guards would prevail. We would be undisturbed for the next fourteen minutes and twenty seconds, which was how long this particular promotional film would run.

On screen, the scene had shifted from the banks of the Hudson to the river itself, where we had filmed Chick Carver standing at the bow of a large powerboat borrowed from one of Garth's friends for the occasion. Carver was narrating a guided tour of the industries along the shores of the river serviced by Carver Shipping, while at the same time describing how he had originally come up with the idea for hauling water from the Hudson to the Middle East; he described how the idea had been eagerly received by the company's executives, and he named each of the individual directors who had come up to personally congratulate him for

195

his initiative; he described the menu at the dinner to which the CEO had treated him, and he listed what he had bought with the five-thousand-dollar cash bonus he had received. He told how he had been made personally responsible for seeing that the captains of Carver Shipping's vessels acceded to the company's decision, and how he had personally delivered cash bonuses to the captains and their crews who agreed to cooperate.

The next-to-last stop on this tour of corporate greed and irresponsibility was the mooring site where he had ordered Julian Jefferson to activate his tanker's main engines while Tom Blaine was in the water below; the last stop was the fisherman's float net where Mary and I had found the bloody pieces of Tom's body.

Chick Carver finished by saying that he deeply regretted what he had done, and apologizing to his father for the damage he had done to the company Bennett Carver had been so proud of. Then the screen went blank.

I turned up the lights, looked down. There was pandemonium below, with all of the shareholders out of their seats, milling about and shouting at each other. The Secretary of the Interior was nowhere in sight. The chairman of the board was up at the lectern, banging his gavel for order, while, to a man, the rest of the directors were staring up at the projection booth, shock on their faces.

I hopped down off my perch, turned to the man who had been sitting stiffly, both feet on the floor and his hands clasped tightly in his lap, in a straight-backed chair throughout the screening. "You're on," I said.

Bennett Carver slowly rose to his feet. He looked much stronger now than when he had visited me in my hospital cell, and he had left his wife's cane at home. He stood straighter, his face was a ruddy color, and his pale green eyes glinted. He looked back and forth between Garth and me. "It sounds like there's a riot down there."

"They'll quiet down when you walk into the hall. I do believe the other shareholders will be looking for new leadership, and you'll have no trouble getting the people presently in charge to submit their resignations."

"I would like the two of you to join me down there."

I looked at Garth, who was standing by the door of the projection booth, his hand on the knob. He hadn't even bothered to rewind the film. There was no need. If anybody wanted this particular print, they were welcome to it.

Garth shook his head. "We'd only be a distraction, Bennett. I've got a wife waiting for me, Mongo has a lover and ex-lover waiting for him, and there's also a little girl we promised to take to the zoo. It's your show now; go break a leg."

"I owe the two of you more than I—"

"You owe us nothing, Bennett."

Garth opened the door, and Bennett Carver, walking steady with his head high and his shoulders back, preceded us out of the projection booth into a narrow vestibule. He went down a stairway leading to the auditorium, and we went down another.